PRAISE FOR KAMI GARCIA'S
THE LEGION SERIES

UNMARKED
2014 BRAM STOKER AWARD NOMINEE FOR SUPERIOR ACHIEVEMENT IN A YOUNG ADULT NOVEL

"A rare sequel that **surpasses the original.**"
—RANSOM RIGGS, #1 *New York Times* bestselling author
of *Miss Peregrine's Home for Peculiar Children* and *Hollow City*

"Get ready to be **scared, surprised, and thoroughly entertained.** A fantastic read."
—MARIE LU, *New York Times* bestselling author of *Legend*

"UNMARKED is both gorgeous and hideous. A frightening and disturbing tale spun with great beauty. **Absolutely riveting.**"
—JONATHAN MABERRY, *New York Times* bestselling author of *Rot & Ruin* and *V-Wars*

UNBREAKABLE
2013 BRAM STOKER AWARD NOMINEE FOR SUPERIOR ACHIEVEMENT IN A YOUNG ADULT NOVEL

"Tense and deliciously twisty, UNBREAKABLE is a breath-stealing midnight run through some of the creepiest locales I've seen rendered in fiction."
—RANSOM RIGGS, #1 *New York Times* bestselling author
of *Miss Peregrine's Home for Peculiar Children* and *Hollow City*

"**A fast-paced race through a world of demons and spirits,** darkness and light....I can't wait for the next book!"
—ALLY CONDIE, #1 *New York Times* bestselling author
of the Matched trilogy

"UNBREAKABLE is **a haunting, chilling tale** that reminded me of Stephen King and Dean Koontz. Creepy places, believable characters with some of the best teen dialogue I've seen, and plenty of suspense. I loved it."
—JAMES DASHNER, *New York Times* bestselling author
of the Maze Runner series

"Paranormal action, secret societies, and romantic suspense! The Legion series is now definitely on my must-read list."
—RICHELLE MEAD, #1 international bestselling author of *Vampire Academy*

* "Edge-of-your-seat paranormal activity keeps this book moving at an astronomical rate.... Garcia brings a fresh new take to the supernatural and the world of secret societies."
—*VOYA*, starred review

"UNBREAKABLE keeps you engaged and on edge. I found myself intrigued in Kennedy Waters' world and not wanting to put this book down. Looking forward to book two!"
—JASON HAWES, cocreator and star of *Ghost Hunters* and a *New York Times* bestselling author

"Strong, engaging characters and a romance to die for."
—RACHEL CAINE, *New York Times* bestselling author of the Morganville Vampires series

"*Supernatural* meets *Buffy the Vampire Slayer*. Kami Garcia is Joss Whedon's talent-sister! I didn't just read UNBREAKABLE; I lived it. When it comes to supernatural suspense, Garcia is the Slayer."
—NANCY HOLDER, *New York Times* bestselling author of *Buffy: The Making of a Slayer* and the Wicked saga

"An eerily fun and emotionally accurate venture into the complex layers of paranormal encounters from both sides. Looking forward to book two!"
—GRANT WILSON, cocreator of *Ghost Hunters* and a *New York Times* bestselling author

"In a fast-paced series opener, Kennedy Waters encounters a ghost, loses her mother and meets a love interest—all in the first few pages.... Garcia shakes it up with an ending that will leave readers reaching for the next book. This vivid, thoroughly imagined paranormal world will draw readers into its icy realm."
—*Kirkus Reviews*

UNMARKED

UNMARKED

THE LEGION SERIES

BY KAMI GARCIA

LITTLE, BROWN AND COMPANY

NEW YORK BOSTON

Text copyright © 2014 by Kami Garcia, LLC
Artwork pages 29, 82, 188, and 362 copyright © Kami Garcia, LLC
Artwork pages 285, 318, and 383 copyright © Chris Berens
Excerpt from *Dangerous Creatures* copyright © 2014 by Kami Garcia, LLC, and Margaret Stohl, Inc.

Little, Brown and Company
Hachette Book Group
1290 Avenue of the Americas, New York, NY 10104
Visit us at lb-teens.com

Little, Brown and Company is a division of Hachette Book Group, Inc.
The Little, Brown name and logo are trademarks of Hachette Book Group, Inc.
The publisher is not responsible for websites (or their content) that are not owned by the publisher.

First Paperback Edition: September 2015
First published in hardcover in September 2014 by Little, Brown and Company

Library of Congress Cataloging-in-Publication Data

Garcia, Kami.
Unmarked / by Kami Garcia.
pages cm — (The Legion ; 2)
Summary: "Kennedy Waters and her companions find themselves in a world where vengeance spirits kill, ghosts keep secrets, and a demon walks the Earth. As they learn more about their ancient secret society, its longtime rivals the Illuminati, and Kennedy's mysterious family, they wonder whether Kennedy is really meant to be a member of the Legion"— Provided by publisher.
ISBN 978-0-316-21022-5 (hc) — ISBN 978-0-316-21023-2 (ebook) — ISBN 978-0-316-33367-2 (library ebook edition) — ISBN 978-0-316-21021-8 (pb) [1. Demonology—Fiction. 2. Ghosts—Fiction. 3. Secret societies—Fiction. 4. Supernatural—Fiction. 5. Identity—Fiction. 6. Love—Fiction.]
I. Title.
PZ7.G155627Unm 2014   [Fic]—dc23   2014004198

10 9 8 7 6 5 4 3 2 1
RRD-C
Printed in the United States of America

For Alex—
May the black dove always carry you.

Hell is empty and all the devils are here.

—William Shakespeare, *The Tempest*

1. CAGED

Iron bars were the only things separating us.

He sat on the cell floor, leaning against the wall, in nothing but a pair of jeans. I glanced at the chain binding his wrists. With his head bowed, he looked exactly the same.

But he's not.

I let my fingers curl around the wet bars. Several times a day, holy water rained down from the sprinklers in the ceiling. I fought the urge to unlock the door and let him out.

"Thanks for coming." He hadn't moved, but I knew he didn't need to see me to sense I was here. "No one else will."

"Everyone's trying to figure this out. They don't know what to do about—" The words caught in my throat.

"About me." He rose from the floor and walked toward me—and the bars separating us.

As he drew closer, I counted the links in the chain hanging between his wrists. Anything to keep from looking him in the eye. But instead of moving away, I gripped the bars tighter. He reached out and wrapped his hands around the metal above mine.

Close but not touching.

"Don't!" I shouted.

Steam rose from the cold-iron bars as the holy water seared his scarred skin. He held on too long, intentionally letting his palms burn.

"You shouldn't be here," he whispered. "It's not safe."

Hot tears ran down my cheeks. Every decision we'd made up to this point felt wrong: the chains coiled around his wrists, the cell doused in holy water, the bars keeping him caged like an animal.

"I know you'd never hurt me."

The words had barely left my lips when Jared lunged at the bars, grabbing at my throat. I jumped back, his cold fingers grazing my skin as I slipped out of reach.

"You're wrong about that, little dove." His voice was different.

Laughter echoed off the walls and chills rippled through me. I realized what everyone else had known all along.

The boy I knew was gone.

The one caged before me was a monster.

And I was the one who had to kill him.

SEVEN DAYS EARLIER

I'm standing in front of the burning building. Ash-covered bedsheets hang from the shattered windows, outside the rooms where people are still trapped. Inside, screams rise over the roaring flames, and my skin crawls.

I want to run through the wall of black smoke and save them, but I can't move. My eyes drift down to my shaking hand, and I realize why.

I'm the one holding the match.

I bolted upright in bed, my heart pounding.

Another nightmare.

They started the night the walls of the penitentiary crumbled around me, and I'd been having them ever since.

I pressed my hands against my ears, trying to silence the screams.

It was just a dream.

And what I'd done in real life was even worse than setting fire to a house full of innocent people.

I had freed a demon.

Andras, the Author of Discords. A demon that had been imprisoned for more than a century.

Until I released him two months ago and he killed my mother and the other Legion members in her generation. Judging from the newspaper articles I obsessively collected, he'd probably killed even more people since then. Some days I thought about it less than others.

This *wasn't* one of those days.

⊣ • ⊢

I spent the afternoon in the library reading articles and printing weather charts and maps.

By dinnertime, I was burned out.

As I trudged across the muddy quad, the rain soaked through the black leather boots my mom gave me the night she died. Between the rain and the Pennsylvania winter temperatures, pneumonia was becoming a very real possibility. But it was worth the risk to wear something she'd given me.

Other girls rushed by in their uniform skirts and Wellies, dodging puddles like land mines while I stomped through every one. It hadn't stopped raining since the night I assembled the Shift—the paranormal key that had unlocked Andras' cage—and the sky still looked as broken as I felt.

How could I ever have mistaken the Shift for a weapon capable of destroying Andras?

The details of that night were branded in my memory, as inescapable as the nightmares.

Sitting on the prison floor, with the Shift's cylindrical casing in my hand and the disks scattered in my lap. Jared, Lukas, Alara, and Priest on the other side of the cell door, urging me to put it together. The paralyzing fear as I slid the last piece of the device into place.

That was nineteen days ago.

Nineteen days since I saw my friends or heard the sound of Jared's voice.

Nineteen days since I fell outside the prison, and the razor wire cut up my legs.

Nineteen days since I sat in the emergency room while a doctor stitched up the gashes and the police questioned me.

The doctor sounded apologetic when he finished. "You're all patched up, but you will have a few scars."

I remember laughing. Scars from a piece of razor wire were nothing compared to the emotional scars that night would leave behind.

Hours later, while I was watching the storm batter the windows in my hospital room, I heard voices outside my door. I only caught bits and pieces of the conversation, but it was enough.

"—from social services. Do you have any idea why your daughter ran away, Mrs. Waters?"

A runaway—that was the story I gave the police.

"It's Diane Charles, *not* Waters. Kennedy's mother is dead. I'm her aunt."

"Your niece has been unresponsive for the most part, Ms. Charles. We need to conduct a psychiatric evaluation to determine her mental state before we can release her into your custody."

"My custody?" Aunt Diane's voice rose. "When I agreed to become her legal guardian, Kennedy was an honor student who'd never been in any trouble. I have no idea what she's gotten herself mixed up in, but I don't want her bringing whatever it is into my house. And what if she runs away again?"

"I understand your concern, but you are her only relative—"

"Who you can locate," Aunt Diane snapped. "Have you even tried to find her father?" The fact that my aunt was willing to hand me over to a man I hadn't seen in twelve years made it clear just how much she didn't want me.

Aunt Diane lowered her voice. "Kennedy's mother and I were not close. My sister had *issues*, which she obviously passed on to her daughter, and I feel terrible about that. But I'm not equipped to deal with a troubled teenager."

On any other night, I would've stormed into the hallway and verbally annihilated my aunt for insulting my mom. But she was right about me, even if she didn't know the real reason why. Letting me live with her would be a death sentence.

"You don't have to take this on alone," the social worker said. "There are programs designed for at-risk teens. Group homes, boarding schools..."

The next morning, Aunt Diane offered me a handful of pathetic excuses. "I only want what's best for you, Kennedy. Winterhaven Academy is a lovely place, and *very* expensive." She rambled on without waiting for a response. "The doctor said you can leave for school as soon as your legs heal. I've already made all the arrangements."

I stared at the TV mounted on the wall behind her as a news station showed clips of golden retrievers and Labradoodles tearing one another apart in a dog park. The headline on the ticker read TWO CHILDREN DEAD AFTER RABIES OUTBREAK IN LOCAL SUBURB. A painful reminder that I had no idea what Andras was capable of or how far his reach extended.

When my aunt finally headed back to Boston that night, I started getting answers.

Electrical storms and torrential rain hit West Virginia nonstop on the first day Andras was free. Lightning sliced through the darkness outside my window, sending the nurses scurrying through the halls whenever the hospital lost power.

By the second day, rain wasn't the only thing falling from the sky. News channels across West Virginia and

Pennsylvania streamed live video of crows dropping out of the sky like black hail.

On day three, while scientists tested dead birds for disease, violence spread like a virus. The killing began in Moundsville, West Virginia, only miles from the hospital and West Virginia State Penitentiary, where I had assembled the Shift. The bodies of a local pastor and his wife were discovered hanging from the rafters of their church, the walls plastered with pages from the Book of Enoch; a retired warden from the prison was electrocuted, an electric razor floating next to his body in the bathtub; and a theology professor from the university was stabbed to death in his office, dozens of books from a locked bookcase stolen. None of the killers were caught.

The violence only increased from there.

The next day, outside of Morgantown, West Virginia, a Boy Scout leader drowned his troop and then himself. In Pittsburgh, a retired firefighter burned down half the houses on his block and then marched into one of the infernos. Three maximum-security prisons were put on lockdown after riots broke out and the wardens were murdered, their bodies left hanging from the guard towers.

On the fifth day, girls started disappearing.

One girl every day for the past fourteen days: Alexa Sears, Lauren Richman, Kelly Emerson, Rebecca Turner, Cameron Anders, Mary Williams, Sarah Edelman, Julia Smith, Shannon O'Malley, Christine Redding, Karen York,

10

Marie Dennings, Rachel Eames, Roxanne North. Their names were burned into my mind without any help from my eidetic memory.

By day six, the doctors had discharged me from the hospital, and on day seven, the headmistress was handing me the same Winterhaven uniform I was wearing now.

And it still itched like hell.

I elbowed my way through the cliques of girls hanging out underneath the massive arched walkway known as the Commons. It was the day after Christmas, and the teary-eyed freshmen were still huddled together crying because their parents hadn't let them come home for the holidays.

A pack of girls with streaked black eyeliner straddled the wall between two of the pillars—sitting half in and half out of the rain—passing a contraband cigarette between them. Across from them, the lip-gloss mafia gossiped near the bathrooms, reeking of envy and imitation strawberry.

I sidestepped my way through the cloying scent and pushed open the bathroom door. With two weeks of winter break looming, I needed to find an alternate route to the library if I wanted to avoid the drama.

Water from my uniform dripped onto the tile as I stood in front of the mirror, wringing out my brown hair. I never bothered to carry an umbrella. The rain reminded me of the night in the prison—and of murdered families and charred homes, drowned Boy Scouts and missing girls.

Things I don't deserve to forget.

As I twisted my long hair into a ratty ponytail, I caught a glimpse of my reflection. I barely recognized the girl staring back at me. My dark eyes were lost in the bluish-black shadows around them, and my olive skin looked pale and washed out against my white button-down shirt.

The past few weeks had taken a serious toll on me. Most days I was lucky if I remembered to eat, and the nightmares kept me from getting more than a few hours of sleep.

An image flashed through my mind. The girl in the white nightgown—the first spirit I'd ever encountered, and the one that would've killed me if Jared and Lukas hadn't saved me. All I needed were the handprints around my neck and I could pass for her now.

The fluorescent light above my head flickered.

Not here.

I froze, my hand instinctively moving to the silver medal on my necklace. The Hand of Eshu, the protective symbol Alara had given me.

A sudden *pop* sent a shower of sparks raining down over me. I ducked and covered my head, my mind scanning through mental pictures of the room. Was there anything in here I could use as a weapon?

Find out what you're up against.

I glanced at the ceiling. Black smoke coated the inside of one of the lightbulbs.

A burnt-out bulb. Not a paranormal attack.

I'd been anticipating one since the night I freed Andras, but nothing had happened. Yet.

What would Jared think if he saw me jump out of my skin over a lightbulb? My thoughts always found their way back to him.

Where was he right now? Was he safe?

What if something had happened to him?

A familiar knot formed in my throat.

He's okay. He has to be. They all have to be.

Jared, Lukas, Alara, and Priest knew how to take care of themselves, and each other. The memory of the last time I saw them, at the penitentiary, lingered in my mind.

Thinking about them will just make you miss them more.

I splashed cold water on my face and groped for a paper towel, blinking away the memories and the water in my eyes.

A blurry reflection passed behind me in the mirror.

I jerked back. "Sorry," I said, embarrassed by my reaction. "I didn't see you."

As I turned away from the mirror, the reflection of the room lingered in my peripheral vision. I looked for the person who had come in.

No one was there.

⊰ • ⊱

Battling vengeance spirits with Jared, Lukas, Alara, and Priest had taught me that paranormal entities could be anywhere. The odds of running into an angry spirit on a hundred-year-old campus like Winterhaven were pretty high for anyone. But the nightmares and my experiences over the last few months left me feeling like there was something more to it.

Whatever I'd seen in the mirror would probably be back. I needed to be ready, and eating blueberry Pop-Tarts three meals a day wasn't exactly the diet of champions. Time to lift my ban on the dining hall.

Ten minutes later, I stood in line, scooping unnaturally orange macaroni and cheese onto my plate. I grabbed a pack of cinnamon Pop-Tarts to switch things up, and scanned the room for an empty table. The dining hall was a breeding ground for everything I hated about Winterhaven—gossip, cliques, self-pity.

Two Black Eyeliners nodded in my direction, inviting me to sit with them. Instead, I took a seat at the opposite end of the table. They didn't realize I was doing them a favor. Getting close to me was dangerous, and I had the track record to prove it.

I dropped my notepad next to the congealed ball of noodles and flipped through the drawings. It felt like watching my nightmares in stop-motion—Priest's hand reaching up from the well, Alara strapped in the electric chair, the spirits of dozens of poisoned children lined up at the ends of their metal beds. There were pages and pages of them, each image more disturbing than the one before.

I reached an unfinished sketch from a few nights ago, a figure looming over me as I slept, just like it had in my nightmare. I hunched over the page, filling in the missing sections. After a few minutes, features emerged—the feral eyes and elongated jaw of an animal, jutting out from a human silhouette.

Andras.

My fingers tightened around the pencil. I'd left out a detail in the sketch, one I couldn't draw. In the nightmare, he'd spoken to me.

I'm coming for you.

It had sounded more like a promise than a threat.

"Another newbie," one of the Black Eyeliners called out from the other end of the table.

A girl with stick-straight blond hair stood in the doorway, her eyes darting around the room like a frightened deer's. She inched forward, her face still puffy and red from crying, a Winterhaven welcome binder pressed against her chest. I recognized that look. Her parents had probably dropped her off this morning.

Winterhaven was the last stop for the troubled daughters of wealthy East Coast families. From runaways and cutters to pill poppers and party girls, Winterhaven accepted them all—including me.

Now the school was responsible for us, which wasn't saying much. None of the teachers cared what kind of trouble we got into behind closed doors, as long as we didn't kill each other in the process. The party girls kept partying and the cutters kept cutting. Only the runaways lost out because the school was buried so deep in the Pennsylvania woods, there was nowhere to run.

Whispers spread through the room in seconds.

"Too young for drunk driving."

"Doesn't look brave enough to be a runaway."

"I'm going with pills. Definitely."

"Final answer?"

I tuned out the voices and shaded in the rest of the sketch. Bits and pieces of the nightmare flashed through my mind—the figure watching me in the darkness, its features emerging from the shadows, the paralyzing fear.

It was too much.

My hand trembled as I fought the urge to rip out the page and tear it to shreds. I was sick of being afraid. I wanted to fall asleep without being tormented. More than anything, I wanted to forget. But I couldn't let myself.

"Is anyone sitting here?" The new girl stood across from me, the edge of her tray shaking. "I mean, is it okay if I sit here?" She looked even younger than Priest—fourteen maybe.

The Black Eyeliners laughed. I had already passed on their invitation to sit with them, the few times I'd eaten in here. They probably assumed the new girl's odds weren't good, which was reason enough to let her sit with me.

I gestured at the empty seat across from me. "Sit down before the vultures start circling."

The girl's shoulders relaxed. "Thanks. I'm Maggie."

"Kennedy." I started drawing again, hoping she could take a hint.

"That's a cool name."

"Not really." I didn't look up.

She stayed quiet for a few minutes, pushing a scoop of orange macaroni around on her plate. I sensed her watching me, but I kept my eyes glued to the page. Eye contact encouraged conversation, something I avoided at all costs.

"So why are you here? Sorry—" She bit her lip. "That's none of my business. My dad says I ask too many questions."

Her dad sounded like a heartless bastard.

Like mine.

"I ran away." At least that was the story I'd told the police and Aunt Diane. Before the new girl had a chance to ask why, I turned the tables on her. "What about you?"

She stabbed at the ball of noodles. "My dad just left me here."

"What did you do to piss him off?"

A tear ran down her cheek. "I exist."

My pencil stopped moving. The anger in her voice was all mixed up with the pain, and it reminded me of the last time I saw my own father. The morning he drove away while his five-year-old daughter watched from the window.

She wiped her face on her sleeve and glanced at my notepad. "That's cool...and a little scary. You're really good. I bet your drawings will be hanging on a gallery wall someday."

A familiar pain tugged at my chest. My mom used to say that all the time.

"What is it?" she asked, still studying the sketch.

"Just something from a dream."

Her eyes lit up. "The easiest way to get rid of a nightmare is to tell someone about it. Then your mind will stop fighting the bad dream, and it'll go away."

My nightmares weren't going anywhere.

"Real life doesn't work that way." I snatched my notepad and stood up, the legs of my chair scraping against the hardwood floor. "There are some fights you can't win."

I walked away without waiting for a response. The last thing I needed was a pep talk from a kid who was crying because her dad dumped her at a fancy boarding school. My mother was dead, and I hadn't seen my own father in years.

My days were full of fear and guilt, dead birds and missing girls.

And it's only going to get worse.

⊰ • ⊱

Guilt ate away at me until I finally dumped my tray and headed for the new girl's room. Her room was easy to find. It was the only door without any messages pinned to the corkboard, which made me feel like I'd kicked a puppy.

I knocked, silently rehearsing the apology I'd practiced on the way over. "It's Kennedy."

After a moment I knocked again, listening for sounds on the other side of the door. Nothing. Either she wasn't in there or she didn't want to talk to me.

I flipped through the sketches at the beginning of the notepad, the ones I'd drawn right after Lukas gave it to me. Instead of the disturbing images from my nightmares, these pictures captured happier memories—half-finished drawings of Priest wrapping paintball guns in silver duct tape, Alara holstering a bottle of holy water in her tool belt, Lukas playing Tetris, a rare smile from Jared. Their specialties—the areas of expertise they had been trained in—were as different as the four of them. Yet each skill complemented the others: Lukas hacked into databases all over the country and used the information to track paranormal surges; Priest engineered the spirit-hunting weapons that Jared commanded with ease; and when weapons failed, Alara used wards and voodoo arts to protect them.

Together, they were a Legion, and for a while, I'd thought I was one of them.

One sketch looked different from the rest—a self-portrait. I ripped it out and pinned it to her board, along with a note.

I'm sorry.
-Kennedy

Clad in military-issue cargo pants and black boots, the girl in the drawing looked brave and determined—like someone ready for a fight. I had already lost my battle, but Maggie could still win hers.

Minutes later, I stood in front of my own door, trying to remember what it felt like to be the girl in the drawing. But I couldn't.

With the Legion, I had faced malevolent spirits and destroyed paranormal entities. Now I was alone, and I wasn't even brave enough to face what was waiting for me on the other side of my own door.

3. BROKEN MIRRORS

When I turned on the light, my reality came into view one terrifying image at a time. Newspaper clippings, maps, crime scene photos, and pictures of missing girls wallpapered my room. Chalk outlines, surrounded by yellow and black police tape, were layered over weather charts and mug shots of people who had been arrested for bizarre or brutal acts of violence.

Every scrap represented an event that could potentially be traced back to Andras.

I started collecting the articles in the hospital. I found the first one while scanning the newspaper for any mention of Jared, Lukas, Alara, and Priest. The headline read: *Lightning Kills Seven in Fire at Holy Martyrs Church.*

What had started as an attempt to track the demon's

movements had developed into an obsession, a kind of self-inflicted penance. I had released Andras, which made his crimes *my* crimes.

Part of me wished there was a way to send all this information to Lukas. He would know how to find the pattern in the madness, a skill I'd underestimated until I tried doing it myself. Even though I searched for their names every time I read newspaper, a bigger part of me was relieved I didn't know how to find them.

They're safer without me.

As I added the finished sketch of my nightmare to the wall, an image that looked like a music stand caught my eye.

Andras' seal.

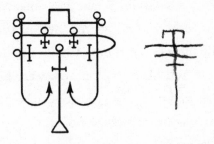

It was the demon's unique signature. Each Legion member's wrist was marked with a different section of the symbol. If they rubbed salt on their wrists and held them together, the marks re-created the seal.

I ran my fingers over the unmarked skin on the inside of my wrist, a permanent reminder I wasn't one of them.

And the reason things would never have worked out with Jared and me.

I scanned the wall for the portrait of his profile, taped above a chart of weather anomalies. The curve of his lips and the long eyelashes that framed his pale blue eyes. For a second, I forgot to breathe. I remembered the way his lips felt against mine, the sound of his voice when he whispered to me in the rain, refusing to leave me behind.

I remembered the promise I made to myself that night. The one I hadn't kept.

I'll find you.

Did he think about that night?

Does he think about me?

Maybe Jared had already moved on, continuing the search for the missing fifth member of the Legion—one thing I would never be.

I peeled off the wool kneesocks I wore every day even though they itched like crazy and made my room smell like a wet dog. A web of white scars snaked across my legs like a tattoo, a permanent reminder of my mistakes. My fingers traced the ridges in my skin. I hated them, but if there was a way to trade my mistakes for even more scars, I would've done it in a second.

I wrestled out of my wet clothes and into dry ones before flipping open my laptop. I skimmed news sites for signs of paranormal activity, the evidence of Andras at work. The Legion taught me that sudden increases in the number of murders and violent crimes were red flags, with suicides a close second.

A photo of thousands of crows flocked on the rooftops in downtown Pittsburgh made me pause. I clicked on it, and a familiar message popped up on the screen: *Unauthorized portal.* Winterhaven limited student Internet access, allowing only approved news sites and libraries. E-mail was nonexistent, and phone use was restricted to calls home—or, in my case, to Aunt Diane. Not that I'd ever call her.

My in-box was probably overflowing with messages from Elle by now. Even if I figured out a way to contact her, what would I say? *I unleashed a vengeful demon on the world, and no one knows how to stop him?* She'd forgive me because that's what best friends do. But this wasn't a failed midterm I could forget about after a pint of ice cream.

The next headline made sure of that: *High School Track Star Disappears Without a Trace.* A brunette with delicate features smiled back from the screen, her name printed under the photo: *Catherine Nichols.*

Number 15.

The article didn't provide any new information: *After the disappearance of fifteen teenage girls, the FBI has issued a statement calling the disappearances "serial abductions," confirming what the public suspected.*

I found a clean page in my notepad and began the ritual that had become second nature by now. My pencil re-created the curves of Catherine Nichols' face, her high cheekbones and brown doe eyes. As I lost myself in the charcoal lines, music blared from the room next door. My hand jerked, and a stray line dragged across her face.

Winterhaven never ceased to annoy me. I pounded on the wall, but the girls laughing on the other side ignored me.

I taped the drawing next to the ones of the other missing girls. The row of sketches looked strikingly similar—dark-eyed girls with delicate features, wavy brown hair, and awkward smiles. Pretty in an average way. There was one more thing—something impossible to ignore.

They all looked like me.

Another reminder that the demon wasn't finished with me, even if I didn't understand why. Maybe he still thought I was the fifth member of the Legion, and I was next on his hit list.

Next door the music cranked up another few notches, followed by scratching sounds.

Are they moving furniture in there?

"Shut up." I banged harder.

Someone finally turned off the music. The scratching intensified at the exact same moment my neighbor's door slammed. The laughter moved into the hallway, and my skin went cold.

The scratching isn't coming from next door.

I whipped around as a jagged line etched itself into the mirror above my dresser. When it hit the bottom of the frame, the line—and the scratching—stopped. Within seconds, another mark dragged its way down the glass.

There was something off about the sound. It didn't have the nails-on-a-chalkboard intensity that would've made it impossible to think it was coming from next door. I inched closer and froze.

The lines were being cut from *inside* the mirror.

My eidetic memory snapped mental pictures as the row of lines hit the frame and changed direction, creating horizontal, diagonal, and curved slashes.

Letters.

Words formed, cut by cut, until the message stared back at me.

HE IS COMING FOR YOU.

The meaning registered slowly, one fragmented thought at a time.

Andras knows where I am.

After all the paranormal attacks I'd escaped in places like a haunted well and an abandoned children's home, my dorm room was the place the demon finally found me? Had it really taken him this long to track me down?

Nineteen days of fear, anger, and guilt turned to rage in a single moment. This was my life now—vengeance spirits and nightmares, missing girls and demons, unanswered questions and paranormal threats. I was tired of waiting for something to happen. I wanted it to happen now.

"I'm right here!" I screamed, turning in a circle with my arms outstretched. "Come on!"

Silence echoed back at me, louder than a hundred screams.

"What are you waiting for?"

The consequences of my mistakes surrounded me—layers and layers of them taped to every surface in a prison of my own making. I hurled myself at the closest wall, tearing down the photos of dead birds and chalk outlines, electrical storms and flooded streets, mug shots and maps.

Slashes of pink and gray peeked out from beneath the bits of paper still stuck to one of the walls—a print of my favorite painting, Chris Berens' *Lady Day*. A girl floating through the air under a glass dome.

I taped it to my wall the moment the boxes marked *School* had arrived—the ones I'd packed before my house turned *Poltergeist* and I took off with Jared and Lukas. She was the last shred of my old room and my old life. It hurt too much to look at her every day, so I buried her under the scraps of what my life had become.

I'd always believed the girl under the glass found her way out in the end. But maybe I was wrong.

I ripped the print off the wall and tore it in half. The dome split down the center, tearing the girl apart along with it. The two halves fell to the floor, lost in a sea of articles about the tragedies my mistake had set in motion.

Someone knocked on the door. "Everything okay in there?"

The first print my mom ever gave me lay in pieces at my feet. I picked up the half with the girl's face on it and folded it before slipping it into my notepad.

"Kennedy, I know you're in there. Open the door."

I recognized the girl's voice, but I couldn't place it.

"I'm not leaving," she said.

I cracked the door. One of the Black Eyeliners stood on the other side, looking bored.

She glanced over my shoulder at what was left of my dorm room. "Rough day?" Her tone dripped with sarcasm.

"What do you want?" I asked, holding the notepad against my chest.

"If you're gonna be a bitch, I'll just tell the hot guy who's looking for you that you weren't interested in his message."

"What are you talking about?"

The girl sighed and rolled her eyes. "I caught him wandering around Anderson Hall. He said he needed to find you. That it was a big emergency or something. You're lucky he ran into me and not one of the dorm mothers." She held up a damp scrap of paper. "He said to give you this."

I unfolded the paper, and my heart felt like it stopped beating. The black ink was smeared, but I still recognized the image—and who had made it.

Jared.

In the center of the page, he'd drawn a black dove. Exactly like the one tattooed on his arm.

Black Eyeliner Girl gestured at the drawing. "So what does it mean?"

"Where is he?"

She crossed her arms, indignant. "Are you gonna tell me who he is?"

I stepped closer, stopping just inches from her face. "Where is he?"

The girl shrank back against the wall. "Relax. Did you skip your meds today or something? He's behind Anderson Hall."

I pushed past her and raced down the hallway.

Nineteen days had passed since the last time Jared and I saw each other, but it felt like forever. I thought about him every day, and every day I fought the urge to take off and look for him.

But now he was here, and finding him was the only thing that mattered.

By the time I reached Anderson Hall, my wet clothes were clinging to my body. Behind the dormitory, the woods stretched into a sea of black. But for the first time since the night I spent hidden in the back of my mom's closet as a kid, my chest didn't tighten from the surrounding darkness.

My only fear was not finding Jared.

"Jared?" I whispered. "Where are you?"

Please be here.

Between the rain battering the roof and the wind rustling the leaves, I couldn't hear anything except the sound of my heart pounding in my ears.

"Kennedy?"

I spun around and collided with Jared's chest. My feet slid out from under me and he caught my wrist. It started to slip through his wet hand, the same way it had nineteen days ago as we ran from the crumbling prison.

But this time I didn't fall.

Jared lifted me and slid his hands under my arms, his thumbs pressing against the tender spot just below my shoulder bones. I let my hands trail up his arms, the muscles tense beneath my touch. He stared down at me, his blue eyes even paler in the sea of black around us.

For a moment, neither of us moved.

"I found you," he whispered, bringing his hand up to touch my face.

The words wouldn't come. I reached out and grabbed the front of the heavy green utility jacket he was wearing on top of his army jacket, clenching it in my fist. Jared's hand slid down my jawline and through my hair. When his fingers reached the base of my neck, he pressed gently, urging me into his arms.

"Talk to me, Kennedy."

I let my forehead drop against his chest and choked back a sob.

"Just tell me if you're okay," he pleaded.

"As close as I'm going to get."

Jared lifted my chin, and I could make out the faint outline of his face. His strong features and long eyelashes, the scar above his eye, and the boyish good looks hidden underneath a *Fight Club* exterior. His lips grazed mine, tentative at first. My breath caught, and he pulled me onto my toes, deepening the kiss.

I felt everything at once—the happiness of seeing him again and shame for allowing myself to feel it, the pain of missing him and the fear of losing him.

He leaned his forehead against mine. "God, I missed you."

"Me too."

Jared guided me toward a cluster of towering evergreens, and we ducked beneath them.

"How did you find me?"

"Elle helped us."

"Elle?" I hadn't spoken to my best friend since the day I called her weeks ago, before my aunt had me shipped off to Winterhaven.

Jared wrapped his arms around me, tucking my head under his chin. "She tried to get your aunt to tell her where she sent you, but the only thing Elle could get out of her was that you were somewhere in Pennsylvania. Luckily, it was enough to get Lukas started. He hacked into the admissions records of every boarding school in the state until he found you."

"There must be dozens."

"Fifty-four. That's why it took so long." He sounded apologetic, as if this was somehow his fault instead of mine. "We started with the most logical schools, and then Luke hit them alphabetically. None of us thought she'd send you to a place like this."

"My aunt thinks I ran away."

Jared took my hand. "Then let's prove her right and get out of here."

I stiffened. "I can't leave."

"Don't worry. We'll be more careful this time."

"I'm not afraid of getting caught." I closed my eyes, dreading the next part. "I don't belong with the four of you."

The real members of the Legion.

32

"You belong with me no matter what," he said.

"I could've gotten you all killed. And who knows how many people Andras has hurt already. Dozens, by my count."

"It's not your—"

"Then whose fault is it?" My voice rose. "Because someone let him out, and I was the only person in that cell."

"You didn't make that decision alone. All five of us were there, and we told you to put the Shift together." Jared's hand tightened around mine. "Come on. You're not staying here."

I wanted to leave with him more than anything, but the stakes were too high. What if I made another mistake and Jared or one of my friends paid the price?

A sick feeling settled in my stomach. "You guys have to find a way to stop Andras. If I screw up again, even more people could get hurt."

Or worse.

Jared let my hand slip from his. "There's something I need to tell you, but I don't know how."

"You can tell me anything."

Jared didn't say a word for what felt like minutes. When he finally spoke, his voice sounded far away. "Your mother's death was a mistake. It never should've happened." He still couldn't forgive himself for accidentally leading the demon to my mom and the other Legion members.

"It was an accident," I said. "You have to let it go."

"You don't understand," he said quietly. "You were right all along."

He wasn't making any sense. "About what?"

"Your mother was never a member of the Legion."

4. DEMON SLAYER

The ground seemed to shift beneath my feet.

"You're wrong." I doubted the words even as they left my lips. "A vengeance spirit killed my mom on the same night the other Legion members were murdered. And she died exactly the same way."

"I wrote your mother's name on the list with the other Legion members' names. That's the only reason Andras hunted her down. It's my fault." Jared slammed his fist into the tree next to him. He punched it over and over, a hit for each word. "Everything. Is. My. God. Damned. Fault."

I caught his arm. "You're not making any sense. Where is this coming from?"

"We figured there had to be a reason why you didn't get your mark after you destroyed Darien Shears' spirit.

So Lukas started digging and realized I made a mistake. When I found your mom's name and she fit the profile of the missing member, I stopped looking. But there was someone else. Lukas found a birth certificate."

I still remembered the first time Lukas and Jared told me she was part of the secret society—and that I was destined to take her place. I had doubted my mom's involvement from the beginning. It felt like I was rubbing salt on my wrist and staring at my unmarked skin all over again.

"At least we finally know why I didn't get a mark."

Because I don't belong.

Even though I'd spent the last nineteen days repeating those words in my head, I wasn't ready to say them out loud.

"Listen to me." Jared grabbed my shoulders. "You didn't get your mark because the fifth member is still alive. It's someone else in your family."

"But there's no one—" The words slipped away as the realization untangled itself in my mind. If my mom wasn't a member of the Legion...that only left one possibility.

It can't be him. Anyone but him.

My knees buckled. "She can't be dead because of him."

"Who?" Jared sounded confused.

"My dad. He left when I was young and we never heard from him again." The words came flooding out. "It killed my mom and broke her heart."

And mine.

"Shh. Listen to me." Jared cradled my face in his

hands. "It's not your father. My uncle said the missing member was a woman."

"There's no one else, Jared. My aunt Diane isn't capable of keeping a secret like this. There's no way she's part of a secret society. And my dad's parents died before I was born." I fought to hold myself together. But I felt the seams I'd stitched together so carefully over the past nineteen days tearing. "He's the only family I have left."

"Your father has a sister."

It was another mistake. "If he had a sister, don't you think I'd remember her?"

"Not if you've never met her. You said he left when you were young, right? What if she's been hiding all this time?"

"Hiding from what?" I practically shouted.

Jared glanced at the back of the building as if he was worried someone might hear me.

"No one knows why the fifth member fell off the grid. But my dad used to say a person who disappears without leaving a trail is someone who doesn't want to be found. Take a look at this." Jared took something out of his pocket and handed it to me, along with his cell phone. "Use the light."

I held the phone over the page. It was a photocopy of a birth certificate.

"Alexander Madigan Waters." Jared recited the information from memory. "Born in the District of Columbia, to Lorelai Madigan Waters and Caleb Quinn Waters."

"A copy of my father's birth certificate? That doesn't prove anything."

"It does if you compare it to this one." Jared handed me an almost identical sheet of paper. The District of Columbia seal was stamped at the top of this one, too. "Lukas searched DC public records to find out if your mom had a female blood relative she could've chosen as her successor. Turns out, your dad is the one with the secret family member."

I scanned the document and found the baby's name: Faith Madigan Waters. Born in the District of Columbia, to Lorelai Madigan Waters and Caleb Quinn Waters, two years after my father's birth.

I held the proof in my hand, trying to reason it away. How could my father have a sister I'd never met? Did he abandon her, too?

"If Faith Waters is the fifth member of the Legion, she might know how to stop Andras," Jared said.

No one wanted that to be true more than me. The last few minutes I'd spent in Darien Shears' cell replayed themselves in my head every day. His story about a Legion member giving him the final piece of the Shift to protect. The look on his face as he lay in the Devil's Trap, begging me not to assemble the Shift. I could still hear his voice.

The Shift doesn't destroy Andras. It frees him.

It was the decision that would change everything—

destroy a demon, earn my mark, and save the world...or unleash a demon and his wrath.

If only I'd made the right choice.

"There's something else," Jared said. "While Lukas was hacking into school servers looking for you, Priest and Alara spent days reading the journals. None of us had ever read ours cover to cover, except Priest. My dad and my uncle never let their journals out of their sight. Then our family members died, and suddenly the four of us *were* the Legion. We were so focused on finding Andras and destroying him before he crossed over that no one knew if the journals explained what to do if it actually happened."

"Do they?" I didn't want to let myself hope.

"We're still looking." Jared took a deep breath. "But we figured out what Andras wants now that he's here."

"What?" I braced myself for the answer.

Jared shifted nervously, the leaves rustling under his boots. "Remember the original entry in Lukas' journal? The one where Markus wrote that Andras wanted to open the gates of hell? He meant it literally."

I thought about some of the vengeance spirits we had encountered and the violence they had been capable of—the girl in the yellow dress and Millicent Avery at the bottom of the well; electrocuted prisoners and Darien Shears; and the dybbuk wearing the magician's skin. I couldn't imagine what might be waiting in hell.

"You have to find Faith Waters." I thrust the documents back into Jared's hands. He reached for me, but I stepped away. "I'm staying here."

"Wait..." Jared stared at me, his expression blank. For a moment, he was silent.

Please don't make me say it again.

Fear flickered in his eyes, and he fumbled with the papers, trying to shove them back in his pocket. He raked a hand through his wet hair. "Kennedy, please. Don't ask me to leave you again. I can't do it." He took a step toward me, erasing what little distance I'd created between us, and rested his forehead on my shoulder.

I wanted to wrap my arms around him, but it would only make it harder to walk away. "I've screwed up enough already. If something happened to Alara, Priest, or Lukas because of me...if something happened to you—"

"Something already did," he whispered. Jared took my hand and slid it under the bottom of his damp thermal, guiding it across his bare skin.

My fingers hit a strip of tape.

I yanked up his shirt and ran my hand over his stomach until I found the bandage above his hip bone. "Oh my god."

"I'm okay." Jared moved my hand away.

"Then why is there half a roll of gauze taped on your stomach?"

"It could've been a lot worse. We were taking down

a full body apparition in an attic. It turned out one of the windows was shattered." He shrugged. "I was distracted and I didn't notice. The spirit had a piece of the glass, and I got cut."

His explanation didn't add up; in a situation involving a paranormal entity, Jared's focus bordered on obsessive. "You can't afford to be distracted in that kind of situation. What the hell were you thinking about?"

He turned away.

"Jared." I grabbed his sleeve, forcing him to face me. "What were you thinking about?"

For a moment, he didn't respond. "You," he finally said, softly. His eyes moved up my neck slowly until they found mine, and my heartbeat sounded so loud that I was sure he could hear it, too. Jared ran his finger down the side of my face, lingering at my jawline to tuck a wet strand of hair behind my ear. "I can't explain it. But when you're not with me, I can't stop wondering where you are, and if you're okay. Andras is out there somewhere, and I keep imagining what will happen if he finds you."

Me too.

But I couldn't admit it to Jared, not when I was trying to convince him to leave me here. Not when all I could think about was the way his touch made me dizzy. "That's crazy."

"Call it whatever you want, but it's not something I can just turn off." He hooked his fingers through the belt loops of my jeans and pulled me against him. "I'm safer *with* you than without you. And you're safer with me. I know you've heard about the missing girls, Kennedy. Are we going to talk about the fact that they all look like you?"

I swallowed hard. "Why me? I'm not even a member of the Legion."

"I don't know, but I'm not letting you out of my sight until we figure it out."

The back door of Anderson Hall banged open, and a path of fluorescent light cut through the rain.

One of the dorm mothers squinted into the darkness. "It someone out here?"

Come with me, he mouthed, tugging my arm.

For nineteen days, Jared had lingered at the edge of my every thought. Wondering if he was safe, and worrying he wasn't. That fear had terrorized me in a place even the nightmares couldn't touch.

I pictured a jagged piece of glass slicing into Jared's abdomen, and his bloodstained hands clutching the wound.

He was thinking about me.

Jared's blue eyes pleaded silently.

Even if I wasn't part of the Legion, I had to find a way to keep him safe.

⛩ • ⛩

When we reached the edge of the woods, I heard voices.

"No one touched your precious demon-slayer belt,

42

Buffy." Elle's voice carried over the rain, irritated and unmistakable.

"Just keep your idle hands off my stuff," Alara snapped.

I squeezed Jared's hand. "Elle's with you?"

He smiled, and I took off through the trees.

"Ladies, let's spend more time worrying about not getting arrested and less time arguing." Priest leaned over the front seat of a beat-up black Jeep Commander, trying to referee.

Lukas' arms were crossed on the steering wheel, his head buried in the crook of his elbow, like a kid who fell asleep on his desk during class.

"Elle," I called.

She spun around, her red hair swinging over her shoulder.

"Kennedy?" She scrambled out of the car and threw her arms around me. "You're okay. I thought they were giving you shock treatments or something in there."

"It wasn't like that." I returned her death grip of a hug.

Elle was exactly the same—from her skinny jeans and vintage leopard-print jacket that only looked cool on her to the red hair and killer smile that drove guys crazy, everything about her was unrestrained and unedited. Two qualities I had always envied. Now the idea of possessing either seemed dangerous.

"Well, you look like hell." Alara had one hand on her

hip and an elbow propped up on Priest's shoulder. The hood of her heavy leather jacket was pulled over her wild brown waves. She'd added a stud next to the silver ring in her eyebrow, undoubtedly piercing this one herself, too. Her leather tool belt—stocked with a plastic soda bottle full of holy water and an EMF, among other things— hung low on her hips over a pair of the army surplus cargos. The black eyeliner that usually winged out at the end to create a perfect cat eye was smudged. Otherwise, Alara was still the prettiest and toughest girl I'd ever met.

"Thanks." The corner of my mouth turned up.

"Real nice." Elle shot Alara a look that would've sent most girls running for cover. "She was practically institutionalized. Let's have a little sensitivity—"

Alara and Priest plowed through Elle. They each hooked an arm around my neck and hugged me.

"Things weren't the same without you." Priest pushed his blond bangs out of his eyes. His signature headphones were hooked around his neck, underneath his orange hoodie. "Alara moped and Jared trashed the hotel room we were staying in."

Jared jammed his hands in his pockets, but instead of staring at the ground, he kept his eyes fixed on me.

"Why don't we move this party before somebody figures out Kennedy's gone?" Lukas walked around the side of the Jeep, wearing a crooked smile—one of the few noticeable differences between the Lockhart twins. Aside from Lukas' smile and his black nylon flight jacket, and the scar above Jared's eye, the two brothers were mirror images of each other.

He caught me in an awkward hug. "It's good to see you."

"So where did you get this thing?" I asked, climbing into the backseat next to Jared.

"Impound," Priest said.

Alara whacked him on the arm. "A friend."

Lukas started the Jeep and pulled off the shoulder. "Alara won't tell us. I think she borrowed it from the Mob."

"Or an ex-boyfriend," Elle said.

Alara scowled at her. "Shut up or I'll call your mom and tell her where you really are."

"Where does she think you are?" Lying to Elle's mom wasn't easy. It required flawless execution, and I was usually around to help cover her tracks.

Elle threw me a smug smile. "Taking a prestigious drama workshop at the Miami Center for the Performing Arts."

"She believed that?" The likelihood of Elle's mother letting her travel to another state without verifying the details was less than zero.

"After she spoke to the director," Elle said.

"How did you pull that off?"

"Alara helped," Elle said, as if that explained everything.

Alara crossed her arms. "Only because you black-mailed us. She wouldn't help us find you unless we agreed to let her come along. If I knew she was such a pain in the ass, I would've left her in DC."

Elle pouted, but I was impressed. She'd always been resourceful but usually limited her talents to torturing guys who liked her. This was a whole new level. "Give it up. I want details."

Alara shot Elle an intimidating glance. "My cousin Thaddeus is the director. The center is one of my family's foundations."

"You worked things out with your parents?" I knew how hurt Alara had been when they asked her to abandon the Legion and come home.

"Not exactly. Thaddeus and Maya have been helping me. Thad dealt with Elle's mom, and Maya has been sending money." Alara pretended to inspect her silver nail polish when she mentioned Maya, the younger sister she'd spared by joining the Legion in her place. "She still feels guilty that I was the one who ended up with my grandmother. And Thad and I were always really close."

"You look cold," Jared said, changing the subject. He rubbed his hands over my arms to warm me up. "Turn up the heat, Luke."

Lukas turned a knob on the dashboard, and the lyrics of Jared's favorite song, "Cry Little Sister," blared from the speakers.

Lukas and Priest groaned.

Alara covered her ears. "Make it stop."

"Change the station." Elle scrunched up her nose.

I couldn't help but smile.

"It's not the radio," Lukas said.

"Someone paid for...whatever that is?" she asked.

"It's Jared's favorite song," Alara said. "From *The Lost Boys* soundtrack."

Elle looked confused. "The lost what?"

"You're all hilarious." Jared tried to reach over the seat and turn it off.

Lukas swatted his hand away. "Come on. Just once for Elle."

Priest, Lukas, Alara, and I joined in for the chorus.

Jared ignored us and unzipped a backpack in the trunk. He handed me an extra shirt. "Here. Since my brother doesn't know how to turn on the heat."

"Stop crying already." Lukas shut off the music, with a crooked smile still plastered on his face, and cranked the heat.

Jared peeled off his wet thermal and slid on a dry one. I tried to ignore the way the sight of his bare skin made me feel.

Nice, Elle mouthed, smiling.

I pulled the extra shirt Jared had given me over my head. Within seconds, I had slipped my arms out of my wet sweater and yanked it through one of the sleeves.

Jared watched as I tossed the sweater over the seat. "I'll never figure out how girls do that."

"It's an innate ability they're born with, like rolling their eyes," Priest said.

I leaned my head against Jared's shoulder, exhausted. "Where are we going anyway?"

Lukas glanced at me in the rearview mirror. "I want to put some distance between your school and us. Then we can hit a truck stop and eat."

Elle stretched her legs between the seats and propped them on the center console. "Promise?"

"Think we should head to West Virginia?" Priest slipped on his headphones. "The prison's not that far."

I stiffened. "Why would you ever want to go back there?" The thought of going anywhere near West Virginia State Penitentiary made my skin crawl.

Priest turned to Jared. "You didn't tell her?"

"Tell me what?"

Jared bit his lip. "After the four of us met up on the other side of the state line, we went back to the prison to find the Shift." He paused for a long moment.

"It was gone."

Do we still need the Shift?" I tried to sound curious, but thinking about it brought back nothing but bad memories.

Lukas glanced at me in the rearview mirror again. "No. The Shift served its purpose. But we figured it was better off with us."

"Just in case," Priest said.

"In case of what?" My shoulders tensed, and Jared pulled me closer. My body fit into the space underneath his arm perfectly. "Did you find something new in the journals?"

"Priest, what's your malfunction?" Lukas shot him a warning look. "She's been locked up in that place for weeks."

"Sorry." Priest frowned and pushed his bangs under his orange hood. "Even if it's useless, a member of the Legion probably designed it. I can't stand the idea of some kid finding it in the rubble a few months from now."

"He just wants to take it apart and see how it works," Alara said from where she was stretched out in the third row.

"It's a badass piece of mechanical engineering," Priest said. "Of course I wanna take it apart."

I settled back into the space under Jared's arm, relieved. Priest was just being Priest. "So what have you guys been doing since…" I didn't want to bring up the night at the penitentiary. "Since we got separated?"

Jared squeezed my shoulder. "Looking for you."

"I have no idea what they were doing before I started helping them," Elle said, gesturing wildly. "But we've been doing all kinds of stuff for the last four days. Searching for birth certificates, making lists of all the towns with crazy weather, making charts of demon trails."

"She means patterns," Lukas said.

"Exactly." Elle nodded, launching ahead. "And Alara lied to a priest. She gave him some sob story about needing holy water to heal her sick dog, so he'd bless a bucket of tap water for us."

"If we run into another vengeance spirit, you'll thank me," Alara said.

"How many vengeance spirits are we talking about?" I turned to Jared without realizing how close his face was to mine.

His blue eyes flickered down to my lips for a second. "Just a few before we picked up Elle. Nothing Andras-level."

Like the mirror in my dorm room?

I couldn't tell them yet. Jared had already been stabbed with a piece of glass because he was worrying about me instead of himself. If he found out about the mirror, he'd be even more distracted.

"I've been tracking crime and violence that might be related to Andras," Lukas said. "All the mass murders have taken place between—"

"West Virginia and Pennsylvania," I finished for him. I pictured the walls in my dorm room, wishing I could show them to him. "I was looking for patterns, too. If we get a map at the gas station, I can re-create some of them."

Lukas gave me a strange look. "Okay."

Priest shook his head at me. "The things I could build with a memory like yours."

Lukas ignored him, his eyes catching mine in the mirror. "That's also the area where all the girls disappeared."

At the mention of the missing girls, I looked away.

"You know, they all kinda look like—" Priest began.

"I know." I cut him off.

"We don't have to talk about it right now." Alara

51

leaned over the seat and silenced Priest with a look. "There's a truck stop before the next town." She pointed at a sign.

"Thank god," Elle said, tousling her dark red waves with her fingers. "I'm in need of a serious caffeine fix."

⧏ • ⧐

"Where is Faith Waters now?" I asked, stirring a cup of burnt coffee. I still wasn't ready to call her my aunt.

Lukas shoved a handful of onion rings in his mouth, washing them down with his second strawberry milk shake. The truck stop was empty for the most part, and the waitress seemed relieved every time he ordered something else.

He shrugged. "We don't know. She doesn't have a bank account or any credit cards, not even a driver's license. No cyber footprint."

Priest pulled one of the headphones away from his ear. "Which means she's probably the person we're looking for."

"Then how are we going to find her?" I asked.

Everyone except Elle—who was busy flirting with a guy sitting at the counter—stared at me as if I already knew the answer.

Lukas flicked a balled-up napkin at Elle. "Think you can concentrate on what's going on over here?"

"I'm capable of doing two things at once, thank you

52

very much," she muttered under her breath, without compromising her smile for a second.

Lukas took his silver coin out of his pocket and flipped it between his fingers. "If we want to find your aunt, your dad is the logical place to start."

At the mention of my father, Elle whipped around in my direction. She was the only person who knew the truth about what happened the day he left—how he saw me watching him through the kitchen window, and still drove away. I never told my mom.

The note my dad left her said enough: *All I ever wanted for us—and for Kennedy—was a normal life. I think we both know that's impossible.*

I picked at the fries on my plate. "I don't know anything about him. He took off when I was little."

"Okay. What do you remember from before he left?" Lukas asked.

"She said she doesn't know anything about him." Elle flashed him a warning look.

Lukas ignored her. "Come on, Kennedy. You have a photographic memory. There must be something."

Elle slammed her glass on the table. "Her father ditched her when she was five years old. He never even sent her a birthday card. He's an asshole. *That's* what she remembers."

Heat spread across my cheeks. "Shut up, Elle."

Jared's hand tightened around mine under the table. I

stared out at the rain running down the windows. Anything to avoid the pity and questions I knew I'd see in his eyes.

"I'm sorry." Lukas sounded sympathetic and uncomfortable, the way my friends had when they found out my mother was dead.

My embarrassment turned to anger. I hadn't seen my dad in twelve years. He didn't even show up to claim me when my mom died. Yet he still had the power to hurt me. "You want to know what I remember about my dad?"

"Kennedy, it's okay—" Jared began.

I held up a hand, silencing him. "My dad smelled like Marlboros and mint toothpaste. More mint or more Marlboros, depending on how well he'd covered up the smell of cigarette smoke. He liked his bacon crispy and his coffee black. He didn't shave every day, so his face was either perfectly smooth or covered in stubble, and he had the greenest eyes I've ever seen. His favorite candy bar was 100 Grand, and he'd let me eat them before dinner even though it drove my mom crazy. He loved Johnnie Walker, Pink Floyd, and Edgar Allan Poe. He hated musicals, collared shirts, and magicians."

I stood up. "And he said he loved me more than the moon and the stars and everything in between. But he lied."

No one spoke as I headed for the dirty glass doors at the front of the restaurant.

"Kennedy?" Jared called after me.

"Give her a minute," I heard Elle say as the doors swung closed behind me.

I leaned against the building under the awning, next to the truckers trying to take one last drag of their cigarettes before they went inside.

Jared's green army jacket flashed in my peripheral vision. He grabbed my hand and pulled it behind him, drawing me close. "When you told me about your father, I didn't realize it was that bad. Why didn't you say anything?"

Because I can still see my dad climbing into his car, and the note, and my mother's tear-streaked face. Because I didn't want you to know that my own father didn't want me. Because I didn't want you to look at me the way you are right now.

"There's nothing to tell. He wasn't around. It doesn't matter." I started to turn away, but Jared kept my arm locked behind him and my body against his.

He lifted my chin. "Is that the reason you think everyone is going to hurt you?"

The familiar numbness I felt whenever I thought about my dad for too long spread through me. "Jared, I don't...I can't talk about this. Please."

"Okay."

We stood side by side in silence, watching the trucks pull in and out of the parking lot. I didn't want to talk about my dad and relive the pain that never seemed to go away. But my memories were the only possible clues we had left, and if Andras was responsible for the crimes on my dorm room walls, he had killed dozens of people.

By the time I slid back into the booth a few minutes later, I was ready. "What else do you need to know?"

Alara turned the sugar dispenser upside down, emptying what looked like half the contents into her coffee cup. "You don't have to talk about this, Kennedy. We can figure out another way to find her."

"We don't have time." I pulled my shoulders back and took a deep breath. "Ask me whatever you want."

Priest fidgeted with his headphones. "Did your father ever talk about his childhood?"

"Not really. I know he grew up in DC, but my grandparents died before I was born."

Priest and Alara exchanged a look.

"Anything else? Like a special place you went together?" Lukas asked.

I started to say no, but then an image flickered in my mind. The photo I'd found tucked into my mirror while I was packing up the house, after my mom died. Me sitting on my dad's shoulders, in front of a gray weather-beaten house. "There was this picture of us...."

I closed my eyes and focused on the details in the photo, things I'd never paid attention to before, scanning them one by one.

A broken gutter on the side of the house.
The half-mowed lawn behind us.

My missing front tooth.

Pink flowers on a dogwood tree.

My dad's silver wedding band.

The quarter-sized hole in the knee of my jeans.

Untied blue Keds.

A green sticker on my Wonder Woman T-shirt.

I zeroed in on the sticker. Blurry letters circled the outside, but the white writing in the center read I VISITED THE WORLD'S LARGEST BOTTLE CAP.

"There's this old picture of my dad and me in front of a house. I have no idea where it was taken, but there's one of those stickers on my shirt that you get when you visit a cheesy museum or landmark."

"Do you remember going anywhere like that with him?" Priest asked.

"No. But the sticker says 'I visited the world's largest bottle cap.' "

"It's better than nothing. Who's up for a road trip?" Lukas asked, just as Alara took a sip of her sugar-laced coffee. She swallowed too fast and ended up in a coughing fit. Elle tried to pat her back, but Alara swatted her hand away.

Lukas' fingers flew across the screen of his phone. "The world's largest bottle cap is located in Massachusetts, at the Topsfield Museum of Revolutionary Taxidermy and Patriots."

Elle scrunched up her nose. "That is so disgusting."

❤ "It's a museum with a giant bottle cap in it. What do you expect?" Priest stole one of my fries. "Just be glad they didn't taxidermy the patriots."

"Your grandparents lived in Massachusetts, right?" Lukas asked.

I nodded. "Boston."

"It's a connection." He sounded hopeful.

Alara crossed her arms. "You aren't actually suggesting we go to Massachusetts because of a sticker? To look for what, exactly?"

"I agree with Alara," I said. "It's a long shot."

Priest took off his headphones and hooked them around his neck. "My granddad used to drag me to all these weird places he loved when he was a kid. Maybe Kennedy's father took her there for a reason."

"Like to see the world's largest bottle cap?" Alara asked.

Lukas pocketed his coin. "The Shift is gone. Andras is orchestrating a murder spree, and we don't even know where to find him. So unless you know something the rest of us don't, this is about as dead as dead ends get."

"I'll pay the check." Alara slid out of the booth.

Lukas nodded at Priest and they followed her, most likely a tag team effort to sell her on the road trip idea. Otherwise, we were looking at ten hours trapped in a car, on the receiving end of Alara's sarcasm.

Ten hours in the car.

"Elle, did you bring any extra clothes?" I asked.

"There's a pair of jeans and some other stuff in my purse." She held up her gigantic black patent-leather bag. "It's totally stocked. Face wash, moisturizer, disposable toothbrushes." She paused as I took the bag. "Makeup."

Definitely a hint.

"Did you bring the prom dress to go with all that stuff?" Jared teased.

Elle put her hand on her hip. I stifled a smile and hauled her purse to the bathroom.

As the door closed behind me, I heard her say, "You obviously never read *Ten Rules for Surviving a Zombie Apocalypse*. Rule number one..."

᚛ • ᚜

When I came out a few minutes later, I heard Elle talking softly to someone. I stopped in the narrow hallway leading back into the restaurant and listened.

"She *watched* him go."

"I don't get it," Jared said.

"I mean literally watched," she said.

"You're not serious?"

"I shouldn't be telling you any of this." Elle sounded nervous. "Kennedy would kill me."

That's right, Elle. So stop talking.

Elle always had my best interests at heart, but this

wasn't the first time she had overshared in an effort to protect me—something I should've considered before I left them alone. I held my breath, praying the conversation was over.

"That's why she won't let anyone get too close," Jared said.

Because I'm screwed up and broken and there's no way to fix me.

"If Kennedy gets scared, she pushes people away," Elle said. "It's what she does. But you can't let her—"

Jared cut her off. "I did everything wrong."

Elle was silent for a moment. "Then I guess you'd better start doing things right."

You need to kill this conversation fast.

I opened the bathroom door and slammed it, as if I had just come out. They stopped talking immediately.

Thank god.

By the time I came out, Jared and Elle had relocated to the front of the restaurant.

They were staring up at a cheap TV mounted on the wall while the waitress tried to close out a check.

"Come on, Henry, I was off at one. I gotta get home."

The trucker pointed at the TV. "Hold on a minute."

A reporter stood in a parking garage, red and blue lights flashing behind her. I couldn't hear what she was saying, but I didn't need to once the girl's photo filled the screen.

The trucker tossed a ten-dollar bill on the counter, shaking his head. "Another one of them missing girls."

Her name was printed under the picture: *Hailey Edwards*.

Number 16.

6. DEAD PATRIOTS

"The museum is closed." Elle cupped her hands around her face and peered through the window.

Priest fished a twisted piece of wire out of his pocket. "I prefer to think of it as temporarily inaccessible."

Alara rubbed her gloved hands over her arms and huddled closer to the side of the house. "Hurry up. I'm freezing."

During the ten-hour drive to Massachusetts, the rain had turned to snow. I couldn't pinpoint the moment when the New England temperature won out, because nineteen days' worth of exhaustion finally won out over my nightmares.

"Think anyone will show up?" Alara glanced down the empty dirt road.

The museum turned out to be a three-story butterscotch-colored Tudor at the end of an unmarked road. We hadn't seen a single car since we turned off the highway.

"Doubtful." Lukas pointed at the brass placard next to the door.

TOPSFIELD MUSEUM OF REVOLUTIONARY
TAXIDERMY AND PATRIOTS
HOURS: 11:00 AM–4:00 PM
TUESDAYS, THURSDAYS & THE FIRST
SATURDAY OF EVERY MONTH
"HOME OF THE WORLD'S LARGEST
BOTTLE CAP"

"What kind of museum is only open twice a week?" Alara asked.

Lukas tapped on the front window. "One that's full of revolutionary taxidermy."

Priest wiggled the wire and a small screwdriver inside the lock. Elle hovered behind him, which seemed to be slowing him down.

"After we destroy the demon and save the world, I totally need a tutorial," Elle said. "I can never get into my locker."

"We're in." Priest opened the door and waved Alara over from where she was standing at the edge of the porch. "Alara, let's go."

She held up one finger, her phone against her ear.

Elle grabbed the elbow of my jacket. "Come on. She's on her cell again."

"Who's she talking to?" I'd never seen Alara call anyone except her parents.

"No idea. But she keeps calling someone."

Inside, the museum looked like a cross between an eighty-year-old woman's cluttered living room and a display at a natural history museum. Glass cases full of Revolutionary War memorabilia were crammed between antique curio cabinets that held everything from pocket watches and thimbles to a shoehorn and a butter dish.

The taxidermy collection appeared to be the only thing that wasn't behind glass. A deer dressed in a wedding gown stood on its hind legs behind a Victorian dollhouse. Inside the miniature rooms, chipmunks positioned in classic fencing stances wielded tiny épée swords.

Elle backed away from a squirrel bronco-riding a saddled rattlesnake. "That is wrong on so many levels."

Priest poked at it. "Some people have too much free time."

Alara made her way toward us from the front of the museum, dodging two white mice with unicorn horns, and a beaver wearing a golden crown.

"Talking to your sister again?" Jared asked.

"When who I call becomes your business, I'll let you know," Alara said.

"So where's this giant bottle cap?" Elle asked in one of her not-so-subtle attempts to change the subject.

"In here," Lukas called from the next room.

Four cables secured the bottle cap to the ceiling.

Elle sighed, unimpressed. "I expected it to be bigger."

Lukas knocked on the red metal. "It's the size of a monster truck tire. How big did you think it would be?"

Elle dug through her purse and pulled out a plastic camera.

Alara started to say something when Elle waved the camera in the air. "It's disposable. I don't need to hear the 'only use your cell to call your mom' speech again." She handed me the camera and stood in front of the bottle cap. "Take my picture. And I want one of those stickers that says 'I visited the world's biggest bottle cap.'"

I snapped the photo before World War III could break out between them.

Priest stared into one of the display cases running along the walls. "You can take your picture with John Hancock's shoelace, too, if you want."

Someone had taped a laminated note to the glass.

Historical artifacts generously donated by the residents of Topsfield, Massachusetts, and their families.

According to the labels, the cases held the personal effects of Revolutionary War patriots: an assortment of muskets and bayonets, tattered flags, broken dishes, a

Bible, and a wooden leg. The highlights of the exhibit were John Hancock's shoelace, a halfpenny that supposedly belonged to Joseph Warren, and a page from Paul Revere's Bible.

Priest pointed at the random items. "All three of those guys were members of the Sons of Liberty and the Freemasons. John Hancock's signature showed up on lodge ledgers way before he signed the Declaration of Independence. My granddad said Paul Revere was a member of the Illuminati, too."

Alara looked over when he said *Illuminati.* "That's a joke, right?"

Priest shrugged. "As far as I know, my granddad's research was always accurate."

"Back up," Elle said. "Does someone want to explain the difference between the Freemasons and the Illuminati for the regular kid in the class?"

Alara looked unamused.

"In 1776, the Illuminati surfaced in—" Priest began.

Elle held up her hand to stop him. "I just want the CliffsNotes."

"My granddad used to say the devil is in the details. Along with the truth." Priest gave her a sheepish smile. "But I'll do my best. The Freemasons and the Illuminati are both secret societies that date back centuries, but they had different agendas. The Illuminati wanted to overthrow

66

the existing governments and churches and create a new world order."

"Then, the Illuminati were the bad guys?" Elle asked.

"Definitely," Lukas said. "And it was the Legion of the Black Dove's job to stop them."

"What about the Freemasons? Good or bad?"

Lukas grinned at her. "They were stonemasons who formed a group in the Middle Ages to protect their trade secrets and pass down their skills. So the Freemasons were good guys."

"Why would Paul Revere be a member of both?" I had a hard time wrapping my mind around the idea that the patriot who made the Midnight Ride to warn the minutemen the British were invading was also a member of the Illuminati.

"The Illuminati were a much smaller group than the Freemasons, and they needed a place to hide from the Catholic Church—and the Legion," Priest explained. "So the Illuminati infiltrated Freemason lodges, and they've been hiding ever since."

"Are you saying they're still around?" I pictured the Illuminati as a bunch of bearded Leonardo da Vinci types who were long gone, like the Knights of the Round Table.

"My granddad had a run-in with a couple of them when he was a student at Yale," Priest said. "One night, he was studying in the Beinecke Library, where they keep all the rare books, and he caught two guys breaking into one of the cases. He tried to stop them, and they beat him up pretty bad."

"How did he know they were Illuminati?" I asked.

Priest held up his ring finger. "Their rings. Not the crap they sell online with pyramids and pentagrams all over them. These were the original design. The Eye of Providence surrounded by the Rays of Illumination. Between those rings and what they stole, it was obvious. At least to a Legion member."

"What did they steal?" Lukas' tone hardened.

"The *Grimorium Verum*." ? look it up online

"One of the oldest and most dangerous grimoires in history." Alara shuddered. "A book of black magic. It deals specifically with methods for harnessing the powers of demons."

"Why would they want that?" Elle asked.

Alara shook her head. "No idea. All I know is that my grandmother didn't trust the Illuminati. She called them 'demons among men.'"

Elle walked over to the last case, labeled *Modern Patriots*. "The Illuminati totally sound like a Legion thing. I'll stick with John Hancock and the patriots." She peered into the case. "I don't believe this junk is real. That shoelace could've belonged to anyone."

Jared grabbed me around the waist affectionately,

and gestured at the case in front of us. "This is definitely a fake." Behind the glass, a framed poem attributed to Edgar Allan Poe hung prominently in the center. "I'm pretty sure Poe didn't use a rollerball."

We had studied the poem in English class the previous year, and my eidetic memory flashed on mental images of the text. As I scanned the actual poem behind the glass, my mind tripped over the last few words.

"Alone"
Edgar Allan Poe
ca. 1829

From childhood's hour I have not been
As others were—I have not seen
As others saw—I could not bring
My passions from a common spring—
From the same source I have not taken
My sorrow—I could not awaken
My heart to joy at the same tone—
And all I lov'd—I lov'd alone—
Then—in my childhood—in the dawn
Of a most stormy life—was drawn
From ev'ry depth of good and ill
The mystery which binds me still—
From the torrent, or the fountain—

From the red cliff of the mountain—
From the sun that 'round me roll'd
In its autumn tint of gold—
From the lightning in the sky
As it pass'd me flying by—
From the thunder, and the storm—
And the cloud that took the form
(When the rest of Heaven was blue)
Of an angel in my view—

"The last line is wrong. It should say 'Of a demon in my view.'"

Jared looked at his brother. "Think it's a code?"

"I need some paper." Lukas was already scribbling on his hand.

Elle riffled around in her junk drawer of a purse until she found an old history test. "Here."

Lukas flipped over the test and held it against the display case. He copied the last line of the poem and began systematically crossing out letters. We watched as he wrote random words down the side of the page, until he had exhausted the possibilities. "It's not letter substitution."

Priest studied the poem. "Try unscrambling it."

Lukas tried different combinations while the rest of us called out words with letters that weren't even in the line of the poem.

"What if you use the right version—'of a demon' instead?" Alara asked.

I stood in front of the poem again. This time, I visualized the words as if they were images in a painting—focusing on the shapes of the individual letters, the shape of the poem as a whole, and the negative space around the words. Nothing jumped out at me, but the label above the poem caught my eye: *Donated by Ramona Kennedy.*

It can't be a coincidence.

Lukas crumpled up the paper and chucked it on the floor. "The person who forged it was probably an idiot and screwed up."

Priest stared at the ceiling. "Or we need the Shift to read the message. It's probably sitting on some firefighter's mantel right now."

"Then we're screwed." Jared slammed his palm against the display case.

I couldn't take my eyes off the label. "My dad wrote that copy of the poem, or he had someone else do it for him."

The script didn't match the handwriting on the note he left my mom twelve years ago, but the forger had obviously copied Poe's style.

Jared interlaced his fingers with mine. "How can you tell?"

I pointed at the label. "I hated my name as a kid. Whenever I complained about it, my mom said the same thing: 'Maybe I should've gone with your father's first choice.' He wanted to name me Ramona, after his favorite band, the Ramones."

Mom was sipping coffee at the chipped round table in our kitchen while my dad stood in front of the stove, in his Jane's Addiction T-shirt, flipping pancakes.

"Ramona is a unique name, and the Ramones were punk rock gods," my dad said over the sizzle of bacon frying in the other pan.

Mom balled up her napkin and tossed it at him, smiling. "You're lucky I let you choose Kennedy's middle name."

"From your list. Rose was your grandmother's middle name." My dad munched on a piece of bacon and winked at me. "Ramona Kennedy would've been my pick."

I forced their voices out of my mind as Alara marched past me. She returned moments later, carrying a taxidermy goat with a mermaid tail from the front of the museum. She walked up to the display case and pulled her sleeve down, covering her hand. "Back up."

Elle covered her ears. "What if someone hears the glass break?"

Alara turned the goat so its horns faced the glass. "Like Lukas said, this place is closed. And it's in the middle of nowhere."

Jared reached for the mer-goat. "Why don't you let me—"

Alara swung the goat by its mermaid tail, releasing it just as the horns hit the case. A crack splintered down the middle of the case, from the spot where the tail was still sticking out of the glass.

"Nice." Jared shook his head at Alara. "I could be blind right now."

"Except you're not." She kicked the rest of the glass out from under what was left of the mer-goat. The poem fell off the wall and crashed to the floor, along with the animal.

"Feeling a little aggressive today?" Lukas picked up the broken frame and handed it to me, trying to keep it from falling apart.

Without the glass to hold it in place, the page slid out. Another piece of paper was folded in thirds behind the poem.

"What is it?" Elle asked as I unfolded it.

Black ink covered the crinkled white sheet of paper. Roads twisted through stick-figure trees and hand-drawn houses that reminded me of scavenger hunts at summer camp.

"A map."

7. CIRCLE OF SALT

MONDAY SEP. 3. 18

I recognized the gray weather-beaten house the moment I saw it. It was the one in the background of the photo I'd found tucked in my mirror the day Elle and I were packing up my bedroom, after my mom died. The details of the picture crystallized in my mind—my dad carrying me on his shoulders, the goofy kid smile plastered across my face.

Faith's house was nestled in the woods about a mile down an unmarked gravel road, like the one that led to the museum. We had passed a few other homes, but none of them were this deep in the woods.

Lukas parked the Jeep on the shoulder of the road.

On one side, there was nothing but a sea of snow-covered trees, and on the other, the forest sloped down, disappearing over the edges of jagged ridges.

I stood at the edge of a wide ridge with Alara and Elle. Faith's house was shrouded by towering pine trees. Without the map, it would've been difficult if not impossible to find.

"I've been there before," I said.

Elle sighed. "Please tell me we didn't hang out in that disgusting museum full of dead animals to find a map we didn't need. Those were two hours of my life I'll never get back."

Alara pushed past her. "And I bet you've wasted more time doing worse things."

"Ow." Elle rubbed her elbow. "Would it kill you to be a little nicer?"

"Yes." Alara headed toward the guys, who were busy drawing routes to Faith's house in the snow.

"Kennedy," Elle whispered. "I have to pee."

I gestured around us. "Choose a spot."

"Just make sure no one comes over here." She stepped away from the edge and trudged through the trees that ran parallel to the slope.

As I stared down at the house through the branches, I wondered what Faith Waters was like. How long had she been living out here? Did she have a family? And the unavoidable question: Did my father live here, too?

"Hey," Elle said, waving from between the trees. "I found a crop circle like the ones on *Ancient Aliens*."

Priest, Jared, and Lukas exchanged amused looks. Alara shook her head as if she couldn't imagine what Elle was going to come up with next.

Jared brushed the snow off his jeans and walked toward me. "There are no crops out here, Elle."

She put a hand on her hip and gave him her you're-about-to-get-dumped-after-two-dates look. "Thanks for enlightening me."

Lukas caught up to her first. His hands were jammed in his pockets and he nudged her playfully with his elbow. "Come on. Let's see it."

Lukas followed Elle to a small stretch of rock that formed a platform overlooking the trees below. When he reached the edge, he froze.

"Anything down there?" Alara asked.

"I told you." Elle stood next to him, smiling triumphantly.

When we caught up to them, Lukas pointed at the house. It was in the center of what looked like a dark gray crop circle. But instead of flattened grass, this circle was made by something else. "Check it out."

Alara squinted. "What is it?"

Lukas looked over at Jared and Priest, who hadn't taken their eyes off the house and the strange ring encircling it. "I don't know."

Jared drove us back down the road until we reached the base of the hill. We'd have to walk the rest of the way. Alara navigated her way between the trees easily while the rest of us tried to keep up.

The house was only about a half mile from the road, and the snowfall had let up a little.

"Does anyone else hear that?" Alara stopped walking and closed her eyes, listening. A delicate, almost musical sound drifted through the woods.

"Think it's the wind?" I asked.

"No." Alara wove through the trees, moving faster now.

With every step, the sound grew louder.

"It sounds like wind chimes," Jared said.

"I think so, too," Alara said.

But before we had a chance to find out, bits of gray wood became visible like puzzle pieces scattered through the trees. A moment later, the house—and a curved stretch of ground—came into view.

"It looks like someone carved the circle into the snow," I said.

"Or melted it into it." Alara stopped at the edge of a cluster of pines. "It's a salt line."

Chunks of rock salt glistened on the ground within the circle's snowy walls.

Jared stood behind me, with his arms wrapped around my waist. "Ever seen anything like it?"

"Not even close." Lukas shook his head and turned toward his brother, then looked away when he noticed Jared's arms around me. It didn't seem like jealousy, but the knee-jerk reaction of someone who was uncomfortable and just wanted the feeling to go away.

I wanted it to go away, too—for the awkwardness between us to disappear.

We stayed close to the tree line, working our way around to the front of the house. When we turned the corner, hundreds of metal wind chimes lined the porch, banging against one another. Some were made from strands of bottle caps, while forks and spoons dangled from others.

Jared covered his ears. "Is she trying to attract every spirit within a twenty-mile radius?"

"Some cultures believe wind chimes frighten spirits instead of attracting them," Alara said.

Priest flipped up the hood of his down jacket, waving his EMF. "The area's clean, paranormally speaking."

"When do I get an electromagnified ghost finder?" Elle asked, pointing at Priest's EMF, butchering *electromagnetic field meter* for the second time today.

Alara bent down and picked up a handful of rock salt. "When you remember what it's called."

When we reached the salt line, I leaned closer to Elle.

"Be careful not to break the salt line," I whispered. I didn't want her to make the same mistake I had.

Priest followed the curve around to the back of the house. "Anyone trying this hard to scare away spirits has to be a member of the Legion."

"Or totally paranoid," Elle said.

Priest stopped a few yards ahead of us. "I'm going with both."

A headstone rose up through the snow, the ground in front of it freshly turned over. Someone had dug a grave at the base of the headstone.

Elle gasped.

A stone dove perched on top of the marker, above looping script that stretched across the face.

FAITH MADIGAN

1972–

MAY SHE SLEEP WITH THE DOVES.

Faith Madigan—the first and middle names from the birth certificate Lukas found. Relief washed over me. She was real.

My dad's not the missing Legion member.

Alara bent down next to the headstone. "Think she dropped 'Waters'?"

"It's the first thing I'd do if I didn't want anyone to find me." Jared pulled my hand into his pocket.

Elle made a face. "Who digs their own grave?"

Priest peered into the hole. "Someone who knows they're being hunted."

Branches snapped somewhere on the other side of the house.

"Is that—?" I glanced behind me.

Alara backed away. "Barking."

A huge Doberman raced around the side of the house and slid into a crouch in front of us, growling.

Elle turned to run, but Lukas grabbed her arm. "Don't. He'll chase you."

"If that's all he does, you'll be lucky." A woman stepped out onto the porch, her face hidden beneath the folds of a hooded olive parka. She was holding a shotgun, the barrel pointed directly at us. "This is private property. I suggest you leave before he gets agitated. Or I do."

The dog barked louder, and Elle scooted behind Lukas.

"I don't see you moving." The woman stepped off the porch and froze when she saw me. She lowered the gun and pulled down her hood, her green eyes familiar and haunting.

My father's eyes flashed through my mind—a deep green flecked with gold, which had always reminded me of Christmas trees when I was young. The woman's eyes were the same unusual shade and almond shape.

"Bear. Come." She called the dog without taking her eyes off me. He stopped barking and padded over to her.

"Do you know who I am?" I asked.

She gave a small nod. "You look exactly like Alex."

My father.

Any lingering doubts about whether she was related to me disappeared.

"I don't know how you found me, but you shouldn't be here." The woman, who had to be my aunt, turned back toward the house. "Your mother wouldn't be happy about it."

"My mother's dead."

Faith stopped short, and her hand tightened around the gun hanging at her side. "Does anyone know you're here?"

I shook my head. "No."

Her eyes darted between us. "Who are they?" she asked me.

"My friends."

"They can wait out here." She scanned the property before turning back to me. "Get inside if you're coming in."

"I'd be dead if it wasn't for them," I said.

"She's not going anywhere without us." Jared pulled our intertwined hands out of his pocket so Faith could see them.

The Doberman growled. Faith snapped her fingers, silencing the dog, and gestured at the door with the shotgun barrel. "Don't touch anything."

At the top of the steps, a hand-painted symbol stretched across the floorboards—a tribal-looking eye.

Alara stopped at the edge of the white paint and looked at Faith. "How do you know about the Eye of Ever?"

"I know about lots of things, and I'd like to forget most of them," Faith said, holding the door open for us.

Priest nudged Alara. "What is it?"

"The Eye of Ever is an abating symbol," Alara said. "It weakens evil in any form."

Faith followed us inside and locked a dozen dead bolts that ran down the inside of the heavy door. She shrugged off her parka, sending a cascade of chestnut waves, exactly like mine, down her back.

From the entryway, the house looked normal enough—meaning it wasn't full of salt rings and wind chimes. The foyer faced a steep oak staircase that reminded me of the one in Lilburn Mansion, and I looked away. To the left of the stairs, a long hall stretched in front of us, with open archways leading into a series of rooms. Faith dropped her coat on a claw-foot bench and rushed into the room on the right.

Elle followed, stopping cold in the doorway. "Maybe someone should suggest curtains."

My aunt stood next to a huge bay window covered in garbage bags held together with long strips of silver duct tape. A pine table stacked with newspapers was the only piece of furniture in the room. Built-in bookcases lined the walls from floor to ceiling. More books littered the floor; some lay half-opened or piled in crooked towers, while others formed pedestals to support larger volumes.

I examined the nearest stack. Grimoires with crumbling spines, balanced on top of seventeenth-century atlases and texts with strange titles like *The Codex Demonotica*, *Documents of Illumination*, *Papal Seals and Ciphers*, and *The Amadeus Code*, as well as a copy of *The Complete Works of Hieronymus Bosch*.

Faith slid one of the shiny bags aside and peeked through the window. "How did you find me?"

"The map," Priest said. "Altering the poem was a smart way to hide it."

"Alex's idea. I move every few months, back and forth between several houses. We needed a system so my brother would always be able to find me." She mentioned my father's name casually, as though he was someone I saw every day instead of the man who had abandoned me.

"Where's Alex now?" Elle asked.

"I'm not sure." Faith gave her a strange look and rushed past us.

Bear trailed after her, unfazed.

The hallway spilled into a great room, where a fireplace crackled in the corner and a sweet floral scent drifted from the kitchen.

Alara eyed the room suspiciously. "This place doesn't look like it belongs to someone who tapes trash bags over their windows."

The same thought crossed my mind, until I saw the rest of the room.

Stacks of canvases depicting apocalyptic scenes leaned against the walls—cavernous holes torn in the ground with hands reaching up from inside them; a guy chained in a cell, with a strange symbol drawn on his back; people being dragged through the streets by metal collars around their necks. The images looked like they were straight out of Dante's *Inferno* or one of Hieronymus Bosch's paintings of hell.

Haunting portraits of spirits with pallid skin and angry eyes were lined up alongside more disturbing paintings of figures with flat, pupil-less black eyes. Faith emerged from the kitchen, her attention shifting nervously between the six of us and the paintings.

I approached one of the larger canvases. A figure writhed in pain behind the bars of a cell. Steam or smoke rose from his body. "You paint? Me too."

Faith glanced at the image, then looked away as if she couldn't stand the sight of it. "Hopefully, your work is nothing like mine."

Priest stood in front of an *Inferno*-style piece. "You've seen some of this stuff, haven't you?"

"Most of them are only nightmares." My aunt leaned against a tall painting and used her weight to slide it down the wall. The canvas moved, revealing a bookcase behind it.

"And the others?" I asked.

"Things you should pray you never see," Faith said, pulling books off the shelves two and three at a time, until she found what she was looking for—a brass doorknob attached to the back of a shelf. She turned the knob and the bookcase opened like a door.

The closet behind it was packed from floor to ceiling with what looked like disaster supplies.

"Your aunt is officially crazy," Elle whispered.

Faith tossed duct tape, rope, batteries, and ammo onto the floor behind her. Once she had cleared a few feet of space, she struggled to drag out a huge burlap sack.

"Need a hand?" Lukas walked toward her, and Bear growled. Lukas stepped back, his hands raised. "Relax, Cujo."

My aunt snapped her fingers and the Doberman loped down the hall and stood guard at the front door. Faith ripped the string across the top of the sack, and rock salt spilled onto the floor. She used a plastic milk jug with the top cut off as a scoop and raced through the house pouring salt lines along the windows and doors, which were already heavily salted.

"I'm sorry about your mother. But you shouldn't have come here."

"If you tell us what's going on, maybe we can help," Alara said in the even tone she usually reserved for volatile spirits.

Faith slid a rubber band from a yellowed newspaper and gathered her hair in a ponytail with it. "You wouldn't believe me if I told you."

"I'm pretty sure we will." Priest scooped a fistful of salt from the sack and pulled up his sleeve. He rubbed the crystals over his wrist and lines carved themselves into his skin.

Faith watched in awe as the cuts formed one-fifth of Andras' seal. The original Legion members had used the seal to summon him, and each of them had branded a section of the symbol into his skin, in an attempt to bind the demon.

Jared, Lukas, and Alara dusted their own wrists with salt. One by one, their marks appeared, each forming another part of the seal.

I stared at my boots and counted the scratches on the toes, anything to distract myself from the envy I hated myself for feeling.

Faith gasped and turned to Elle and me.

I didn't give her a chance to ask the question. "If we're right about who you are, then you know I don't have a mark."

Elle threw up her hands. "Don't look at me. I don't have any demon tattoos. I'm just here to make sure my best friend doesn't get herself killed."

My aunt turned back to the real Legion members. "I've never seen the marks together before."

"Wanna see all five?" Priest asked.

Faith held her wrist over the sack and rubbed it with salt. Lines carved themselves into her skin, revealing the final section of Andras' seal.

I had imagined holding my wrist where Faith's was now—being the missing piece of the Legion puzzle and the person to finally complete it.

When the demon's seal faded, Priest brushed off his wrist. "Now that we know we're all on the same side, I'm Priest. It's my name, not my occupation."

Lukas didn't bother with formalities. "I'm Lukas, and this is my brother, Jared. You're not an easy person to find."

Faith stared at them like she was just now registering that they were identical twins. Then she switched back into survival mode, digging through a box full of flashlights and changing the batteries at a dizzying speed. "That's the idea, Lukas."

Jared took an extra screwdriver from the toolbox and helped her. "Miss Madigan, right?"

"Just Faith."

"Think you can take a break?" Alara asked. "We came a long way to talk to you."

"And you would be?"

"*Just* Alara."

Elle waved. "Hi. I'm Elle."

I took a deep breath. Telling her my name made the fact that I was standing in front of my father's sister feel real. "I'm—"

"Kennedy." She stopped digging through the box. "I was there the day you were born."

For a moment, I didn't know how to respond. How many times had she seen me before? Were she and my mom close? "I have a picture of my dad and me in front of this house. But I don't remember you."

"You were young the last time I saw you. Maybe five or six."

"Five. I was five." Certain things stay with you, like how old you were the last time you saw your father. "Why haven't I seen you since?"

Faith hauled a box of batteries out of the closet. "I was in hiding, and your father had—"

"Ditched me by then."

Faith's expression clouded over. "Alex did what he had to do."

Tears pricked my eyes, but my aunt had already gone back to whatever it was she was doing.

Lukas noticed my reaction and jumped in. "We didn't come here to fill out the missing branches of Kennedy's family tree. There's something you need to know. Except for you, we're all that's left of the Legion."

"The other four—our family members—all died on the same night two months ago," Alara added.

"And my mom," I said.

"Why Elizabeth? Kennedy's mother wasn't part of the Legion." Faith emphasized every word as though the idea was unthinkable.

"The demon made a mistake," Lukas said, covering for his brother.

Jared stared at his hands. No one except Lukas and I knew that Jared's innocent search for the Legion members had led Andras right to their doors. Any mention of our dead family members seemed physically painful for him.

After what I'd done, I finally understood the weight of that kind of guilt. The way one mistake could feel like ten thousand. I carried that feeling with me every minute of every day.

Priest pulled at the strings of his hoodie. "It was an execution. And Andras' vengeance spirits have been hunting us ever since."

"That's why we came," I said. "We need your help."

Faith looked back at us. "You don't know what you're up against. This is a fight you can't win. Split up and disappear like I did. Before it's too late."

"It's already too late." I let the truth spill out before I could change my mind. "Andras is free."

She shook her head, dismissing the idea. "It's easy to mistake a demonic entity for the demon himself. Andras can't break free from the prison holding him. It's not easy to explain, but there are safeguards in place."

"You mean the Shift?" Priest took out his journal and flipped to the diagram.

Faith stepped closer. "I've never seen it before, only a piece."

"The one you gave Darien Shears?" Lukas asked.

She turned around slowly. "Where did you hear that name?"

"From Darien's spirit. We had a little run-in with him at the prison." Alara studied my aunt, measuring her reaction. "He told us a woman gave him the cylinder—the last piece of the Shift—and asked him to keep it safe."

"Shears said it was his chance at redemption," Lukas said.

My aunt stared at them in shock.

"You and my grandmother were the only women in the Legion," Alara said. "You're the woman who gave him the cylinder, aren't you?"

"There's no way you would know about that unless you found it." Her eyes went wild. "Where is it? You have no idea what that device can do."

I didn't want to tell her the next part.

"I assembled it."

8. THE BLOOD OF ANGELS

Then Andras is free." Faith slumped against the wall, her shoulders sagging. "And the clock is ticking."

"Until what?" Priest asked when she started to turn away.

"Andras opens the gates and invites the rest of the demons to his party up here." Faith stifled a bitter laugh.

"How do we stop him?" Jared asked.

She took a deep breath and rubbed her neck. "Andras isn't some vengeance spirit you can destroy with salt rounds. He is a marquis of hell. The incarnation of evil. He's everywhere and nowhere, and he *will* find us."

"With all five members of the Legion, we stand a chance," Priest said.

Faith gave him a strange look. "You honestly believe I even the odds against a demon?"

Lukas slipped his journal out of his jacket pocket. "My dad always talked about how much stronger the Legion would be if all five members were together."

She shook her head. "And you think that means we have some kind of superpowers?"

"Of course not." Lukas frowned.

Faith sighed. "When the Legion members are together, they *can* raise a protective barrier. Priests used grimoiric magic and seals to protect themselves from evil for centuries. The barrier is an extension of that principle, but it can't help us hurt Andras. It keeps him from hurting us."

"That's it?" Priest picked at the silver duct tape on his headphones. "The five of us get together and it makes what—a force field?"

"I'm sorry you thought it meant something else. But we aren't talking about catching a stray dog and dropping it off at the pound." Faith stopped pacing and looked him in the eye. "Do you know your Legion history? What happened the night our ancestors in the Legion summoned Andras?"

"Markus Lockhart drew the Devil's Trap. But he screwed it up, and they lost control of Andras." Priest sounded like he was tired of recounting the story. "We know everything except the part about what happened to the angel."

My aunt stiffened. "Your families certainly didn't tell you much."

Alara hooked a thumb under the edge of her leather tool belt. "Then why don't you fill us in?"

Faith slipped back inside the hidden closet behind the bookshelf and came out carrying a brown leather-bound book embossed in gold.

"Is that your journal?" Alara sounded hopeful.

Faith dismissed the possibility with a wave of her hand. "Of course not. Someone who's been running as long as I have knows better than to keep anything irreplaceable with them. This book belonged to my father. The journal he inherited was in terrible condition, so he transcribed the older entries into this book. He died before he finished, but he did transcribe the most important entry—the one from the night Andras was summoned."

Priest's eyes widened, and Alara looked like she was holding her breath. The story none of them knew—the missing puzzle pieces—were written on the pages in my aunt's hand.

"What exactly were you told?" Faith asked.

"My journal has an entry about the plan." Lukas held it up.

Jared shoved his hands in his pockets. "The one in mine was written after everything went bad. A lot of stuff about unleashing the beast and Markus taking the blame for whatever happened to the angel. He said her blood was on their hands."

"Which makes it sound like she died that night," Alara said.

Elle gave her a strange look. "Angels can't die."

"How do you know? Have you ever met one?" Alara shot back.

Faith rested the book on one of the taller stacks so we could see it. "You should read it for yourselves. There's nothing more dangerous than going to war without knowing your enemy."

15th December 1776
Nathaniel Madigan

As I write this, I fear God will not forgive us for what we have done. I know I will never forgive myself. But our errors on this night must be recorded, even if our sins cannot be erased.

With only candlelight to guide him, it is no surprise Markus' hand betrayed him. Julian read from the grimoire, and the five of us spoke the words to summon the demon. In my darkest dreams, I never imagined seeing the true face of evil—a creature that was not man nor beast but something in between.

Markus prepared the angelic summoning circle, and we called the angel Anarel to control the beast. She appeared, her tattered wings reaching out like crooked fingers on an old woman's hand. Anarel's ferocity rivaled that of the beast himself. With features cut from the finest stone, she did not resemble the winged protectors painted on the ceilings of the city's wealthiest churches. She seemed as angry to be called as Andras. But unlike the angel, the marquis of hell was amused.

Julian spoke first, facing the beast without fear. "Andras, Author of Discords, we call you to do our bidding in the name of His Holiness. We command you to seek out the men who call themselves the Illuminati and—"

The demon laughed. "You dare to command me? I command six thousand legions in the Labyrinth, and you stand before me, five men, and this"—he faced the angel with disdain—"castoff, as if you have the power to control me?"

The angel showed no emotion as she responded to the beast. "This would not be the first time I have commanded you, Andras. Or the first time you have bent to my will."

In that moment, all things happened at once.

Andras crossed the circle and looked into Markus' eyes.

Then he stepped inside our friend's body, and Markus' chest expanded, as though he were taking a deep breath. His back stiffened, and he stood straighter than any man I had ever seen.

When Andras had filled him, Markus turned toward the angel, cracking his neck as though his bones were stiff from days of sleep. The demon's shining ebony eyes replaced Markus' green ones.

Markus opened his mouth, but the voice that spoke to us was not his own. "I should thank you all for inviting me into this world.

96

The Devil's Labyrinth is crowded, with fewer souls to harvest. I prefer my space." He turned to Anarel, whose terrifying and tattered wings flickered in and out of view like a candle flame.

From her belt she drew a sword, clear in places and stained with dark streaks in others. "Killing you will be a great honor. One for which I will be greatly rewarded."

Konstantin stepped forward, his rosary and Bible in hand. "Markus is an innocent, possessed by the darkest of evil. You are an angel, a messenger of God."

Anarel's tattered wings rippled in the candlelight, and she faced Konstantin with the same disdain she had shown the demon. "A messenger? That is what you believe me to be? I am a soldier for a father you do not know. My loyalty is to him, not you. Soon enough, _the sins of man will rival those of the demons in hell_." The angel raised her sword. "There are no innocents among you."

In futile desperation, Konstantin began to recite the Rite of Exorcism. Julian, who knew the words by heart, ripped the crucifix from his own neck and joined him:

"I cast you out, unclean spirit,
along with every Satanic power of the enemy,
every spectre from hell,
and all your fell companions;
in the name of our Lord Jesus Christ."

In a flurry, the angel lunged with her sword at the demon inside Markus' body. Another blade, infinitely smaller,

97

forged from steel by the hands of men, shot forth from Vincent's hand.

This ordinary blade cut through Anarel's glistening chest plate.

The angel seized, and blood as black as coal soaked the floor of the church.

Vincent dropped the dagger.

The man who killed an angel.

It is the name they will give him in books written hundreds of years from now.

Andras reared back his head, thrashing and jerking as Konstantin and Julian continued the rite, their voices unwavering.

The angel held her wound with one hand and drew something from beneath her chest plate with the other. Anarel raised the object above her head, her wings hiding it. "From the gallows of hell you emerged, and in the prison between that world and this one, you shall be exiled. Command your legion there, Andras. The only way I would send you back to hell is skinned like the beasts that serve you."

A blinding light burned my eyes.

"With this key, I open the door to your prison," the angel said, holding her wound.

A shrill sound ripped from Markus' throat and pierced my eardrums.

I turned away and covered my ears, knowing that if I survived this night, that sound would haunt my every waking hour.

May the black dove always carry you—and us all.

⸙ I closed the book and handed it back to my aunt. "Thanks for letting us read it."

"Unfortunately, that isn't the end of the story." Faith paced in front of us, stopping in exactly the same spot each time before she turned and followed the path back in the opposite direction.

"OCD much?" Elle whispered.

"The Legion went back to the Vatican that night. But when the pope learned they had lost control of Andras and failed to deliver the Illuminati members, he deemed them enemies of the Church. As excommunicated priests, the Legion members were well versed in the way the Church dealt with its enemies. So they fled through the tunnels under Vatican City. But they didn't leave empty-handed. They took the *Diario di Demoni*—the private journals of the Vatican's exorcists."

"Exorcism records?" Alara asked. "Seems like a weird choice."

"Not weird. Smart." Faith paced faster. "No one knew more about demons than the Catholic Church's exorcists, and the *Demoni* was filled with their firsthand accounts."

"Were they trying to exorcise Andreas?" Elle asked.

My aunt scowled at her.

"It's Andras," Lukas whispered.

Elle rolled her eyes. "Whatever. It's not like he's here to be offended."

Faith waited to make sure Elle didn't have any more

stupid questions, and then she continued. "*The Art of War*: 'To know your Enemy, you must become your Enemy.' If you want to destroy a demon, you have to know everything about them. According to the *Diario di Demoni*, demons don't want to live in hell any more than we do. They like it here."

Lukas shook his head. "More good news."

My aunt ignored him, lost in her own manic train of thought. "But when demons cross over, they aren't strong enough to take their true forms."

"I don't like where this is going," Priest said under his breath.

"Until they consume enough souls to regain their strength, demons need human bodies to possess."

"Consume?" Elle winced as she said it.

"Demons feed off violence, so they entice people to kill or brutalize each other. If a person racks up enough sin, when they die—or kill themselves, which is often the case when the devil's soldiers are involved—the demon consumes their soul."

I thought about the Boy Scouts leader who had killed his troop and the fireman who set his neighbors' homes on fire. In the past nineteen days, most of the mass murderers ended up killing themselves.

Faith glanced at the canvases in the next room. "If Andras opens the gates of hell, the people whose souls the demons don't consume, or whose bodies they don't use as

100

temporary housing, will be enslaved or tortured for their amusement."

I pictured my nightmares and the images in Faith's paintings. "Our world will become the new hell."

Jared's expression hardened. "I'm not okay with that."

"Unless you have a magic wand or the Vessel, you won't have a say in the matter," Faith said. "The Vessel is the only prison that can hold Andras."

"Where do we find this Vessel?" I asked.

No one had ever mentioned it before, which seemed strange. Jared, Lukas, Priest, and Alara listened, waiting for her answer.

My aunt stared at us like we were idiots. "No idea. You're the ones who lost it."

"She's talking about the Shift," Priest said.

Faith nodded. "And without it, there's no way to stop Andras."

Lukas stepped in front of Faith before she could start pacing again. "How do we keep him from opening the gates?"

She stared at him for a long moment, sadness passing over the green eyes that looked so much like my father's. "Once he gets strong enough, you can't."

9. BULLETS AND BEAR TRAPS

The closet door slammed behind Faith, and within seconds, the doors upstairs began slamming one by one, like falling dominoes.

Bear crouched at the base of the steps, snarling.

Faith raced to the windows and checked the salt lines. When she turned around, the blood had drained from her face. "None of them are broken."

Lukas yanked a paintball gun from the waistband of his jeans. Instead of paint, the casings were filled with Alara's holy-water cocktail. "I'll check upstairs."

Alara followed him, taking the steps two at a time.

Faith pointed at the second landing. "Bear. Search."

The Doberman vaulted up the steps.

"How can I get a dog like that?" Priest asked.

"Spend five years putting one through combat training." Faith hit a button on the wall with the side of her fist. The fire sprinklers above us hissed, and salt water rained down from the ceiling.

The lights flickered, and the dead bolts on the front door unlocked themselves from top to bottom, in rapid succession, and then locked again in reverse order.

"None of the salt lines are broken up here, either," Alara called from the upstairs landing.

My aunt kicked back the corner of the braided rug on the floor and worked one of the floorboards free. A modified assault weapon, right out of a video game, was hidden inside. When she flipped a switch near the trigger, green lights illuminated across the top of the barrel.

Priest's eyes widened. "That's a masterpiece of badassery."

"It's a crowd-control—" Faith started.

"A semiautomatic air-burst crowd-control weapon, with a laser range finder," Priest finished. "In the military, they call it the Punisher."

Jared wiped his eyes with his sleeve. "I don't care what they call it, as long as it works."

Salt water continued to hiss from the sprinklers, flooding the first floor and coating everything in a sticky film.

"There's nothing up here." Lukas headed back down the stairs with Alara.

Bear leapt ahead of them. When the dog reached the bottom stair, he froze, and Lukas almost tripped over him. Bear stared up at the ceiling, transfixed, a low growl rumbling in his throat.

"He probably doesn't like the sprinklers," Alara said.

Faith followed the dog's gaze and raised her weapon. "That's not it."

Every light in the house switched on simultaneously.

I waited for the lights to flicker. Instead, they changed from a dingy yellow to a deep crimson.

"What's happening?" Elle whirled around, her skin bathed in the same bloody tint as the rest of the room.

Red bursts bled into my peripheral vision like a strip of film that had been removed from the darkroom too soon. Cherry-stained streaks ran down the walls like blood. My stomach lurched, and I stumbled back.

Priest caught my elbow.

"Is it a poltergeist?" I remembered the way my house had come to life a few months ago.

"No." Alara shook her head without tearing her eyes away from the walls. "A visual haunting."

The room seemed to tilt, and Faith gripped the banister. "This house was clean before the six of you showed up. What did you bring in here?"

"Nothing," I said.

The sprinklers spluttered as the last of the salt water choked its way out.

"A vengeance spirit couldn't make it through my door unless it attached itself to one of you." The words had barely left my aunt's lips when a clock chimed upstairs. A second later, an oven timer went off in the kitchen and the doorbell started ringing over and over.

"Did you come straight here from the museum?" Faith shouted over the noise.

Lukas pressed the heels of his hands against his eyelids. "Yes."

"What about inside? Did you touch anything?"

Jared backed away from the bleeding wall. "Of course we did. How do you think we found the map?"

My aunt splashed through the ankle-deep water in the hallway. "The map can't be haunted. I made it. Anything else?"

Priest shrugged. "A giant bottle cap, and I might've touched a few of those dead squirrels with the swords."

"But you didn't take anything from inside?"

"No." Priest sounded annoyed.

"Um..." Elle stalled. "I didn't *take* anything. But I did *find* something on the floor." She pulled up her sleeve. A gold art deco cuff clung to her wrist.

"Take it off." Faith held out her hand, and Elle complied.

All at once, the doorbell stopped ringing and the room fell silent. The color flashes subsided and the red hue blanketing the rooms faded, working its way down from the ceiling.

Elle let out a long breath. "It's over."

Jared, Lukas, Alara, and Faith scanned the room, less convinced.

"You never remove crap from a place like that," Alara said. "Museums are almost as bad as yard sales. I bet half the junk people buy at those things is haunted."

I didn't realize objects could be haunted, which meant Elle definitely had no idea. My experience was limited to dybbuks—demonic entities trapped in sealed containers—the real-life version of Pandora's box.

By now, the ceiling and upper two-thirds of the walls were white again, and the crimson stain filtered toward the floor. Bear growled, his gaze fixed on the waterline along the baseboards. As the stain seeped into the water, the flooded hallway turned into the Red Sea. The stain spread across the surface like an oil spill, moving unnaturally fast.

Jared sloshed down the hall. "We need to burn the bracelet. It might not be enough to destroy the spirit, but maybe it will banish it." He found a steel bowl full of batteries and emptied it.

Faith stumbled back, looking terrified. "The windows are salted, and there's a salt circle around the house. The spirit is trapped in here with us. We need to get out of the house."

A crack snaked its way down the wall next to the front door the moment she spoke the words, and Bear's growl turned feral. Drywall exploded and a thick black wire ripped itself out of the wall.

"Get out of the water!" Lukas yelled.

Priest caught Elle around the waist and hurled his body against the steps, taking her with him.

Jared stood in the hallway and scanned the room, his muscles tense, until he saw me standing safely on the staircase. He jumped and caught the banister, letting his body hang over the side of the staircase.

Faith splashed toward us.

"Take my hand." Alara reached for her.

Just as their fingertips touched and my aunt's boot hit the step, the wire reared back like a viper. It struck the water and a spray of sparks erupted from the point of contact.

Electricity splintered through the water, the salt acting as the ultimate conduit.

The force threw Faith forward and her body slammed against the wooden staircase. She moaned and rolled onto her side, cradling her wrist.

Alara knelt down and helped her sit up. "We have to get that bracelet out of the house."

The wire hovered over the water, then struck again.

"I need your pouch. Can you empty it?" Faith pointed at the bag of salt tucked in Alara's tool belt.

Alara dumped out the salt and handed it to her. "What are you going to do?"

"I'm not even sure it will work." My aunt dropped the gold cuff from the museum into the bag and tied it closed with her uninjured hand. "Bear. Come."

The Doberman darted to her side, awaiting my aunt's next command.

Faith pointed at the window covered in trash bags. "We need to shoot out the glass."

Alara slid a paintball gun from the waist of her cargo pants. "Done."

My aunt turned to me. "Are you a good shot?"

"I can hit the window, if that's what you're asking."

"Give Kennedy the Punisher," she said to Priest.

He lifted the heavy weapon. "I've got it. This thing's gonna have some hard-core kickback."

Faith threw him a hard stare. "My mother used to say that girls should be seen and not heard. I say we should be seen and *feared*. Give Kennedy the gun."

Priest handed me the weapon, and my aunt explained the basics. The ammo was packed with holy water and rock salt. To ensure an accurate shot, I had to lie on my stomach sniper-style and fire from the landing.

The wire jabbed at the water again, a few feet from the staircase.

"On three," Alara said, as we aimed together. "One. Two. Three."

I squeezed the trigger. The butt of the Punisher rammed against my shoulder, round after round. Glass exploded from the panes, sending sheets of black plastic fluttering into the air.

"That's enough," Faith called out.

Even after I stopped firing, my muscles kept vibrating and the sound from the shots echoed in my ears.

Lukas grabbed the back of Jared's jacket and hauled him over the railing.

Faith bent down and offered Bear the pouch. The dog took it in his mouth and waited. She slid a small metal flashlight out of her pocket and shined the light on the bench in the hallway. Bear snapped to attention, his eyes locked on Faith.

"Jump," she said.

The Doberman leapt from the stairs. He landed on the bench and turned toward Faith, awaiting the next command.

This time, she shined the flashlight on the dining room table, in front of the window we had just destroyed. "Jump."

The dog crouched and focused on the pale circle of light in the center of the table. I held my breath as he sprang. Bear's paws hit the wood, and he skidded across the table.

My aunt didn't waste any time. She pointed the beam through the bay window and into the yard beyond it.

One of the dining room walls cracked, and another wire began to work itself free.

Faith didn't hesitate. "Take it outside, Bear."

The dog focused on the circle of light and catapulted himself toward the glass jutting from the frame. Bear's lithe body sailed through the glass jaws, and he disappeared into the darkness.

The electrical wires twisted in the air. By now, every inch of the floor was soaked—including the staircase we standing on. The wires reared back, their black plastic coating pulsing like a paranormal heartbeat inside them.

I held my breath.

The wires dropped into the red water like stones, and the pigment began to fade.

"Bear must've crossed the salt circle," Faith said. "He'll take the bag into the woods and leave it there, the way I trained him." She leaned against the wall and exhaled slowly. "You're lucky a random vengeance spirit attached itself to that bracelet, and not Andras, or this would've been a lot worse."

Jared looked at the water on the floor. "Think it's safe?" he asked Priest.

Priest tossed a cold-iron round into the flooded hallway. When nothing happened, he jumped down, his green Nikes splashing in the water. "We're good." He opened the basement door and a rush of clear water ran down the stairs.

"You okay?" Jared stood in front of me with damp hair and anxious eyes.

I only nodded, watching as he knelt next to Faith and examined her wrist.

"I'm fine," she said, snatching her hand away. "There are towels upstairs, second door on the left."

My aunt walked down the stairs and waded through the water until she reached her survival closet. Faith unearthed an emergency splint buried underneath a stash of first-aid supplies, including dental extraction instruments and a suturing field kit. She reached for a box of ammo, and the box slipped from her fingers, sending the rounds clattering to the floor. One hit the edge of my boot, and I picked up the shell.

The shell in my palm wasn't a salt round.

It was a bullet.

"Bullets won't stop a demon." Alara picked up another shell and handed it to Faith. "You're better off with salt rounds."

"Thanks for the tip," Faith said. "But I'm not planning to use them on a demon."

Goose bumps pricked my arms.

From the wind chimes and the salt ring to the stockpiled supplies and apocalyptic paintings, Faith's paranoia marked every inch of the property and her every action. But until now, she had seemed sane.

Maybe she isn't.

"Are you saying you're going to shoot someone, Faith?" I asked, afraid of her answer. She was my only connection to the Legion and my father—no matter how much I hated him. Eccentric and antisocial and paranoid I could handle, as long as she wasn't crazy.

My aunt finished winding a strip of tape around the splint and headed for the kitchen. She paused in the doorway.

"The demon isn't the only one hunting me."

EP. 6.18
09

We should give her a little space," I said after my aunt retreated into the kitchen. "She seems more stressed out than when we first got here."

"If by *stressed out*, you mean *crazy*, then I agree." Alara sat down on the steps.

"She's been on the run, moving from house to house, for more than a decade," Priest said. "Cut her some slack."

Jared shook his head. "It's more than that. She was loading her gun with bullets."

Bear poked his head through the broken bay window. Alara whistled, and the dog jumped over the jagged pieces of glass and trotted over to her. He sat down next to Alara, and she scratched his head.

Elle glanced at the door. "Maybe we should leave. I don't think she wants us here."

"We can't." Lukas appeared at the top of the stairs and dropped a few towels over the side of the railing. "She's still the fifth member of the Legion. Even if she won't help us, we need to find out what else she knows about Andras." He ran a faded gray towel over his wet hair. "And what Faith is hiding from."

Elle wadded up her towel and threw it at him. "The demon. Even I know that."

He caught it with one hand and smiled at her. "Andras has been free for less than a month. Kennedy's aunt has been in hiding for years."

"So we hang tight and wait until she comes back out," Priest said, a towel still draped over his blond hair.

All of a sudden, a loud bang came from the kitchen, like someone had smashed two heavy pots together.

"Or not," I said.

Priest walked into the kitchen first and almost slipped. The floor was covered with black trash bags, with at least a dozen bear traps scattered on top of them.

"Be careful." Faith stood by the sink, wearing a welder's apron and a yellow dishwashing glove on her uninjured hand.

The floral scent I'd noticed earlier was overpowering in here.

"Is that wintersweet?" Alara asked.

My aunt carried a soup can over to one of the traps and painted the teeth with a sticky pink substance that looked like raspberry preserves. "You're a smart girl. Most people wouldn't recognize it."

Alara held out her arm so none of us could get any closer. "Faith, people call that stuff 'bushman's poison' for a reason. If it spills, the sap will kill you."

My aunt dipped the brush in the can and painted another trap. "Then I guess I'd better be careful."

Elle pushed up on her toes to get a better look. "What are you gonna do with those anyway?"

"Protect us." Faith wrapped one of the traps in a plastic tarp and carried it outside, before returning for the others one by one.

We watched as she positioned the traps around the perimeter of the house. Jared offered to help, but Faith refused. I held my breath each time she unwrapped a poison-tainted trap.

When she came back inside, Priest didn't waste any time. "Bullets and bear traps? None of this stuff will protect you from a demon. Who are you really hiding from, Faith?"

When she realized we were all waiting for the answer, her irritation turned to shock. "You really don't know."

"So tell us," Alara said.

"The Illuminati."

Priest staggered back a few steps. "Are you sure, Faith?" he asked. "Because I think my granddad was the

115

last Legion member to see any of them, and that was over forty years ago."

My aunt pressed her lips together and swallowed hard, steeling herself. "If they kidnap me again, I'll ask for identification. But they interrogated me for three days, so I think I'm qualified to make that call."

For a moment no one moved or said a word.

"Why did they kidnap you? What did they want to know?" Alara finally asked.

"Something they didn't find out. Something I'll take to the grave. But when I go, I'm taking a few of those bastards with me."

"If Andras opens the gates, I'm pretty sure he'll kill them all for you," Lukas said. "I know it's a long shot, but if you help us, maybe we can stop him."

"I'm not going to help you kill yourselves." Faith's stoic expression and her rigid posture made it clear she wasn't going to change her mind.

"I'll take your place," I said automatically.

Faith spun around. "It doesn't work that way, Kennedy. The duty rests with me until I die or pass it down to a successor."

"Then pass it down to me." If anyone warranted a life sentence of defending the world from demons and spirits, it was me.

My aunt's face turned ashen. "Your father would never want you to be part of this."

Rage exploded inside me. "My father left me. He didn't even bother to show up after my mom died. I don't care what he'd want, and I'm already part of this."

Faith stared at me, speechless. "He made mistakes, Kennedy. But there are things you don't know. I will not put his only child in harm's way."

"And letting Andras get strong enough to open the gates isn't putting me in harm's way?"

Faith peeled off the yellow glove and tossed it in the sink, then shouldered past me without a word.

When my aunt reached the doorway, she stopped. "Your father isn't the man you think he is, and even if the sky came crashing down around me, I would *never* pass this godforsaken curse on to you."

⇥ • ⇤

I stood in front of Faith's bedroom door, summoning my courage. There were so many things I wanted to ask her, so many questions she might be able to answer.

As I raised my hand to knock, the door opened.

My aunt stood on the other side wearing jeans and a flannel shirt, her hair braided down her back. One look around her bedroom convinced me the outfit was probably Faith's version of pajamas.

The Eye of Ever was painted on the ceiling above a four-poster bed, sandwiched between rows of overflowing metal shelves—with everything from plastic milk jugs of holy water and mason jars packed with rock salt to dog-eared road atlases and enormous crucifixes that looked like they belonged above church altars.

On the lower shelves, she had enough weapons to arm a small village. I couldn't look at them without wondering how many of those guns were loaded with bullets instead of salt rounds. Bear slept beneath the shelves, his bed wedged between cases of ammo and stacks of unfinished paintings.

"Do you need something?" Faith asked.

"I wanted to ask you a few things. If that's okay."

Bear lifted his head from the dog bed, as if he was waiting to see if she would invite me in. She glanced over her shoulder, frowning.

"My room is a little—"

"My room is messy, too," I blurted out. "At least, it used to be."

Faith stepped back and opened the door. "I was going to say *private*."

This is going well.

"I can go." I started to turn around.

"It's fine." My aunt opened the door wider and gestured for me to come inside. "You must have a lot of questions. I never thought your mother would wait this long to tell you the truth." She looked away.

"I guess she never got the chance. Now you're the only

family I have left, except for my mom's sister, and she and my mother weren't close."

Faith crossed the room and leaned against one of the shelves. "I remember Diane. Bitchy and annoying."

I laughed, and a smile tugged at the corner of Faith's mouth.

"Diane isn't your only family," she said.

"Don't." I raised my hand to stop her. She was talking about my father. "Please."

Faith busied herself in front of the shelves, checking the labels on the containers to make sure they were all facing the same direction.

"I was wondering about the kidnapping. You went into hiding after that, right?" I couldn't ask her what I really wanted to know—if her kidnapping was the reason my dad left.

She took a deep breath. "I went into hiding for other reasons."

And my dad left for other reasons.

Faith stopped turning the jars. "My life wasn't always like this. Everything changed when I met Archer. He was handsome and charming, and I was young and stupid. Your parents had been married for about a year, and your mom disliked him right away. She told me you couldn't trust a man who didn't like dogs."

Bear's ears perked up.

"But I was already falling in love with him by then, and I didn't listen." She looked back at me. "I should have."

"So she was right about him?"

"I met Archer at the farmers' market, but it wasn't an accident. He knew I'd be there, just like he knew I loved chocolate chip cookies and disaster movies—and that I was part of the Legion. He was a member of the Illuminati, a sleeper." She paused, as if the subject was too painful to talk about. "His assignment was to earn my trust and find out everything he could about the Legion. And my dreams."

"Your dreams?"

"I have what are called prophetic dreams. I see things, and some of them end up happening." She rubbed her eyes, the shadows beneath them even darker than mine.

I remembered what she said when we saw her paintings.

I hope your dreams are nothing like mine.

"Your paintings."

She nodded. "After we learned the truth about Archer, Alex sent me into hiding. I didn't want anything else to do with the Legion."

My chest tightened at the mention of my father's name.

"Unfortunately, the Illuminati caught up with me. But only once."

"What gave Archer away?" I asked.

"Your mother was the one who finally put it all

together. I should have realized then—" Faith stopped and blinked back tears. "Some bones should stay buried."

"Thanks for telling me what happened." As much as I wanted to know more, it didn't seem fair to ask any more questions after I had dredged up such painful memories.

"Good night, Kennedy Rose."

I stopped, my hand on the doorknob. Hearing her say my middle name—the one my father had chosen—made me wonder what else she knew.

"Why did my dad leave?" I kept my hand on the knob and my back to her. Asking the question out loud was hard enough.

"It's complicated, and it's not really my story to tell. But if it makes you feel any better, he didn't want to go."

I pushed open the door. "It doesn't."

11. PROMISES IN THE DARK

As I climbed the rickety stairs to the attic, the railing swayed. Or maybe it was me. After my conversation with Faith, everything felt off balance.

The room didn't help.

Crossbows and rifles hung from metal hooks on the attic's Peg-Board walls—along with knives, Tasers, chains, and a pickax. Another reminder of the war we were fighting.

Jared sat on top of a sleeping bag in the middle of it all, with his elbows propped on his knees, staring out the window.

Alara and Elle had claimed the remaining bedroom in the house, outfitted with a fold-out sofa hidden behind a wall of bundled newspapers. When I saw the sofa, I wondered if my father had ever slept there. Priest and Lukas ended up in my aunt's great room, surrounded by her paintings. They seemed that to sense that Jared and I needed time alone, or they didn't want to get stuck in the attic with the two of us.

Seeing Jared sitting there with his hands clasped behind his neck, something he only did when he was worried or uncomfortable, reminded me how vulnerable he really was—and how well he hid it.

He turned around as if he sensed me watching him, and his face broke into a smile. "Hey."

"Hey." I smiled back and walked toward him.

Jared pulled me down in front of him, and my legs slid into the empty space underneath his, leaving us barely a foot apart.

"I can't believe you're really here." His thumb ran down the side of my face, pausing to tuck a strand of hair behind my ear. He lifted my chin, never taking his eyes off me. When his lips finally grazed mine, I felt it everywhere.

A soft sigh escaped my lips as his hand slid around to the back of my neck. The next kiss was hungrier. Fingers trailing over my skin. Teeth tugging at my bottom lip. Hands tangled in my hair. I had forgotten the way the rest of the world melted away when he touched me.

"God, I missed you," he murmured against my lips.

I nodded, unable to say the words. Because as much as I'd missed Jared, I felt damaged and broken in ways no one could fix.

Jared held my shoulders gently and leaned away from me, studying my face. "You're shaking. Did something happen?"

"I'm just cold." I tried to keep my expression unreadable.

He wrapped his arms around me, heat radiating from his body into mine. For a moment, I let myself feel it. The warmth and safety I only felt with him.

"I still can't believe you're here and I'm holding you." He tugged me closer, burying his face in my neck. "I thought about you all the time, Kennedy."

"I tried not to think about you." The words slipped out before I could stop them.

His shoulders tensed.

"Not because my feelings changed." Tears pricked my eyes. "Because it hurt too much. I—"

"What?" Hope edged its way into his voice.

I shook my head and closed my eyes.

Jared pulled me against his chest, his heart beating fast. "Talk to me, Kennedy. You're scaring me."

Tell him.

"I was afraid I'd never see you again."

He stiffened. "You didn't believe I'd come back for you." Jared still thought he wasn't good enough for me—that his mistakes eclipsed everything else about him. He didn't realize I was the one who wasn't good enough for him.

Jared let his fingers slide down my arms. "You don't know how hard—" He inhaled deeply. "It killed me to leave you behind that night. You were hurt, and I just walked away."

"You didn't have a choice."

"Yeah." He sounded disgusted. "That's what I told

myself, for about five minutes. Then I circled back to the interstate and hitched a ride to the closest hospital."

I lifted my head off his chest and stared at him. "Are you kidding? What if you'd gotten caught?"

"I didn't care. I needed to know you were okay. But when I got there, you were already in the emergency room. I tried sneaking back to see you, but the cops were all over the place."

I remembered lying on the hospital bed, praying he was okay.

If I'd known he was so close...

"Eventually, they moved you. I watched them wheel you into the elevator. Your face was still muddy and you had this look in your eyes." Jared bit his lip. "I don't know how to describe it. You looked so alone, like you didn't care what happened to you. It took everything I had in me not to go over there. Watching those elevator doors close with you inside—" He shook his head. "Felt like it broke me."

Every part of me ached for him. I rested my palm on his chest, above his heart.

Jared laid both of his hands on top of mine and held them there. "You're the only thing I thought about, Kennedy, I swear. I didn't care about the demon or the dead crows or the end of the world. I know it was selfish, but all that mattered was finding you."

The back of my throat burned. "I thought about you, too. I wanted you to find me. I just—"

He squeezed my hand. "What?"

I struggled to find the words. "I know you said you were thinking about me, but after everything that happened, I didn't think you'd want me anymore."

And I don't deserve you.

Jared looked stunned. He pulled me into his lap and pressed his forehead against mine. "You're the only thing I want. But it's more than that. The way I feel about you..."

"What?" I didn't know what he was about to say, but I wanted to hear it.

"I need you," he whispered. "More than I've ever needed anything."

I tugged on the collar of his thermal and kissed him like I might never get the chance again. When we finally came up for air, Jared pulled the sleeping bag around us. "I've never said that to anyone before."

I wanted to tell him I felt the same way, but I stopped myself. "Are you sorry you said it?"

"No." He shook his head in the darkness. "I'm just not used to talking about the way I feel. I was always the guy who never let anyone get too close, because I didn't want to care. Not like this."

"And now?"

He tightened his arms around me, the only answer he could give. I rested my head against his chest and listened to the sound of his heartbeat.

As I drifted off to sleep, I heard Jared whisper something else. "I don't even remember how to be that guy anymore."

12. BLACK-EYED GIRL

Thursday 09/05/18

I awoke with Jared's body curled around mine, his chest rising and falling against my back in a gentle rhythm. His lips grazed my neck each time he took a breath, sending a shiver up my spine.

I forgot about where we were and all the things that had led us here, until a streak of light fell across the wall of weapons.

I untangled my body from Jared's and tiptoed down the attic staircase.

We needed Faith, no matter how crazy she seemed. She knew more about Andras and the Legion than the rest of us, and if she was right about the Illuminati, we were in the dark on yet another front. As much as I hated the thought, if I promised to sit on the sidelines, maybe she would reconsider and help us.

I padded down the hallway. The bare white walls and the emergency lighting along the baseboards reminded me how different my aunt's life was from mine—and how much lonelier.

When I reached Faith's door, I stood there with my fist poised in the air.

You can do this.

A strange sound came from inside. Was she crying? The sound grew louder, and I recognized the insistent whimper.

Bear.

"Faith?" I called through the door, knocking over and over. "It's Kennedy. Is everything okay?"

A door opened down the hall, and Alara poked her head out. "What's going on?"

"Something's wrong." I pounded harder. "Her door is locked, and Bear's in there whining. She's not answering."

Alara jammed her feet into her black tactical boots and buckled her tool belt around her waist as she walked toward me.

"Can we break down the door or something?" I asked.

"It's not as easy as it looks in the movies. You have to kick it in just the right spot."

Alara pushed me out of the way. "Back up. This is a one-woman job."

I stared at the layers of chipped white paint coating

Faith's door. It had been painted at least a half dozen times, each new shade slapped over the peeling layer below it.

Something terrible is waiting on the other side.

Alara kicked the middle of the door with the bottom of her boot. The wood cracked and splintered. The second time Alara's boot made contact, the lock snapped and rusty screws rolled across the floor.

The door swung open slowly, and I stumbled into the room.

A sweet scent clung to the air. At least it wasn't sulfur, the telltale sign of a demonic presence.

Bear whimpered, and my eyes drifted to where he sat next to the four-poster bed.

Tiny green pods the size of olives were scattered all over the floor.

"Oh my god." Alara clamped a hand over her mouth.

Faith was slumped against the headboard.

My mind flashed back to the night I found my mother's body—her empty stare and her pale arm hanging over the side of the bed.

I just wanted her to wake up.

I inched closer to my aunt, unable to stop myself.

Wake up, Faith.

Faith's eyes were closed, her face smeared with the pink stain she'd been painting on the bear traps earlier. A metal bucket was tipped over next to her bed, a pool of poisoned sap oozing across the floor.

Wintersweet.

Above the headboard, crushed green pods streaked the walls in the same intense shade of pink. They formed jagged letters exactly like the ones that had etched themselves into the mirror in my dorm room. But the message was different.

HE IS HERE.

Voices drifted down the hallway. Jared, Lukas, Priest, and Elle were talking about something—maybe breakfast and hot showers or crazy aunts who tape garbage bags over their windows. They didn't know Faith was dead—that I'd lost another family member, even if I barely knew her.

"We're in Faith's room," Alara called out, sounding strangely calm. She looked up at the Eye of Ever painted on the ceiling above my aunt's body. "The Eye wasn't strong enough to protect her."

Maybe nothing would've been.

Lukas stopped just inside the doorway. "Hey, what are you guys—"

Elle took one look at Faith's body and the dripping wall, and screamed. "Is she dead? She's dead, isn't she?"

Priest's eyes darted from my aunt's bound wrists to the green berries scattered across the floor. "What the hell happened?"

130

Jared stared up at the message on the wall, transfixed.

"A vengeance spirit or something poisoned her." Alara stepped away from the bed, trying to distance herself from the body and the message.

"*Something?*" Elle backed into the doorjamb and jumped. "What kind of something?"

For once, I was the one with the answer. "A demon."

⊰ • ⊱

Lukas, Jared, Alara, and Priest guided me and Elle out of Faith's bedroom, their weapons drawn.

"We should bury her." I couldn't stand the thought of leaving her lying under the sinister message.

"Not until we sweep the house." Priest tossed Jared an EMF, taking command.

"Stay here with Elle." Jared kissed my forehead and handed me a semiautomatic with silver duct tape wrapped around the barrel. He slid his hand up the side of my leg until he reached the pocket of my jeans. The metal clinked as he dropped salt rounds inside. "Just in case."

"In case of what?" Elle flattened herself against the wall.

"I'll stay with Kennedy and Elle." Lukas' eyes flickered over Elle's face when he said her name, but she was too terrified to notice.

Instead, she clamped her hand around his arm in a death grip. "You won't leave us, right?"

He pushed a strand of red hair out of her eyes. "It's gonna be okay."

She nodded over and over like a battery-operated toy with a glitch.

"I'm going to check the salt lines." Alara headed for the stairs with her nail gun drawn and a rifle leaning against her other shoulder.

Bear followed, racing to get ahead of her.

I stood next to Lukas and Elle, listening to the familiar chirping sounds of the EMFs.

Elle stared at Faith's door with a dazed expression, and scooted farther away from it. "I can't believe she's dead. And the way it happened...I never should've taken that bracelet from the museum."

"This had nothing to do with the bracelet." My hand tightened around the grip of the gun. What happened in my aunt's room was connected to the message scratched into my mirror at Winterhaven.

"Kennedy's right," Lukas said. "When objects are haunted, the vengeance spirit is attached to the item itself. And the bracelet is buried out in the woods somewhere. Trust me, I've dealt with a lot of vicious spirits. This is something else."

Elle looked up at Lukas, her chocolate brown eyes still dazed. "Why do you do it?"

"What are we talking about exactly?" He shifted his gaze between Elle's face and the spot on the floor between them, as if he suddenly realized how close together they were standing.

Elle rubbed her face, smearing a trail of black eyeliner across her cheek. "I know you're trying to keep a demon from opening the gates of hell and turning the world into his personal playground. And I get that. But Kennedy said you've been fighting these killer spirits since you were a kid, *before* the demon even escaped." Her thoughts spilled out in a crazy stream of consciousness. "Why would you risk your life like that?"

I remembered asking Jared and Lukas the same question when I first met them, wondering why anyone would take those kinds of risks.

Lukas wiped the smudged eyeliner off her face. "Because I want to protect people."

Elle nodded as if she understood.

After that, the hallway was quiet. No flickering lights or wires ripping themselves out of the walls, only the sound of familiar voices and normal EMF readings, until Priest and Jared returned.

"The house is clean." Priest propped the Punisher against the wall next to him.

Jared slid his fingers between mine like it was something he'd done a thousand times.

Bear trotted up the stairs with Alara behind him. "Salt lines are all intact."

"I want to bury her." After all the terrible things that had happened to Faith, she deserved some peace.

⇥ • ⇤

We buried Faith in the fresh grave she had dug herself.

Alara recited a prayer, and we took turns tossing handfuls of dirt into the hole. I kept picturing my mother's gravesite, the details as clear as a photograph.

Standing behind a mound of overturned earth. Staring down at the white roses—some bent or broken—and the dirt-covered petals scattered over the glossy coffin.

I looked away when Jared and Lukas refilled the hole. I couldn't watch. Instead, I kept my eyes fixed on the headstone, where Jared had chiseled the year of her death.

Had Faith known the end was coming all along? Did she see it in one of her dreams? I added them to the list of unanswered questions piling up in my head.

I still didn't know why my mother had kept the Legion a secret from me, or if she had ever planned to tell me the truth. Was she afraid of the Illuminati—of men like Archer who might hurt us?

My eyes skimmed over the epitaph: *May she sleep with the doves.* Faith had probably chosen it herself. I tried to imagine writing my own. What would it say?

The girl who destroyed the world.

I followed everyone back into the house. They stopped to talk in what would've been the living room in a normal home.

Standing there, surrounded by my aunt's prophetic paintings, I was vaguely aware of the conversations around me.

"How did he get inside?"

"Andras can't cross a salt line."

"We don't know what he can do."

Until I heard something I couldn't ignore.

"Do you think this means Kennedy is one of us now?" Alara sounded hopeful.

"You heard what my aunt said about not wanting me to be part of the Legion." I tried to act like it didn't bother me.

"Who else would she choose? Your dad?" Priest asked. "He's not exactly the next generation."

"Did you really just say that out loud?" Alara hissed at him under her breath before turning back to me. "Adults spend half their time lecturing us about the things they won't let us do, then they end up changing their minds."

I thought about everything my aunt had shared with me about the Illuminati, Archer, and her past. She wouldn't have told me her secrets if she didn't trust me, and Faith had seemed less guarded when we were alone.

What if Priest was right, and Faith had changed her mind and chosen me?

"Maybe." I didn't try to sound convincing.

"We should get our stuff together and get out of here," Priest said to Jared, or maybe Lukas. I wasn't paying attention anymore.

I focused on the silver buckles that ran up the sides of

my boots, the loose thread on the bottom of my shirt, a brown smudge on my hand. It took me a second to realize what it was.

Dirt. From my aunt's grave.

My stomach lurched, as if the smudge was blood. After the past twenty-four hours, it was close enough, and all I could think about was getting it off.

Jared looked up when he saw me rushing toward the hallway.

"I'm just going to wash my hands." I could tell he was worried by the way he was tracking my every move.

Before he had a chance to respond, something hit the roof with a thud.

Elle's head shot up. "What was that?"

Within seconds, another heavy object hit the front of the house. Bear bounded down the stairs and crouched below the shattered bay window, growling. Two more loud bangs followed, in rapid succession.

"It sounds like rocks," Alara said.

Jared bolted for Faith's supply closet and returned carrying an armload of crossbows and semiautomatic weapons. He dropped a few boxes of salt rounds on the steps. "Check them and make sure they aren't loaded with live rounds."

Every few seconds, the house took another hit. Lukas shoved a handful of ammo in his jacket pocket and walked toward the window, where the dog's bark had turned feral.

Priest made it to the window first. "Guys, we have a serious problem."

A brown blur sailed through the broken window.

"Watch out!" I grabbed Alara's sleeve and yanked her out of the way just before it hit the floor.

Elle skidded to a stop. "Is that—?"

"A brick." Alara kicked it across the room.

Outside the window, dozens of reddish-brown bricks littered the yard. Beyond the salt circle, a crowd had gathered—an old woman wearing an apron, with her slippers on and curlers still in her hair; a burly guy wearing denim overalls and a checkered hunting cap; a thin woman in a dingy dress, surrounded by four children, each one skinnier and dirtier than the next; an elderly lady leaning on a gnarled walking stick.

Each person had a pile of bricks at his or her feet.

In the distance, more people with bricks wove their way through the trees, as if Faith's house was calling them.

"They must be your aunt's neighbors, or whatever you call the other people living out here in the woods," Alara said.

The old woman in curlers hurled a brick, and it whacked against the front door.

Lukas peered out the window. "Whatever they *were*, I don't think they're her neighbors anymore."

A child, who looked about five or six, took a step forward with her eyes glued to the ground. Her hair hung in frayed braids and her tattered dress was ripped in more places than I could count. She carried a brick in one hand as she trudged methodically through the snow, like she was in a trance.

The little girl walked to the edge of the salt ring and bent down, dipping a finger in the white crystals. As she stood up, she raised her head.

Her eyes were as black as tar.

Elle staggered back. "What's wrong with her eyes?"

"She's possessed." Alara sounded terrified. "I think they all are."

The child stared at us through unblinking eyes. She tilted her head to the side and licked the salt off her finger. Then a slow, menacing smile spread across her face as she stepped over the salt line.

13. SONS OF LIBERTY

One by one, my aunt's neighbors stepped over the salt line, their movements rigid and awkward.

"We have to get out of here now." Alara grabbed Elle by the arm.

Lukas dumped out a box of salt rounds and loaded his paintball gun. "Priest, get the gear. You've got four minutes. Then go out the back door."

"It's already packed." Priest ran for the hallway.

The black-eyed girl raised the brick and hurled it through the broken window. It smashed on the floor, sending bits of clay and mortar chasing after Priest. My aunt's possessed neighbors raised their bricks without breaking stride.

"Jared! Are you waiting for an invite?" Lukas yelled at his brother, who was still staring at the child.

Jared tore his attention away from the girl and grabbed his paintball rifle.

"Kennedy, go!" Lukas shouted, aiming his gun.

Lukas had said those words to me once before, inside Lilburn Mansion. But this time, I listened. Bear ran behind me, barking if I slowed down for a second.

Salt rounds exploding replaced the sound of bricks smashing against the house.

When I reached the hallway, Priest was on the landing, tossing bags down the staircase. He gathered up our coats and leaned over the railing. "Catch. I'm gonna grab the Punisher. Weapons are in the bag with the duct-taped handle."

I dug through the duffels and found a paintball gun, then shoved the coats inside. Bear barked, urging me to keep moving. As I ran through the great room, the walls vibrated from the hailstorm of bricks pelting the house.

They're still out there.

How many? A dozen?

I caught a glimpse of Alara and Elle before they ducked into the kitchen. Bear stayed behind me, herding me toward the back door. As we cut through the kitchen, the lingering smell of wintersweet made my stomach turn.

Bear darted in front of me and slid to a stop at the door, snarling.

"Move, Bear." I squeezed in front of him and threw open the door. Icy air hit my lungs and I gasped.

Empty black eyes stared back at me from every direction—a gray-haired woman with an ax balanced on her shoulder; a girl not much older than me, wearing jeans and a stained apron, holding a brick in one hand and a black-eyed toddler's overall strap in the other; a guy in mechanics' coveralls brandishing a wrench; old men carrying bricks as they hobbled on canes through the falling snow.

Alara and Elle stood only a few feet away from the pack working to surround them. Bear darted in front of the two of them, snapping.

The toddler lunged at Bear, hissing like a feral cat and straining against his mother's hold.

"Keep moving!" Priest yelled from somewhere behind me.

I heard his sneakers skid across the linoleum as Alara raised her paintball gun and fired.

Elle screamed and covered her ears.

The salt round hit the toddler's mom right between the eyes. Her head snapped back and her feet slid out from under her.

Alara kept firing round after round, but my eyes were glued to the woman lying in the snow—the one she had shot.

The one who was sitting up now.

"Look."

A white mark was branded in the center of the mother's forehead, between her glassy black eyes.

Andras' seal.

"Get out of the way." Priest dropped onto his stomach, lining the Punisher up in front of him.

Alara grabbed Elle and dove to the side. Bear ran after them, circling the spot where they lay huddled in the snow. Elle had stopped screaming, her frightened expression replaced by a thousand-yard stare.

Priest unleashed the crowd-control weapon on my aunt's possessed neighbors, hitting them with a hailstorm of nonlethal ammo that sent them flying. But after a few moments they rose, one at a time, with Andras' seal branded on their foreheads.

Lukas barreled through the kitchen door. "We need to move."

I waited for a glimpse of Jared's green army jacket, but it never came. "Where's Jared?"

"I thought he was ahead of me." Lukas reloaded and turned to go back inside, when the door flew open.

Jared stumbled out, sweaty and gasping.

Lukas grabbed his brother's arm. "Where were you?"

Priest fired off another flurry of ammo, drowning out their voices. Not to be outdone, Jared and Lukas raised their own weapons, sending liquid-salt rounds rocketing at the few people still standing.

People.

Somewhere trapped inside those zombies, they were still people. Weren't they?

"Run!" Priest shouted.

Alara dragged Elle to her feet, and Bear took off in front of them, paving the way through the ash-covered snow.

⊰ • ⊱

Jared gunned the engine, and the Jeep slid across the ice and onto the road.

I leaned back against the seat and shoved my frozen hands into my coat pockets. My fingers brushed against a scrap of paper and I reached over to stuff it in the seat pocket, already overflowing with Priest's candy wrappers. But it wasn't trash.

The tight square of paper was folded too carefully, like the notes Elle and I used to pass each other during class. I unfolded it, revealing messy script. My mind cataloged every curve, including the ones that were almost illegible.

Jared glanced at me in the rearview mirror. "What are you reading?"

"I think it's a note from my aunt."

Priest hooked his headphones around his neck. "What does it say?"

"It's really messy, but I think it says 'A story buried. A shoelace tarried. A King Jane page'—"

143

Priest leaned closer and pointed at the word. "It's *James*. Like the Bible."

"Right." I held up the note so everyone could see it.

A story buried.
A shoelace tarried.
A King James page.
A halfpenny wage.
While these remain trifles at best,
Something more precious in the stone
is at rest.
Between 39 and 133.

"What does it say at the bottom?" Elle asked.

" 'May the black dove always carry you.' " I squinted at the smudged ink. " 'And the angle'—no, that's probably 'angel'—'guide you.' "

"I hope there's a translation," Elle said.

"It's a riddle. 'A story buried...'" Alara leaned closer.

Priest studied the page. "A shoelace tarried. A King James page. A halfpenny wage. They're all things from the taxidermy museum. John Hancock's shoelace. The page from Joseph Warren's Bible—"

"It was Paul Revere's Bible," Jared said.

"Okay, Paul Revere's Bible and Joseph Warren's halfpenny. Maybe we need to go back to the museum and get all that stuff."

It didn't make sense. If we led the demon to Faith's house, there was no way to predict how long he'd been following us—something Faith would know. "Faith wouldn't send us back there. She was too paranoid."

"I don't think we need the actual items." Lukas spun his silver coin between his fingers, still working it out. "Priest, what do those three things have in common?"

"A shoelace, an old Bible page, and a halfpenny?" Priest shrugged. "Is it a trick question?"

"Not the items themselves," Lukas said.

"They all belonged to patriots," I offered.

"And Freemasons," Alara added.

"Three Revolutionary War patriots who were all members of the Sons of Liberty." Jared glanced at us in the rearview mirror. "Guess I learned more from the Philadelphia public school system than I thought."

"What about the next part?" Alara asked. " 'Something more precious in the stone is at rest.' "

"Based on Faith's trusting personality," Lukas said, "I'm guessing she hid something, and she wanted Kennedy to find it."

"Why does everything have to be a poem or a riddle?" Elle rubbed her face, looking exhausted. "Couldn't she just tell us whatever insane thing we're supposed to do?"

"Writing things down is dangerous," Lukas said. "Vengeance spirits, demons, and—if Faith was right— the Illuminati could use the information to find us." He exchanged a glance with his brother, but no one else seemed to notice.

Alara stretched her legs across the third row, leaving room for Bear. "So where do we start?"

"Places related to Paul Revere, John Hancock, and Joseph Warren." Lukas took out his cell phone. "The Sons of Liberty held meetings and votes at the Old South Meeting House. And it looks like they were all buried in the same cemetery in Boston."

Recognition flickered in Priest's eyes. "Granary Burying Ground."

"Graveyards are definitely full of stones," I said.

Priest grinned. "We need to check it out."

Alara threw her arm over her eyes and sighed. "Of course we do."

I want to see John Hancock's grave before we leave," Elle said, stomping through the mud-streaked snow of Granary Burying Ground.

"You did enough sightseeing on the way here," Alara snapped, zipping her jacket to ward off the cold.

Boston was only an hour and a half from my aunt's house, but it felt like it had taken forever to get to the cemetery. The streets were blocked off for a festival, and we'd sat in traffic for forty-five minutes before we finally gave up and parked. We ended up walking for over an hour in the snow, and Alara's mood had gone downhill fast.

Once we passed through the cemetery gates, Alara

stayed on the main path, even though it meant braving the icy pavement. She didn't want to risk stepping on one of the overgrown plots.

Jared glanced at a tour guide dressed in Revolutionary War–period costume. "I think we might be on the wrong track. I can't picture Faith hiding anything here. This place seems like it gets a lot of traffic."

It was the second guide we'd seen in fifteen minutes.

"Whose grave are we looking for?" Alara asked as Bear trotted alongside her.

"Paul Revere was the only one of the three who was a Freemason and a member of the Illuminati," Priest said.

Elle stopped. "It's gonna be a quick search."

A modest marker covered with rocks and pennies jutted out of the snow. Next to it, a small footstone was flanked by two American flags. Someone had left three stuffed bears in front of the grave marker, each one dressed in Revolutionary War garb and carrying a tiny drum. The oxidized plaque on the rectangular tomb read:

PAUL REVERE.
BORN IN BOSTON,
JANUARY. 1774:
DIED
MAY. 1818.

Jared knelt in front of the mound. "Unless your aunt left you something in one of these bears, this doesn't look good."

"Think she buried it?" Priest slipped off his headphones, Nine Inch Nails' "Head Like a Hole" still blaring.

Alara looked disgusted. "Go ahead and find out, but I'm not digging in a cemetery. That's the definition of bad luck."

I stared down at the soggy stuffed bears. I'd known my aunt for all of twenty-four hours. I had no idea what we were looking for, or why she wanted me to have it.

This is a dead end.

Lukas studied the map again. "Revere has a family tomb." He pointed at a row of tombs, shrouded by evergreens. "Back there."

Everyone followed Lukas across the graveyard—except Alara, who lagged behind with Bear.

Priest elbowed me and nodded in her direction. "She's on the phone again."

"Who do you think she's talking to? Her sister?" I asked.

"No one calls their sister that much," Elle said. "I told you, it's a guy."

When we reached the family tomb, Jared cleared the fresh snow off the stone with his sleeve. REVERE was etched across the top. "This is it."

The corners were chipped and weathered, and a tangle

of tree roots had wrapped themselves around the tomb. Only a few tiny cracks cut across the stone.

Lukas bent down and checked the base. "There's nowhere to hide anything here."

Priest opened his mouth to say something, but I held up my hand to stop him. "Forget it. We're not looking inside."

"It would be pointless anyway," Elle said. "Based on the width of these roots, they've been wrapped around this thing for decades. So unless your aunt hid this mystery item over twenty years ago, it's not in there."

"Where did that come from?" Jared asked.

Elle stared at him from beneath the furry hood of her faux-leopard jacket. "Botany, which I took after AP Biology and Geology. Not all pretty girls are stupid."

"She's right on both counts." Priest turned on his EMF and circled the tomb.

"You're testing for spirits in a graveyard?" I wasn't sure how that worked.

"Just this tomb," he said, turning off the device. "The needle barely moved."

Alara made her way toward us, navigating between the snow-covered grave markers. According to the cemetery map, there were a little over two thousand tombs and markers in the graveyard, but closer to five thousand bodies were actually buried here. I didn't have the heart to tell Alara that she'd probably stepped on more than a few of them already.

"Talking to your boyfriend again?" Lukas teased, once she was in earshot.

Her expression was somber. "Another girl disappeared this morning."

My stomach twisted and I pictured the row of photos in my dorm room. "What was her name?"

Alara gave me a strange look. "Lucy Klein. Why?"

"Just wondering." I added her name to my mental list. I'd look up her photo later and sketch her portrait in my notebook.

"Maybe they're alive somewhere," Elle offered.

I waited for someone to agree, but there was only silence.

⊰ • ⊱

Priest was sure that Faith had hidden whatever I was supposed to find at the Old South Meeting House, and he tried to convince the rest of us on the way there.

"The Sons of Liberty held public debates and votes at the meeting house," he said. "It's also the place where they gave the signal that started the Boston Tea Party. The Sons of Liberty marched out of there and led colonists straight to the wharf."

By the time we reached the brick building, with its towering steeple and a door painted the color of a redcoat's uniform, the snow had turned to cold rain.

A group of tourists stood out front, huddled under their

151

umbrellas. A tour guide dressed like Paul Revere, complete with a brown tricorn hat, gestured at the red door.

Alara rolled her eyes. "Seriously? Another one? Who goes on a tour in this weather?"

"I wonder if they get a discount on those hats," Priest whispered as we walked by.

"The cornerstone was an important symbol to Freemasons like Paul Revere and John Hancock." The tour guide's voice carried over the rain.

Priest stopped on the front steps. "Hold on a sec."

The guide pointed at a gray weathered stone that stood out from the surrounding red brick, and the tourists craned their necks. "For early masons, the cornerstone was the first stone set into the foundation, and it was often inscribed with the date and initials of the builder," he continued. "Freemasons considered the stone a symbolic element and continued the tradition, but they usually added it to the outside of their buildings. *Unless* you were patriot and Freemason Benjamin Franklin."

Alara stood in the doorway. "Maybe you can take the tour later, Priest. I'd rather watch paint dry."

"Now this is for all you *Jeopardy!* fans," the guide rambled on. "Benjamin Franklin cared more about what was *inside* the cornerstone than what was inscribed on the outside. In his diaries, Franklin revealed that he hid important documents related to the Sons of Liberty behind the cornerstone of his house."

A pudgy guy wearing a plastic poncho raised his hand like he was in elementary school. "If the documents were so important, why'd he write down where he hid them?"

"An excellent question, sir." The guide jumped at the opportunity to elaborate. "Freemasons were known for their flawless and *seamless* workmanship and often hid valuables inside the things they constructed. Those items could only be accessed by leveraging a specific angle—just like the cornerstone of Franklin's house."

Lukas turned to me. "Let me see the note again."

Priest scanned the scrap of paper in my hand and turned to Lukas. "Are you thinking what I'm thinking?"

Lukas flashed him a crooked smile. "Maybe."

Elle squeezed between them, trying to avoid the rain. "Can we think about whatever it is *inside*?"

Priest flipped up his hood. "We need to go back to the cemetery."

Alara groaned. "We didn't find anything there."

Lukas grabbed her elbow and steered her down the stairs. "That's because we were looking in the wrong place."

"So what do the numbers mean?" Jared asked, falling into step next to Lukas.

"I think they're angles," his brother said.

I pictured Faith's handwriting on the note she'd left in my coat pocket.

And let the angle guide you.

It said *angle* all along, not *angel.*

Priest looked around. "We need to find a drugstore."

Alara stopped walking and stood in the middle of the sidewalk with her arms crossed. Bear sat down next to her.

"What are you doing?" Priest asked.

"Waiting for someone to tell me what's going on," she said.

Priest pointed at the drugstore at the end of the street. "How about we explain inside, where it's dry?"

Alara stalked past him and headed in the direction of the store.

That was a yes.

⇥ • ⇤

The five of us stood in the school supply aisle of the drugstore, scanning the shelves and dripping all over the cheap carpet, while Jared waited out front with Bear.

Priest found a compass and a ruler and opened them, while Lukas unfolded the note. "If I'm right—"

"If *we're* right," Priest said.

Lukas pointed at the bottom of the page. "If we're right, these two numbers are angles."

"And you know that how?" I asked.

"The tour guide said Ben Franklin's cornerstone could only be moved if someone leveraged a specific angle."

Lukas tapped the numbers on the note. "But there are two numbers here. I think the intersection of these two angles is the spot that opens the cornerstone where Faith hid whatever you're supposed to find."

Elle opened a roll of paper towels she'd nabbed on our way down the aisle and wiped her face. "Back up. How do you know Faith didn't hide this mystery item behind the cornerstone at the Old South Meeting House?"

Lukas shrugged. "I don't. But the meeting house is in the middle of a busy street. I can't see Faith climbing over the fence and prying stones out of a historic building without anyone noticing. Granary Burying Ground seems like an easier place to hide something."

"If he's wrong, we'll have to wait until it gets dark to go back to the meeting house anyway," Priest said.

Elle wiped off the smudged black eyeliner under her eyes. "You guys really know how to show a girl a good time."

Lukas slung his arm around Elle's neck. "How do you feel about breaking into a tomb?"

The three soggy bears were still standing in formation as we passed Paul Revere's grave. When we reached his family tomb, Priest examined the base. "The cornerstone should be over here."

In the northeast corner, the initials *P.R.* were carved into the stone.

Lukas positioned the compass at the ninety-degree angle at the bottom of the cornerstone. "This point would be zero." He drew an arc to thirty-nine. "What's the other number?"

I double-checked the note. "One hundred thirty-three."

He measured the second angle and drew an arc that bisected the first.

"Is it just supposed to open or what?" Alara asked, holding her umbrella over Lukas while he worked.

Jared scrolled down the display on his cell phone. "According to everything online, if you hit the spot where the lines intersect, the cornerstone should open."

Priest pulled a screwdriver out of his back pocket and elbowed Lukas. "Scoot over. Mathematical genius required."

"You know you're about to steal from someone's grave, right?" Alara looked nervous.

"Relax. The EMF didn't pick up any spirits." Priest positioned the screwdriver and picked up a broken brick, holding the brick over the end of the screwdriver like a hammer.

Alara stepped back like she wanted to be sure the spirits of Paul Revere's relatives knew she disapproved.

Lukas pointed at the stone. "Make sure you hit it right where the lines intersect."

"Got it." Priest tapped the end of the screwdriver with the brick.

Elle hovered behind him. "Nothing's happening."

"Give it a minute. It's not a magic trick." Priest tapped it again. This time, the cornerstone shifted, and the edge across from the screwdriver pivoted toward us. Priest worked the rectangular stone free, revealing a dark space behind it. "Who's sticking their hand in there?"

Alara held up her hands and stepped back. "Don't look at me. I don't do grave robbing."

"We're not stealing anything from the dead people," Jared said. "Whatever's in there belonged to Faith, and she wanted Kennedy to have it."

I pushed up my sleeve. "I'll do it." I slid my hand into the hole, trying not to think about all of the disgusting and dead things that were probably inside. I walked my fingers forward one at a time until they hit a smooth, rectangular surface. "I found something."

"What is it?" Priest asked.

My knuckles scraped against the stone as I eased it out. "It feels like a box."

A book emerged, the pages protected by silver-plated covers. Dirt had settled into the symbols and scrollwork engraved on the front.

Alara held the umbrella above me, shielding the book as I opened it carefully. Despite the tears and water damage, it only took me a moment to recognize the story on the first page and realize what I was holding.

My aunt's journal.

Alara smiled. "Unbelievable."

Priest nudged her. "How do you feel about grave robbing now?"

"You know what this means, right?" Lukas watched me expectantly. "Your aunt's passing the torch."

I wanted to believe it, but I'd been disappointed so

many times. "Faith wouldn't even discuss letting me replace her. You were all there."

"Maybe it was some kind of test to see if you really wanted in," Alara said.

"I'm not sure." After spending less than twenty-four hours with my aunt, I didn't know her any better than my friends did.

Elle wedged herself between Alara and me. "If Faith didn't pick you to replace her, then why would she give you that crazy math equation and leave you her journal? Isn't she supposed to pass it down to the next person in line?"

Alara stared at Elle like she'd just proven the earth was round. "Seriously? You're gonna throw that out there like it's no big deal? Have you actually been paying attention this whole time?"

Elle flashed her a self-satisfied smile. "Remembering the name of your electromagnet ghost-finding gadget isn't a measure of intelligence."

Alara shook her head. "You were so close."

"Close only counts when it comes to horseshoes and hand grenades," Priest said. "Which means the next paranormal entity that messes with us belongs to Kennedy." He turned to me. "We'll stand back while you draw a symbol and destroy it. Then you'll get your mark."

I touched my wrist.

Was there still a chance?

Jared brought his lips to my ear. "I knew you were part of the Legion," he whispered.

Don't get your hopes up again. But I had Faith's journal, which made me feel like one of them.

"Maybe she left you a note," Elle said.

I scanned the first entry, which outlined the plan to summon Andras. It matched the one Faith's father had copied, word for word. But there was something different about seeing the writing on the aged parchment.

One line stopped me cold.

There are no innocents among you.

The angel had spoken those words to Konstantin—an angel who couldn't stand humans. I flipped to the next entry, which consisted of two lines centered on the page.

May the black dove always carry you.
And the white dove set you free.

"You guys never mentioned a white dove," I said.

"I've never heard of one before." Lukas looked at Priest and Alara. "Have you?"

Alara shook her head.

"Negative," Priest said.

"Everything means something." The last few months had taught me that.

Lukas slid the cornerstone back in place. After he brushed away the bits of loose rock, it blended seamlessly into the tomb again.

As I skimmed a few more entries, my eidetic memory created snapshots of the pages and filed them away. Another line caught my attention. "Faith was telling the truth about the protective barrier."

Raising the Barrier
Only when all five members of the Legion join hands, and speak these words as if their voices are one, can they raise the barrier and hold it fast:
May the bonds of blood and the marks we bear protect us.
As the wings of the black dove carry us.

"Yeah." Priest sounded strangely disappointed. "We can make a force field."

Alara glanced down the path at another Paul Revere look-alike heading our way with a fresh flock of tourists. "We can figure it all out in the car."

I slid the journal under my jacket and thought about my mom. The journal made me feel a step closer to destroying the demon responsible for her death. I tried not to think about the other person the pages connected me to, or where he had been all this time.

As we walked along the slushy streets, I held the journal against my chest and tried to pretend I didn't care. But my father's shadow still lurked in the back of my mind, like a different kind of ghost.

⊰ • ⊱

After trekking back to the Jeep in the rain, everyone was wrecked.

"I'll drive," Jared said.

Lukas tossed him the keys, and I climbed into the passenger seat next to Jared. Alara and Bear had permanently claimed the third row, so Priest got stuck with Lukas and Elle.

Elle pulled off her boots and rubbed her wet socks. "I think the bottom of my foot is one huge blister."

"If you had real boots instead of those fashion statements you're wearing, you wouldn't be so miserable," Alara said, peeling off her coat.

Elle unearthed a brush from her gigantic bag and dragged it through her hair. "Not everyone shops at the army surplus store."

"Not everyone can pull it off," Alara shot back.

"Let's save the catfight for pay per view." Priest sounded a little too hopeful.

"We're all just tired," Lukas said. "I vote we find a hotel. I need to get more info about the girl who disappeared—"

"Lucy Klein," I said. She deserved to have someone remember her name.

Lukas gave me a strange look. "And I want to get online and see if I can figure out where the hell Andras is now."

Priest dried off his headphones and MP3 player. "I should probably check out the weapons and make sure we're good on ammo."

"You don't have to convince me," Jared said. "I'm freezing and starving."

"Me too." Elle coughed, phlegm rattling in her chest. "I think I'm getting sick."

"Why are you still here?" Alara asked.

"Excuse me?" Elle looked offended.

"Lay off, Alara," Lukas snapped, before I had a chance to bite her head off.

"Calm down, Romeo," Alara said. "I didn't mean it the way it sounded."

Lukas blushed.

"What I meant was you don't have to be here," Alara said to Elle. "If I could leave, I'd be gone."

Priest turned around in his seat. "You'd walk away from the Legion?"

"I said if I *could* leave. Like if tomorrow we destroyed Andras and this whole thing was over."

Priest frowned as if he'd never considered the possibility.

Alara leaned forward and propped her elbows on the back of the seat, between Elle and Priest. "If we took down Andras tomorrow, I'd pack my bags and backpack around Europe for a year. Maybe two. And Asia. I'd hang around cafés all day and drink coffee, and walk the Great Wall of China. I'd get a stamp on every page of my passport. What would you do, Lukas?"

Lukas thought about it for a moment. "Go to college, I guess?"

"Where?" Elle asked, egging him on.

Lukas smiled at her sheepishly. "Virginia Tech. My calculus teacher always said I could get in if I stopped cutting class."

Jared looked surprised. "When did she say that?"

"When you were in Algebra I with all the freshmen," Lukas said.

"What would you major in?" I asked.

"Applied mathematics. But it wouldn't matter, because I'd get recruited by the Department of Defense or Homeland Security right after I hacked their system during senior year."

Priest crossed his arms and shifted in his seat. "You mean after they let you out of jail for threatening national security?"

"They only throw you in jail if you're an actual threat. Otherwise, hacking their mainframe is basically the job interview. I bet half the guys working there are former

164

hackers. How about you, Priest?" Lukas asked. "You could probably walk right into a mechanical engineering class at Harvard and ace it without cracking a book. You'd probably have your PhD before I even graduated."

Priest pressed his lips together in a tight line. "I'm not interested in going to some pretentious university to earn a worthless degree I don't need."

Alara slung her arm around his neck. "I'm with you. Screw the system. Go straight to NASA or revolutionize an entire industry with one of your inventions."

"Like that guy who invented the star for Christmas trees that sprays water all over the tree if it catches on fire," Elle said.

"Of course, you'd deejay on the weekends at some exclusive club," Alara said. "And I'd have to show up every once in a while to scare off all the girls who'd be stalking you."

Priest shrugged Alara's arm off his shoulder. "If I invent anything worth remembering, it'll be for the Legion. We can't just walk away if we destroy Andras. What about all the vengeance spirits and dangerous paranormal entities out there? Someone has to protect people, and it's *our* job."

"Our job is to protect the world from the malevolent spirits Andras influences, and to keep him from finding a way into this world." Alara glanced at me awkwardly. "I mean...it was. Now our job is to destroy him. If we do that, it's over. I'm not sticking around to be one of the Ghostbusters."

Priest cringed at the reference, his eyes flickering over the faces of the other Legion members. "Is that how you all feel? You'd just bail?"

Alara twisted her eyebrow ring, and Lukas took out his coin and flipped it between his fingers.

"Jared? Is that how you feel, too?" Priest asked.

Jared rubbed the back of his neck. He seemed almost as uncomfortable with the conversation as Priest. "I'm not sure what I'd do if I wasn't part of the Legion. But I don't want to fight vengeance spirits if I have a choice."

Priest stared at him, speechless. Then he put on his headphones and yanked up his hood. "Good to know. I didn't realize I was the only one who actually believed we had a calling. That we were in this for the long haul."

"Over two hundred years is a pretty long haul," Alara said, referring to how long the Legion had been in existence. "I don't want to spend the rest of my life toeing that line."

"Yeah. I got that," Priest snapped, turning up the music.

Lukas reached over and squeezed Priest's shoulder. "Come on. It was a hypothetical conversation. We don't even know where to find Andras, let alone how to destroy him. It's not like the band is breaking up tomorrow."

Priest relaxed a little, but he didn't respond.

I couldn't imagine wanting to lead a life like his forever, not if I had the chance to have a normal one. But to Priest, the Legion probably was normal. His grandfather had raised him and trained Priest from the time he was young. He was homeschooled. I didn't even know if he had any friends before he met Jared, Lukas, and Alara, less than six months ago.

He wanted to belong.

Something I understood better than anyone.

16. HEROES AND MONSTERS

'm not sleeping with the dog," Elle said, flopping down on one of the double beds in our hotel room.

Alara unbuckled her tool belt and dropped it on the other bed. "Don't worry. He doesn't want to sleep with you either." She scratched Bear's ears. "Do you?"

"I hope you're nicer to Elvis," I said to Elle, prying off my wet boots.

Elle had unofficially adopted my cat when I took off with the Legion. After being possessed by a vengeance spirit, he'd been traumatized enough when she found him.

"Whatever." She waved a hand in the air. "I treat that cat like the king that he is. I'm definitely a cat person."

Alara opened a pack of complimentary oatmeal cookies and fed one to Bear. "That explains a lot."

One of the guys knocked on the door between our adjoining rooms. When neither Alara nor Elle moved, I got up and opened it.

"Why is your room bigger than ours?" Priest asked as they walked in. He was finally talking again after the awkward conversation in the car.

Alara popped a cookie in her mouth. "Because I'm the one paying."

Jared sat down on the bed next to me. He noticed my aunt's silver journal on the nightstand and picked it up. "I still can't believe we found it."

"I know." I opened the cover, and my fingers brushed his. "Faith wasn't exaggerating when she told us it was in bad shape. Some of the pages are so faded you can't even make out the letters anymore."

"You have it now. That's what matters." He closed it, keeping my hand beneath his.

Priest stretched out next to Alara, who was watching TV, and Bear sandwiched himself between them.

"What do you think?" she asked Priest as the host of the show challenged viewers to predict if a punch from a heavyweight boxer was more powerful than one from a mixed martial arts fighter. "I'm going with the MMA fighter," Alara said.

"How do they know who wins?" Elle asked.

Priest pointed at a group of scientists in white lab coats on the screen. "The experts use a robotic dummy that measures all kinds of variables when the fighters hit it."

Lukas stood in the doorway. "Hey. I'm going down to the vending machine. Anyone hungry?" He looked over my shoulder at Elle.

"I'll go with you," she said a little too quickly.

"Of course you will." Alara turned up the TV. "I'll take chips if they have salt and vinegar. And a Coke."

"Just give me a minute to change," Elle told Lukas before disappearing into the bathroom with her huge bag.

"Wipe that dopey grin off your face," Jared said, teasing his brother.

"What?" Lukas looked at me like he was checking to see if Jared's comment bothered me—and hoping it didn't.

I smiled at him, and he relaxed.

"Make sure she calls her mom while you guys are down there." Alara didn't look up from the TV. "According to my cousin, her mom is super high maintenance."

Lukas nodded. "Got it."

The moment Elle came out of the bathroom, I knew we had a problem.

"You *cannot* wear those in here." Alara stared at Elle's pink sweats like she was wearing raw meat.

Elle glanced at her outfit, trying to figure out what Alara was talking about.

"They're pink." Priest pointed at her sweatpants, as if that explained everything.

170

"And?" Elle asked.

"And that color represents death and bad luck. I'm not sleeping in a room with anything pink in it," Alara said. "Including you."

Elle stared at Alara, waiting to see if she was joking. She wasn't.

"You have serious issues," Elle said. "No one told me about the color rules. Are there any others I should be aware of?" Lukas dragged her out of the room, but Elle was still ranting. "Red? Gray? Blue? Let me know."

"Wow. She's sensitive." Alara popped another cookie in her mouth as the mixed martial arts fighter threw a punch and knocked the head off the robotic dummy. "Told you."

"Want to go in the other room?" Jared whispered.

I nodded and followed him.

"Don't do anything a priest wouldn't do," Priest called out.

I curled up on one of the beds under Jared's arm. "Can I ask you something?"

He pulled me closer. "Anything."

"If you destroyed Andras tomorrow, what would you do?" Jared was the only Legion member who hadn't answered the question. "Travel around like Alara? Or go to college?" I didn't know anything about his dreams— the regular things he wanted that had nothing to do with demons and vengeance spirits.

He frowned. "I'm not college material. Luke is the smart one out of the two of us."

"Don't say that." I sat up and looked down at him. "You have instincts I'd kill for. And you're brave and loyal, and you'd do anything for the people you care about. My mom used to say, 'There are always choices.' It was kind of her way of asking me if I thought I was making the right one." I rested my hand on his chest, right over his heart. "When it counts, you make the right ones."

Jared's heartbeat sped up under my hand. His lips parted like he was about to say something. But he stayed silent. He watched me, his heart hammering.

Finally, he reached up and slid his hand behind my neck, pulling me toward him.

I closed my eyes, anticipating the kiss.

"Look at me, Kennedy." His voice was thick and heavy. "You're the only person who's ever said anything like that to me. The only person who sees me that way."

Our faces were a foot apart, but it felt like Jared was so close he could hear what I was thinking.

"That's not true—"

"Shh." He moved his hand and brought his finger to my lips. "I don't care if anyone else thinks those things, as long as you do. The way I feel about you…" He bit his lip, as if he couldn't find the right words. "Sometimes, when I look at you, I can hardly breathe."

I pressed my lips against his, trying to make the space

between us disappear. It felt the way it always did when our lips finally touched. I sensed how much he wanted me—how much I mattered to him. Like a need I'd never be able to fill.

But I tried until every part of me ached with exhaustion and with something I only seemed to find with Jared.

Happiness.

⊰ • ⊱

When I woke up the next morning still tangled in Jared's arms, I felt stiff—and desperately in need of a shower. I wiggled out from underneath his arm and tiptoed past Priest, who was sleeping in the other bed.

The adjoining door was still open. Alara was buried under the covers in one bed, with Bear sprawled across the bottom, and Elle and Lukas were asleep on top of the covers in the other bed. Lukas was propped up and Elle was using his chest as a pillow. At some point, she'd changed out of the offensive pink sweats, and now she was wearing red ones.

I dug through her clothes until I found a pair of skinny jeans and a T-shirt that wouldn't look like a dress on me, and carried them into the bathroom.

The water barely had time to heat up when I stepped into the shower. As the soap slid down my back, I wished the guilt would wash away as easily.

I needed to stop feeling responsible for the horrible

things happening around me for at least a few minutes. I flipped through mental snapshots of my life, searching for a happy memory.

My house.

The smell of macaroni and cheese cooking—not the orange kind from a box, but the kind my mom always made, with bread crumbs sprinkled over the top.

A door closes upstairs, and I wait for her to come down. But it isn't her. My father smiles at me, all green eyes and dimples and five o'clock shadow.

"How's my sunshine?" He takes something out of his pocket.

I know what it is before I even see the writing on the red and white candy wrapper.

No—

I pressed the heels of my hands against my eyelids, forcing the images to fade.

Not him.

My father wasn't allowed to be my happy memory, or anything else.

The water suddenly felt heavier, like the syrupy filth inside the well in Middle River. I didn't need those awful memories coming back, too. I moved my hands away from my eyes, and the shower floor slowly came into focus.

First the tiles. Then the round silver drain. Black lines were still blurring my vision. I blinked a few times and looked down again.

Black streaks cut across the tile and the letters printed on the drain: MADE IN THE USA.

Drops of inky liquid splattered onto my skin and around my feet.

I scrambled backward, my hands slipping over the smooth glass walls. The showerhead was directly above me now. Dark water ran down my body, the sticky consistency of motor oil.

I opened my mouth to scream, and the black liquid burned its way down my throat. Cigarette butts and gasoline was my first thought. I stumbled out of the shower, gagging.

My black handprint dripped down the glass.

I snatched a towel and reached for the doorknob. The moment my fingers curled around it, I froze. A drop of clear water ran down the perfectly clean skin on my wrist. I turned back to the glass.

The handprint and the black streaks were gone.

The burning sensation in my throat and the nauseating taste in my mouth—even the smell—had all vanished. Clear water sprayed from the showerhead.

I threw on the T-shirt and jeans and tore out of the bathroom.

"Something's in here!" I yelled, slamming the door behind me.

Lukas, Elle, and Alara were awake now, watching TV.

Alara jumped out of bed. "What do you mean?"

Jared and Priest ran into the room. "What happened?" Jared asked.

I struggled to catch my breath. "Black stuff came out of the shower. It was all over me. Then it just disappeared."

"Was it thick?" Lukas asked.

"Yeah." I could still feel the slimy liquid running down my body.

Jared and Lukas exchanged a knowing look, and Priest darted into the other room. He returned moments later with a nail gun in one hand and a kitchen fire extinguisher in the other, which I knew was filled with a rock salt and water solution.

"That black stuff is a sign of demonic activity," Lukas said.

Alara walked around the room with her EMF. Priest shadowed her, with his weapon ready.

As she stepped into the bathroom, I held my breath.

"Nothing," she called from inside.

"I want to get out of here." I pulled on my boots and twisted my wet hair into a ponytail.

Elle shoved her stuff back into her bag and grabbed her coat. "Me too."

⊰ • ⊱

We waited in the Jeep while Alara checked out of the hotel and Priest took Bear down the stairs the same way we'd brought him in the night before. Priest made it to the Jeep first.

Lukas turned on the radio and switched between stations. "I want to see if anything weird is going on nearby. It might explain what happened to you in the shower."

Meteorologists continued to weigh in on the unusal weather, citing everything from global warming to acid rain as possible causes.

"Pretty soon, these geniuses will be saying the polar ice caps are causing it." Priest changed the station.

Alara jogged across the parking lot and climbed in just as the weather report cut to breaking news: "The body of Father John O'Shea was discovered this morning when a parishioner at Blessed Sacrament arrived for eight o'clock mass to find the priest hanging from the rafters above the altar. The police have ruled out suicide, due to what they are calling the *bizarre* details of the crime."

"That was an hour ago," Lukas said, pulling out of the parking space. "Where's the church?"

"Downtown. Ten minutes away." Priest had already pulled up a map on his cell.

I tried not to picture a priest hanging from the rafters of his church or the slimy black handprint on the glass in the shower. But the more I fought to keep the images away, the harder my mind held on to them.

"Think it's Andras?" Lukas asked.

We weren't far from the church, but the police had blocked off the street thanks to the morbid crowd of onlookers gathered at the corner.

"Yes." Alara didn't hesitate. "Park on the next block. We can walk."

Lukas guided the Jeep into a parking space, and Priest hauled one of the duffel bags out of the trunk.

The Boston sidewalk was teeming with people rushing to escape the rain. Before we turned the corner, I noticed something strange.

On the block across from us, one man stood in the middle of the crowd, unmoving.

People pushed past him, yet he remained stock-still, water dripping from the visor of his Red Sox baseball cap. He stared through the sea of people, his black eyes zeroing in on me. When I looked at him, crippling sensations rolled over me like waves.

An icy chill racing up my back—

Black slime sliding over my body in the shower—

The smell of ash and sulfur—

I tried to look away, but I couldn't.

Other people were staring at him, too, now—and at one another. A woman huddled beneath a designer umbrella bumped into him, then froze for a moment. The woman's composed demeanor changed, and she shoved an elderly man walking beside her. Within seconds, they were screaming at each other. As people tried to squeeze past them, they accidentally brushed against the black-eyed man. Anger spread through the crowd, radiating from him and rippling from one person to the next.

But he was the source.

Alara tugged on my jacket. "Kennedy, what are you staring at? We've gotta go."

"Watch."

A couple rushed toward him holding hands, huddled together under the guy's jacket. The girl brushed against the black-eyed man as they passed. Within seconds, she let go of her boyfriend's hand and shoved him away. They stood in the icy rain arguing, as if they didn't remember being happy moments before.

The chilling chain reaction repeated itself over and over.

"Guys," Alara yelled. "You need to see this."

I didn't turn around when I heard Jared, Lukas, Priest, and Elle come up behind us, or when Bear started growling.

"Is there a reason we stopped walking?" Elle's teeth chattered. "I'm freezing."

"What exactly are we looking at?" Priest searched the crowd.

"The guy in the Red Sox hat," Alara said. "But I don't think he's a guy."

"He looks like one of those possessed people at Faith's," Elle said.

"But he's not acting like a zombie," Lukas said.

The crowd around the black-eyed man in the Red Sox cap grew more agitated by the second, as people pushed and shouted at one another. A fight broke out between two businessmen trying to hail a cab and spilled into the street. A car swerved to avoid hitting them, but both men were so enraged neither seemed to notice.

Alara turned to Jared, Lukas, and Priest. "Look at the way the aggression is spreading through the crowd. Have you ever seen anything like it?"

Lukas shook his head. "Never."

Jared didn't say a word.

The black-eyed man tilted his head slowly to the side. There was something familiar about the way he moved and the gesture itself. He took a step forward and focused his gaze on me. His eyes narrowed in what looked like concentration. After a moment, he jerked his head back, as if something had taken him off guard.

He looked almost impressed.

Why?

The man's pupil-less black eyes changed, transforming into brown ones that could've belonged to anyone on the street.

Including me.

17. MAKER OF NIGHTMARES

A slow, menacing smile spread across the demon's face—because I was sure that's who I was looking at now. I remembered that smile. It was the same smile the little girl who crossed the salt circle at my aunt's house gave me.

The demon raised his hand slowly, as if he were going to wave. Instead, he touched his fingers to his lips and blew me a kiss.

"It's Andras." There was no doubt in my mind.

"He doesn't look like a demon to me," Elle said.

"Were you expecting a tail?" Alara asked.

Lukas studied the man in the Red Sox cap. "How do you know?"

"The way he looked at me...his smile." I pictured the scene at Faith's house, focusing on the details. "The little girl at my aunt's had the exact same smile. Even her mannerisms were the same. And remember the way she licked the salt off her finger? She was the only one who wasn't acting like a zombie." I looked over at Lukas. "Did you see the way his eyes changed color? They looked human."

"Demons can change their eye color," Lukas said, without taking his eyes off Andras. "It helps them hide in human bodies."

When they possess people.

"Kennedy's right. That's him." Alara unzipped her coat and reached for the paintball gun on her tool belt.

Jared caught her wrist. "What are you doing? You can't pull out a gun on a busy street. The cops will be here in two minutes, if we don't get our butts kicked by a mob first."

Alara kept her hand on the grip. "We can't let him get away."

"Um...I don't think he's trying to get away," Elle said. "It looks like he's coming over here. Sort of."

The man in the Red Sox cap walked toward us, zeroing in on a blonde a few feet ahead of him. She stopped when she saw him, her eyes locking on his. The man's body jerked forward. A second later, the blonde lurched backward as if someone had bumped into her, and the man in the Red Sox cap collapsed on the wet sidewalk. Two people stopped and helped him up. From the dazed expression on his face, it was hard to tell if he remembered anything.

The woman stood frozen, ignoring the sea of people pushing past her. Everything from her rigid posture to the way she stood motionless in the rain mirrored the way the man in the baseball cap had looked minutes ago.

The blonde stared right at us, and the familiar smile spread across her lips.

Within seconds, it happened again. A kid, clutching the straps of his backpack, rushed by her and stopped the moment her black eyes found his. The woman's body jerked forward, then went slack, like someone had yanked the string on the back of a marionette. Something hit the kid's backpack, forcing him backward. He started to fall, but caught himself before he hit the sidewalk. When the kid stood up, he was wearing the same menacing smile.

The demon drew closer, only half a block away now.

The kid watched a girl skateboarding toward him. The moment the skater noticed him and their eyes met, she stepped off her board. It rolled into the street, just as the boy's body jerked. The same invisible force smacked against her, and the skater caught herself mid-fall. The boy wasn't as lucky. He hit the ground hard and curled into a ball, clutching his arm.

The skateboarder pulled her shoulders back until she was standing impossibly straight. Then she smiled.

Priest watched with a morbid fascination. "He's moving from body to body."

Lukas looked around. "We need to get out of here."

Alara still had her hand on her gun. "We can't lose him."

"We can't unload salt rounds and cold-iron bolts out here in the open," Lukas said. "And if he can jump from body to body like that, it's easier for him to get away if we miss. We need him to follow us somewhere more secluded."

"The wharf isn't far." Jared pointed up the street. "I bet the longshoremen don't work when it's pouring rain. It's probably deserted."

The skateboarder Andras had jumped into was only a quarter of a block away.

"Go," I said, pushing Jared.

He grabbed my hand and we took off.

The sky darkened the way it had in the prison yard the night I assembled the Shift. Icy rain pounded down on us, and thunder rumbled in the distance. The traffic lights next to the demon shorted out, spraying sparks onto the street.

A transformer blew ahead of us and every light on the block went black.

"Make sure we don't lose him," Priest said.

I glanced behind us. The demon was still there, strolling casually down the street in the body of the skateboarder.

The sky grew darker. Even in the failing light, I saw them—the source of the rumble I had mistaken for thunder.

Birds.

Thousands of them.

Black rain. That's what Alara called it.

Bear barked, but he was drowned out by a sky full of dark wings.

The demon jumped again, this time into a woman carrying an armload of shopping bags. She looked right at him, then dropped the bags. Her back arched until she was standing impossibly straight, like the others. Something hit the ground next to her, splashing in the puddle at her feet. Another object dropped, and then another.

Birds fell from the sky all around her, crashing against the sidewalk like rocks.

People screamed and covered their heads.

The demon strode toward us, still animating the woman's body. The carcasses of dead crows, pigeons, and sparrows littered the ground as more birds thudded against the roofs of nearby cars. She stepped over the feathered bodies and crossed the street.

A man in a blue hoodie rounded the corner, and the demon changed direction and stepped in front of him. The woman's black eyes met his. Her body sagged for a split second before she dropped to her knees, and the man lurched forward, barely breaking stride.

The traffic lights swung dangerously from the wires on the street alongside us. A wire snapped, and one of the lights smashed against the asphalt like a warning.

We elbowed our way through the mob of frightened

people, some rushing to get out of the street while others were too stunned to move. We turned onto Pearl Street, where the sky hadn't turned completely dark yet. I fought the urge to look back, terrified that Andras might be right behind us. Judging from the rate at which he was jumping from body to body, he could be anywhere.

Or anyone.

Jared ran down an alleyway that led to the waterfront.

When we reached the wharf, Bear charged ahead of us, dodging forklifts and rows of metal shipping containers arranged like a giant maze. He stopped before every turn to be sure we were still behind him.

Priest pointed at an unchained warehouse door at the end of the row. "That way."

Inside, there were more shipping containers, surrounded by pallets of lumber and sheet metal stacked against the walls. Cables hung from the ceiling above sawhorses and makeshift worktables, outfitted with rusted table saws and heavy machinery.

The metal door slammed behind us, the sound vibrating between the containers.

I turned around slowly, my heart thudding in my chest.

Instead of Andras, a rough-looking dockworker, wearing a hooded canvas coat and matching tan coveralls, stood just inside the door. He lit a cigarette with a blue plastic lighter and took a long drag, like he'd been waiting for a smoke break all day.

"We gotta get rid of this guy," Priest whispered.

The dockworker looked up, the cherry of his cigarette glowing in his shiny black eyes.

Jared tightened his hand around mine and tried to pull me behind him, but I held my ground. I was the reason Andras was here, instead of trapped somewhere between our world and hell, where he belonged.

I'm not hiding behind anyone.

Jared opened the duffel bag and pulled out a semi-automatic paintball gun. Priest grabbed the Punisher and dropped to the floor like a sniper, aiming the massive weapon at the demon.

Andras took another drag and walked toward us, his brown leather work boots squeaking across the concrete floor.

Lukas and Alara scrambled for the bag, but Jared and Priest didn't hesitate. They both fired, and a hailstorm of ammo ripped through the air. Paintball cases exploded against the demon's chest, the salt and holy water cocktail burning right through the canvas coat. The Punisher's crowd-control rounds pummeled Andras' torso, and he stumbled back.

Lukas reached for his crossbow and a handful of cold-iron bolts.

"You can't use those," I yelled over the ammo. "You'll kill the guy Andras possessed."

"Right." Lukas shook his head as if he should've known better and tossed the weapon on the floor.

Priest peered over the top of the Punisher's sight. "He's not going down."

Andras glanced down at the smoking holes in his shirt. "I hope you have something more than this." His voice didn't sound anything like the demonic voices in horror movies. It was deep, and deceptively human.

Bear charged in front of us, snarling.

The demon flicked his cigarette across the floor and responded with a growl of his own. The dog dropped onto his belly, whimpering.

Alara knelt on the floor and used the black marker that never left her tool belt to draw a pitchfork. I recognized the beginning of the protective voodoo symbol that was etched into the medal around my neck.

The Hand of Eshu.

Between my eidetic memory and artistic abilities, I could draw the symbol more accurately than Alara. The demon watched, mildly interested.

Elle and I sprinted toward Alara and dropped down next to her. "Let me do it."

She held out the marker, her hand shaking. I worked fast, drawing perpendicular lines, and the slanted cross in the center.

"In the Labyrinth, names have power," the demon said.

He's talking about hell.

"Alara." The demon pronounced her name slowly. "Means 'ruler of all.' I command six thousand legions, and you do not even rule this Legion of black doves. Tell me, Alara, Ruler of All, when the nightmares come, what do you fear?"

Footsteps echoed from somewhere beyond the shipping containers.

"Alara?" a girl's voice called out.

Alara's eyes darted around the room. A girl a few years younger than her stepped out from between the dented metal aisle of shipping containers. She was tall and thin with dark corkscrew curls, and she shared her sister's striking features.

"Maya," Alara whispered. She stumbled toward her younger sister, the person she had sacrificed everything for.

My eyes darted to Andras, but he was gone. A moment later, he stepped out from between the containers where Maya was standing.

The demon's eyes were blue again, disguising his true nature. "Hi, Maya. I'm a friend of your sister's." His formal tone and speech pattern had changed, replaced by a more casual one.

Maya gave him an open smile. "Hi."

"Don't go near him!" Alara yelled, racing toward her sister.

Lukas and Jared were closing in from the sides.

When Maya saw the terrified expression on Alara's face, she took a step back. But she wasn't fast enough. Andras was behind her in seconds, and the huge hands of the man he'd possessed closed around the girl's throat.

Lukas raised his crossbow as Maya struggled for air.

"I wouldn't do that," Andras said. "You won't hurt me, but one of those bolts could kill her."

Lukas lowered the weapon slowly.

Jared inched closer. Andras noticed, and tightened his hold on Maya's neck.

"Please don't hurt her," Alara pleaded.

"You never answered my question, Alara," Andras said. "When the nightmares come, what do you fear?"

Alara fell to her knees, tears running down her cheeks. "I'll tell you anything you want. Just don't hurt her."

The demon's irises turned black, the color seeping out from the center of his eyes like ink. "Wrong answer."

Andras lifted Maya off the ground by her neck and looked right at Alara as he twisted his hands in a sharp motion. Maya's neck turned unnaturally between his palms, and her body went limp.

Jared and Lukas charged Andras as he let Maya's body drop onto the concrete.

"No!" Alara let out a piercing scream so raw and guttural it made my skin crawl. She collapsed onto the floor sobbing, and I threw my arms around her.

Elle's eyes went wide. "Oh my god. He killed her."

Andras stepped away from the body, moving slower than before.

Jared knelt next to Maya's body and reached out to close her eyes. When his hand touched her skin, it slipped right through her. Jared swept his arms over the spot where Maya's body had fallen. Her faded silhouette remained for a moment and then vanished.

Alara stared at the chipped wall behind us, her

expression blank. I grabbed her shoulders, forcing her to look at me. "It wasn't real. Andras created some kind of illusion. Maya was never here."

"She's right." Priest pointed across the room. "There's no body."

It took a moment for the words to register before Alara stole a glance at the spot where Maya had fallen. She rubbed her swollen red eyes and looked again. "Where is she?"

Jared and Lukas rushed back to where we sat huddled on the floor. Bear chased after them.

"It wasn't real," I repeated.

"Somehow he manifested your fear," Lukas said.

Alara stared at Lukas for a long moment. "How are we going to fight him?"

"If our physical weapons won't work, let's see how he handles a spiritual weapon." Priest opened his journal and flipped through it. When he found the page he was looking for, he recited the words:

"I cast you out, unclean spirit,
along with every Satanic power of the enemy,
every spectre from hell, and all your fell companions.
In the name of our Lord."

I recognized the Rite of Exorcism from *Rituale Romanum*. I'd seen it written in Priest's journal once, and it was the same passage Konstantin had recited in the entry from Faith's notebook.

Priest kept reading:

"Tremble in fear, Satan,
you enemy of faith,
you foe of the human race,
you begetter of death, you robber of life,
you corrupter of justice,
you root of all evil and vice."

The demon laughed. "I have shed blood on the sword of an angel and battled demons in the cages of hell. I do not fear you."

Priest's voice rose.

"I adjure you, ancient serpent,
by the judge of the living and the dead,
by your Creator,
by the Creator of the whole universe—"

"I am the Author of Discords, and I have faced exorcists stronger than you. But in the cages of hell, they called me by another name. Maker of Nightmares," Andras said. "Allow me to make yours, Owen Merriweather."

Jared, Lukas, Alara, Elle, and I looked around. It took us all a moment to realize the demon was talking about Priest.

Andras raised his arms in the air, and a spray of black liquid the consistency of motor oil rose toward the ceiling. The liquid splashed against the rafters above our heads, twisting into thick ropes on its way back down.

Not ropes.

Snakes.

Another trick.

Priest looked up in time to see the writhing black mass coming at him. The journal slipped from his hands as the shower of snakes hit, their bodies draping over him like a net. I could tell from the terrified look on Priest's face that he didn't realize the snakes were an illusion.

"They're not real!" I shouted.

Priest deflected the smaller serpents with his body and clutched frantically at the larger ones, hurling them away. "Get them off me! Get them off!"

I stumbled toward him and reached for a black snake draped over Priest's shoulder. When I touched it, my hand slipped right through and the snakes disappeared.

"Priest. Look at me." I grabbed his face in my hands. "The snakes aren't real. Don't you remember what Andras did to Maya?"

Priest stared back at me, his expression dazed. After a moment, the fog lifted. "Kennedy? Did you see them?"

"They were some kind of illusion," I said, trying to reassure him.

Priest nodded. "I kept trying to tell myself that, but it

was like my mind wouldn't listen. It was so real. I could feel them slithering all over me." He shuddered.

Jared, Lukas, Alara, and Elle crowded around us, and the demon laughed. But Andras' shoulders sagged and his movements were slower, as if manifesting Alara's and Priest's fears had drained him.

"Enough games," the demon said.

"We can't fight him," Lukas said. "He's too strong."

Elle's eyes darted to the door. "There's no way to outrun him."

I have to trust Faith.

"We can raise the barrier," I said. "Maybe it will buy us some time."

Lukas held out his hand. "It's our only shot."

"What about Elle?" I asked. "She can't be part of the circle."

Lukas stepped behind her. "Stay in the middle and hold Kennedy's journal so the rest of us can see it." By now, he knew I only needed to see something once to remember every detail.

Elle wrapped one arm around Bear. We joined hands and followed the instructions in my aunt's journal.

I recited the words from memory, while the other Legion members read from the page: *"May the bonds of blood and the marks we bear protect us."*

Andras laughed, but our voices remained strong.

"As the wings of the black dove carry us."

A surge of energy cracked against us and hurled our bodies across the floor. My cheek hit the concrete, and I struggled to push myself onto my knees.

The barrier didn't work.

My friends lay scattered around the room, and Andras stood in the center of it all. His sadistic expression looked frighteningly human.

Faith was right. This is a fight we can't win.

"From where I'm standing, these odds don't look even," a male voice that didn't belong to Andras called out. "A marquis of hell preying on a bunch of kids? Times must be tough, Andras."

A tall man I'd never seen before stood at the far end of the warehouse smoking a cigarette. His sandy-blond hair was neatly trimmed, and dark sunglasses covered his eyes. Between the cigarette hanging from his lips, his SWAT-style clothing, and the black tactical boots sticking out underneath his coat, he didn't look like the kind of guy you wanted to mess with. He dropped a leather doctor's bag and a red plastic container on the floor next to him.

Andras stared back at him through the dockworker's eyes. "I am happy to prey on you first."

A second man, dressed in matching sunglasses and tactical gear, stepped out from behind one of the metal shipping containers with a black canvas bag. Something was looped around his other hand. His dark features and a few days' worth of stubble made him look even more formidable than his partner.

He opened his hand, releasing what looked like a whip. He snapped the ivory-colored weapon, and it arced in the air, the individual sections clicking forward one at a time like links in a bike chain.

The whip—or whatever it was—struck Andras.

The demon arched his back and roared in pain. He tried to pull it off, but the whip began to move without any help from the man wielding it. The ivory sections latched on to the demon's back, pulsing and writhing like rats.

"It's alive." Priest watched in awe.

"What the hell is it?" Lukas asked.

Priest shook his head. "I don't know, but I want to meet the guy who made it."

The man guiding the whip flicked his wrist and retracted the weapon. Andras dropped to his knees as the individual parts of the whip ripped from his back.

Elle squinted at the jagged pieces of ivory. "Are those bones?"

Alara recoiled. "They look like vertebrae."

The whip struck again, and Andras let out another enraged cry.

"You must've wasted a lot of energy on whatever you were doing before we got here," the man holding the whip said.

I remembered how drained Andras looked after he manifested Maya. Then he brought Priest's fear to life. Had the *Rituale Romanum* rite affected the demon, too? Did he have to fight it somehow?

The taller man in the long coat lifted the red plastic container and walked toward Andras.

A gas can.

"Do you think he's gonna set Andras on fire?" Priest sounded hopeful.

"Not unless he wants to burn up the rest of us, too." Lukas glanced at his brother. "I'm thinking it's not gasoline."

Jared nodded. "Makes sense."

"Why does he have a gas can?" Elle's eyes darted between Lukas and Jared. "Will someone tell me what's happening?"

"Relax." Lukas pulled her against his shoulder. "I'm guessing it's holy water."

"You're *guessing*?"

The tall man hoisted the can in the air and dumped the contents over Andras. Clear, odorless liquid splashed onto the dockworker's body. Steam rose from the areas where the liquid hit his skin, leaving behind red burns.

The guy with the whip rushed toward them, hooking the weapon through a loop on the back of his pants. The ivory bones, or whatever they were, coiled through the loop like a sleeping snake. He opened a black canvas bag similar to the duffels Priest packed his gear in, and dragged out a heavy chain. The two men worked together, winding the chains around Andras' neck, wrists, and feet in a strange configuration and securing them with a padlock.

"I will tear off your skin and strip your bones," the demon said.

"That gives me something to look forward to," the man with the whip said, hauling Andras to his feet and half-dragging him out of the room by the padlock. The demon bared his teeth, snapping at his captor like a rabid dog.

"Are you all right?" The tall stranger wiped the holy water off his hands with the edge of his black coat, then removed his sunglasses and tucked them in his jacket pocket.

"I think so," I said.

Priest helped Alara up and examined her eyes. "You hit your head pretty hard. You might have a concussion."

"I'm fine." She swatted his hand away, sounding like herself for the first time since Andras brought her worst fear to life.

"Who are you guys?" Lukas asked.

The stranger raised an eyebrow. "A little appreciation would be nice. We did just save your lives."

"How did you know we were in here?" Jared asked. "This place isn't exactly on Boston's Freedom Trail tour. Were you following us?"

"We were following Andras, but apparently he was following you."

"How do you know about Andras?" Priest sounded shocked.

"I've spent the better part of my life monitoring Andras, though I never expected to come face-to-face with him." He extended his hand to Priest. "My name is Dimitri, and that was my associate, Gabriel."

Priest reached out to shake his hand.

Jared caught his arm. "Look at his ring."

A heavy signet ring encircled Dimitri's finger. A triangle with an eye on top, like the one on the back of a dollar bill, was engraved in the silver. Lines resembling sunbeams radiated from the eye. The ring looked exactly like the one Priest's grandfather had described.

"He's Illuminati," Jared said.

Dimitri smiled. "The Eye of Providence is popular these days. I see it online all the time."

"But you didn't buy that ring online, did you? Or it wouldn't have the Rays of Illumination on it," Priest said.

"And you would've called the symbol the All-Seeing Eye," Alara added. "Only Illuminati members refer to it as the Eye of Providence."

Dimitri's hazel eyes flickered with amusement, and he raised his hands in surrender. "Well played, Miss Sabatier."

Alara stepped back, stunned. "How do you know my name?"

"I know all your names. Jared and Lukas Lockhart. Alara Sabatier. Kennedy Waters." Dimitri ticked off our names until he reached Priest. "And you're Owen Merriweather. But I understand you prefer to be called Priest." He stopped in front of Elle. "Now, you I don't know. Have they added a sixth member to the Legion?"

"No." Elle swung her red hair over her shoulder and folded her arms. "And my mother told me never to talk to strange men."

"Good advice for a young lady." Dimitri didn't sound condescending, but that didn't stop Alara from being offended.

She took a roll of pennies out of her tool belt and curled her hand around them. "Strangers aren't an issue for young ladies who hit hard enough."

"I stand corrected." Dimitri looked around the warehouse. "I'm surprised Andras followed you in here. In his weakened state, he needs a body at all times. I would've expected him to stay in crowded areas."

I shuddered, remembering the way the demon had jumped from body to body while he'd chased us through the streets. "He has to possess someone all the time?"

"Don't ask him questions," Alara snapped. "He's Illuminati. We can't trust him."

Dimitri studied Alara for a moment. "We're on the same

side, Miss Sabatier. Whatever stories you've heard about the Illuminati are probably from hundreds of years ago."

Priest turned to Dimitri. "Like the story my granddad told me about two guys wearing rings just like yours, who beat him up in college and stole a grimoire from a library at Yale? That wasn't hundreds of years ago."

Dimitri unwrapped a pack of Dunhills. "I'm familiar with the incident, but I didn't realize your grandfather was involved. I understand he was a brilliant inventor and mathematician." Dimitri lit the black cigarette. "Those men were part of a rogue sect of the Illuminati—one that was not acknowledged by the Grand Master. Your grandfather was attacked at Yale shortly after the Order was formed. But Gabriel and I are not affiliated with the Order or its members. We want to stop Andras as much as you do."

"You guys never offered to help the Legion before. Why now?" Jared asked.

"Andras is free, and that affects us all," Dimitri said. "If he opens the gates, the world as we know it will cease to exist."

Jared eyed Dimitri, suspicious. "You guys show up out of nowhere and give us some speech about how we're all playing for the same team, and expect us to just take your word for it?"

Dimitri walked over to Jared. "We saved all your lives.

If we harbored any ill will toward you, we would've let the demon finish you off."

"We were doing fine on our own," Priest said.

Dimitri laughed. "Are you referring to what you were doing when we arrived? Holding hands while you waited for your Wonder Twin powers to activate? You don't even know why it didn't work, do you?"

Jared's eyes darted from Lukas to Alara and Priest.

"You need all five members of the Legion to raise the barrier," Dimitri said. "Without Kennedy's aunt, you're one person short."

"My aunt is dead." Considering how much he knew about the five of us, I probably wasn't telling him anything new. "I took her place in the Legion."

Dimitri's smile faded and a worried crease formed between his eyes. "Well, then that explains why your little hand-holding demonstration failed." He looked right at me, his eyes searching mine. "You can't be the fifth member of the Legion, Kennedy."

I was sick of people telling me what I could and couldn't do—and tired of being judged because my family had kept the Legion a secret from me. "Why is that?"

Dimitri's eyes clouded over, and he hesitated as if he was choosing his words carefully. "You can't be a member of the Legion, because you're one of us."

A lara stepped in front of me protectively, her tool belt rattling around her waist. "If you want to con someone, do your homework first. Kennedy didn't know anything about the Illuminati until she met us."

Hearing Alara defend me took some of the sting out of Dimitri's accusation. Why was he lying about me?

Dimitri watched me over Alara's shoulder. "That might be true, but her mother certainly did."

"I already know the story," I said, heading him off. "My aunt told me how the Illuminati sent some guy to pretend he cared about her, when he was really spying on her. My mom was the one who figured it out."

"But your aunt didn't tell you the rest of the story, did she? About what happened after she left the Legion?"

"I don't know what you're trying to—"

Dimitri cut me off. "The best way to hide your own guilt is to point the finger at someone else. Especially if the person you're pointing it at *expected you to blame him*, because it was part of a larger plan. Faith's boyfriend wasn't the only Illuminati member spying on her."

I wasn't sure where he was going with this. "What are you saying?"

"When your mother revealed the truth about Archer, she earned your aunt's trust. Your mom was a smart woman, one of the Illuminati's top operatives."

"Liar!" Elle shouted at Dimitri, pulling me away from him. "Don't listen to him, Kennedy. He's messing with your head."

Dimitri took a step closer. "Didn't you ever wonder why your father left?"

The words cut through me, reopening my oldest wound. Judging from the look on Dimitri's face, he knew it, too. "He left when you were five, if I'm not mistaken? Out of the blue, without any explanation? Your father figured out the truth, Kennedy—that not one but two Illuminati spies had infiltrated his family. Archer was the first, the sacrificial lamb.

"Your mother was the second operative, the one the Illuminati were counting on all along. The plan was genius." Dimitri dropped his cigarette on the floor and ground it into the concrete with his boot. "What better way to get close to Faith than by marrying her only brother?"

I didn't know why this guy was lying about my mom, but I was too angry to care. "My mother would never do anything like that. She loved my dad, and it destroyed her when he left."

Elle squeezed my hand.

My mind pulled up an image of my mom sitting on her bed, surrounded by a sea of tissues. She was holding a framed photo of my dad, her eyes swollen and red.

"I have no way of knowing how your mother felt about him, but I do know that she was Illuminati." Dimitri turned to Priest. "Which, correct me if I'm wrong, means Kennedy can never be a member of the Legion. What is it you say in the Legion? 'No ties to darkness or Illumination'?"

Priest looked at Jared for answers.

"You're pretty impressed with yourself, aren't you?" Jared asked. "But Faith knew that better than anyone, and she left Kennedy something a Legion member passes down to the person they choose to take their place. Faith never would've done that if Kennedy's mom was Illuminati."

Priest nodded at me as if he was saying, *I've got your back*.

Dimitri walked toward me. "Then maybe you can answer a question for me, Kennedy. If you are truly the fifth member of the Legion, why couldn't the five of you raise the barrier? It should've been easy."

A sinking feeling settled in my stomach because I was thinking the same thing.

"We probably screwed something up," Priest said. "We do it all the time."

Alara shot him a warning look.

"She hasn't earned her mark yet," Lukas said. "I'm sure that has something to do with it."

Alara crossed her arms. "If that's all the proof you have, then none of us believe you, any more than we trust you."

Dimitri shook his head. "You kids are loyal, I'll give you that. You would've been valuable additions to the Illuminati."

"I'd rather be dead," Priest said with a hatred I'd never heard from him before.

Dimitri walked over to the leather doctor's bag. "There's only one way to find out if I'm telling the truth."

He reached inside and took out a mason jar with what looked like voodoo symbols painted on the outside of the glass. A thick layer of red wax covered the lid and dripped down the sides. Dimitri held the jar in front of Alara. "You know what this is, don't you, Miss Sabatier?"

"Where did you get that?" Alara whispered, backing away.

"We use Battle Cruets all the time. The Illuminati embrace the knowledge of any culture that has surpassed us when it comes to dealing with spirits and demons."

"What the hell is it?" Lukas asked Alara.

"We call it a War Jar." She didn't take her eyes off the wax-covered glass. "Bokors, who practice dark arts and sell their services, use them. One of the most common services they offer is hexing people. There are different ways to do it—dolls, spell bags, or using photos or items that belonged to the person you want to hex. But the War Jar is one of the worst."

"Your grandmother taught you well." Dimitri smiled.

"My grandmother would never have touched one of those. Torturing people isn't part of our religion."

"I should've clarified." Dimitri sounded apologetic. "I retrieved the contents of this cruet from the home of a person who was being tormented by it."

Elle eyed the jar suspiciously. "What's in there exactly? I don't see anything."

"If he's telling the truth, there's a vengeance spirit inside." Alara held her arm out in front of Elle to keep her from getting any closer to Dimitri—or the jar. "You trap the spirit in a glass container and take it to the home of the person you want to hex. To release the vengeance spirit, you break the glass and bury the pieces nearby, usually in the person's yard. The spirit can't leave the place where the pieces are buried, unless people like us come along and destroy it."

Dimitri raised the jar higher. "Or someone like me brings another Battle Cruet to trap it."

"How will your black magic jar prove anything?" Elle asked him.

But I already knew.

"Someone has to destroy the vengeance spirit inside, or the innocent victim of its wrath will never have any peace," Dimitri explained. "Kennedy's area of expertise is symbols and invocation. All she has to do is draw a symbol that will destroy the spirit. If she's a member of the Legion, she'll earn her mark."

"That's the demon tattoo, right?" Elle whispered to Alara.

Priest stared at Dimitri, dumbfounded. "How do you know that?"

"It's my job to know as much as possible about the Legion of the Black Dove. As I said, we're fighting for the same cause."

Jared stepped in front of me protectively. "She's not doing it. She doesn't have to prove anything to you or anyone else."

But I could tell from the way Alara, Lukas, and Priest were looking at each other that I did. Dimitri had planted a seed of doubt in their minds.

Worse, he'd fed the one already planted in mine.

"I'll do it," I said.

Jared cradled my face in his hands. "Kennedy, you don't have to do this."

Priest's eyes dropped to the floor.

Gabriel emerged from between two metal shipping containers, his clothing completely soaked. "He's chained up, and I doused him with enough holy water to drown an elephant. But they're still prepping the sanctuary, so we can't move him yet."

Dimitri patted down his pockets, most likely searching for more cigarettes. "That was supposed to be done days ago."

"There was some confusion about the cross," Gabriel said. "It wasn't an actual altar cross."

"Idiots." Dimitri riffled through his pockets, clearly agitated. "We can't afford mistakes like this. If Andras hadn't wasted so much energy terrorizing these kids, chains and holy water wouldn't have been enough to hold him. And without knowing how many souls he's consumed, there's no way to predict how long it will take for him to regain his strength."

"Consumed?" Elle whispered to Lukas. "As in..."

"Possessed and killed," Gabriel said. "The more souls Andras consumes, the stronger he gets."

Gabriel peeled off his wet sweater. Dozens of black tattoos covered his right arm—the Eye of Providence, a hooked X, and other symbols I didn't recognize. His left arm appeared to be bare until he turned, revealing a strange tattoo on the inside of his forearm.

A medieval cross with a hawk in the center and Latin script running down the bottom.

I pictured the letters and scrolled through lists of words in my mind for English root words to translate the Latin. But for some reason, I couldn't call up the last few letters of the tattoo.

Something was wrong. I had just looked at it a second ago, which meant my eidetic memory had already recorded the image, but I couldn't picture it in my mind. I glanced at Gabriel's arm again. The symbols looked exactly the same, but he was standing too far away for me to see the script clearly.

My eyes must be tired.

I closed my eyes for a second and opened them again, but I still couldn't read the writing. I realized something even more disturbing. Gabriel hadn't moved since he took off his sweater.

How did I see them before?

"What are you staring at?" Alara asked.

I looked away, embarrassed she'd noticed. "The weird cross on Gabriel's arm."

"It's another Illuminati symbol," she said.

Gabriel noticed the jar in Dimitri's hand. "Looks like I interrupted something."

Dimitri shook the jar. "Kennedy still believes she's a member of the Legion. I offered her a way to find out for sure."

"Why torture yourself, kid?" Gabriel asked.

I swallowed hard. "Open it."

"Not yet. You need to be ready." Dimitri pointed. "Draw a symbol to destroy the spirit, then I'll give you the cruet."

Alara took the black marker out of her tool belt and handed it to me. "Show them what you've got."

I nodded and knelt on the cold concrete floor, picturing the symbol I was about to draw.

The Devil's Trap—the symbol I'd used to destroy Darien Shears, the spirit who had warned me not to assemble the Shift.

I should've listened.

I drew the outer circle first, then a heptagram with a seven-pointed star inside it. My mind had recorded every detail—the symbol in the center of the star, the names around the innermost circle: Samael, Raphael, Anael, Gabriel, Michael...

When I finished, I stood up and tossed the marker at Dimitri's feet. "Done."

He walked around the symbol, nodding. "Impressive. You certainly have the gift."

"It's her specialty." Jared sounded proud.

"We call them gifts," Dimitri said. "Some Illuminati members have them as well."

"Open it." My throat felt like sandpaper. I wanted this to be over.

Dimitri held out the jar. "The cruet has to be broken, not opened. You should be the one to release the spirit."

"That leaves no room for doubt," Gabriel said, from where he stood watching.

My hand closed around the glass, and I carried the War Jar into the center of the Devil's Trap.

"Stand on the outside," Alara called out.

Of course. An amateur mistake.

I moved outside the symbol and leaned over, stretching toward the center. A gray mist swirled behind the glass. The wax slid beneath my fingers as I let the jar drop and yanked my arm back.

The glass shattered, and waxy shards spun across the floor.

My pulse raced as the vengeance spirit materialized. Dirty sneakers and worn jeans covered with mud...bloody hands gripping a wooden handle...the dull, bloodstained blade of an ax. The woman's face took a moment to solidify, her features twisted into a deadly expression. The hate in her eyes was unmistakable.

And all that blood.

"I told him if he hurt me again, I'd kill him," she said, looking right at me. The woman walked toward me, balancing the ax on her shoulder. "You were supposed to protect me, but none of you cowards did a damn thing."

When she reached the outer circle of the Devil's Trap, her body convulsed as if she'd touched an electrified fence. The force threw her back into the center of the symbol.

Just like it did when Darien Shears tried to cross one.

But she wasn't as strong as Darien. As she struggled to get up, her form began to fade. She pointed a bloody finger at me. "I'll see you in hell."

The spirit cried out in pain, and her body flickered one last time before it exploded into millions of tiny particles.

Don't wait. It'll only make it harder.

I reached into my pocket and scooped out a handful of salt and rubbed the crystals over my wrist. I stared at the scuffed toes of my boots. The next few minutes would change my life, one way or another.

What if the mark didn't show up and I wasn't the fifth member of the Legion? Would my friendships vanish like the tiny bits of the vengeance spirit I had just destroyed? Who else would Faith have chosen? My deadbeat of a father?

I kept my eyes fixed on the concrete, my boots, the edge of the Devil's Trap—anything to avoid my friends' faces as they waited for the moment that would determine my fate.

It's been long enough.

I turned my wrist over and flexed my fingers.

The moment was here.

20. LION'S DEN

I raised my eyes slowly, wanting to know the truth and not wanting to know at the same time. I stared down at my wrist.

Unmarked.

I held my breath, afraid to move.

I'm not one of them.

This time there were no loopholes left.

I'd drawn the Devil's Trap that destroyed the spirit in the War Jar, and I'd watched Jared and Lukas bury my aunt, the fifth member of the Legion.

I remembered waiting for my mark inside the West Virginia State Penitentiary. I'd been so sure the lines were carving themselves into my skin.

But they weren't.

That night broke me. At least, I thought it did. But it was nothing compared to how I felt right now—shattered, empty, and alone.

Please let this be another nightmare. Let me wake up.

"Kennedy?" Jared sounded nervous, which meant he saw it, too.

"I'm sorry, kid," Gabriel said.

I spun around, still cradling my wrist. "Are you?"

Dimitri lit another black cigarette. "You needed to know the truth."

The truth.

"Even if she isn't the fifth member of the Legion, that doesn't prove her mother was Illuminati." Jared wasn't giving up on me.

The fifth member.

Faith must've picked my father, her only other option.

Dimitri rubbed his temples. "Your mother didn't have much family, did she, Kennedy? Just one sister, and I'm willing to bet they weren't close. The Order of the Enlightened never chooses operatives with close family ties. It's one of the criteria for selection."

"What did you call them?" Alara sounded stunned.

Dimitri flicked his ash on the floor. "The Order of the Enlightened. Do you recognize the name?"

Alara tensed behind me. "No. I thought you said something else."

She was lying.

"The Order of the Enlightened operated outside the laws of our organization," he continued. "They were engaged in dangerous behavior, which the Illuminati weren't even aware of. After your father left, we sent someone to speak with your mother and try to reason with her."

I squared my shoulders. "I don't believe you."

Dimitri turned to Gabriel. "Please confirm that Elizabeth Waters was one of us."

"She was part of the Order, but I wouldn't call her one of us," Gabriel said.

"A shepherd is responsible for all his sheep, Gabriel. Even the lost ones."

He threw Dimitri a hard look. "Some sheep want to stay lost."

"Tell Kennedy how you knew her mother," Dimitri said.

Every muscle in my body tensed. I was still trying to figure out what was wrong with my memory. The last thing I wanted was to hear about how Gabriel supposedly knew my mom.

Gabriel didn't move for a moment, and I thought the conversation was over. Then he took a deep breath. "I was a member of the Order of the Enlightened, until I figured out what they were really up to, which had nothing to do with the garbage they were feeding us. I told the Illuminati what I'd learned, and they welcomed me back. Eventually, I convinced the Grand Master your mother was worth saving, too.

"So I went to your house in Georgetown, the one with the green door. Your father was gone by then." He smiled to himself, as if recalling a fond memory. "Your mom cooked me dinner a few times. She made a killer lasagna, and the best marinara sauce I've ever had in my life."

Marinara. Mom's signature recipe.

"Anyone can drive by Kennedy's house and see what color her door is," Elle said, her tone venomous.

Gabriel's smile faded. "I knew that house inside and out. Elizabeth lived there before she married Kennedy's father." He turned to me. "I stained those wood floors and built the shelves in the library. Are they still there?"

I didn't react. Anyone who'd ever set foot in my house would know about the floors and the library shelves.

"I also built a few things you probably never saw," he said. "Your mom had this hidden door in the back of her closet."

The words slammed into me, and I couldn't catch my breath.

The crawl space.

I'd never told anyone about the tiny crawl space in my mother's closet, or the night I spent hidden inside. Not even Elle. My friends knew about my crippling fear of the dark, but no one knew how it started.

Gabriel was still talking, but the memory was already taking over.

"Someone's in the house," my mom whispered, pulling

a board away from the wall to reveal a small opening in the back of her closet. "Stay here until I come back. Don't make a sound."

Don't make a sound or the bad guys will hear you. That's what she meant.

I squeezed inside as she replaced the board, drowning me in darkness. Not the kind of dark where you could see silhouettes, but a blackness that swallows everything. I closed my eyes and tried to pretend I was still in my bed.

Then I heard the sounds—the stairs creaking, furniture scraping against the floor, muffled voices. I wished my dad hadn't left us. He would've scared away whoever was in the house. I held my hand against the board, praying for my mom to come back. Eventually, the wood gave beneath my palm and a thin stream of light flooded the space.

Black splotches exploded in front of my eyes as they adjusted to the light again. I saw the closet floor through the opening—my mom's red high heels and her fuzzy bedroom slippers. Then her face peering into the crawl space and her arms reaching for me.

And something else...

I fought to hold on to the memory I'd spent my whole life fighting. Usually the memory ended the moment my mom pulled me out of the closet. But there was more—pieces my mind had repressed.

As she pulled me out, I glanced back at the terrifying

space. An image blurred past—painted on the wall, black like the darkness.

Don't look.

But I already had, I just never remembered until now.

A medieval cross with a hawk in the center and Latin script running down the bottom—the letters I thought I'd seen on Gabriel's arm, before I realized he was standing too far away for me to actually see them. The rest of the tattoo—the part I *had* seen—must've broken through whatever wall my mind had built around that night.

Which means they're telling the truth about my mom.

The realization was worse than not being a member of the Legion. My mom's whole life was a lie.

"I'm sorry," Gabriel said. "We shouldn't be the ones telling you this. I wanted your mother to leave the Order and start over."

Elle pushed past us and strode up to Dimitri. "Even if your friend here did wax Kennedy's mom's floors and raid her fridge, it doesn't mean she was Illuminati."

"Maybe they were friends, and Kennedy's mom had no idea Gabriel was a member of the Order," Jared said. "None of this proves anything." He didn't believe Gabriel's story. But he didn't know about the crawl space or the symbol.

He didn't know they were telling the truth.

"Maybe you were a spy like that guy Archer," Lukas said. "And you just pretended to be her friend."

My mom lied to me and betrayed my dad. She was a member of the Illuminati.

Jared stormed across the room and grabbed my hand. "She's not one of you," he told Dimitri. "She's one of us."

I glanced at my friends' faces. Lukas and Elle were staring at Dimitri like they wanted to kill him, but Priest's and Alara's eyes were fixed on the ground.

They know I'm not one of them.

Jared tightened his grip on my hand. "You're wrong."

My knees buckled. I felt myself falling, the room and the darkness closing in on me.

Jared caught me and eased me down to the floor. "Are you okay?"

"Of course she's not okay," Elle said. "Look at her face. She's as white as a ghost."

I looked up, and Gabriel was staring at me. "You know I'm telling the truth, don't you?" he asked.

"Kennedy?" Jared's eyes searched mine.

I couldn't lie to him—not now.

"My mom was one of them."

'm going to check on our guest," Gabriel said, heading toward the containers.

Dimitri nodded. "Never underestimate—"

"What an animal will do to free itself from a cage," Gabriel finished. "I know."

Jared ignored them and pulled me up. "What's going on?"

"Gabriel's tattoo." I could barely get the words out. "The cross."

Elle rushed over and threw her arms around me.

"What about it?"

"I remember seeing the same one on a wall in my mom's closet."

Priest and Alara hung back, but they were listening.

"That doesn't mean—" Jared began.

"Don't say it doesn't mean anything." I shook my head. "You think my mom just happened to have a cross with a hawk and Latin writing on the wall of a secret room in her closet?" Tears burned my eyes, but I didn't let them fall. "It means everything."

"Dimitri." Gabriel's voice called out from behind the containers. "I need help in here."

"We can talk about this later," Jared said, watching Dimitri.

Without another word, all of us followed Dimitri as he ran between the rows. At the end of the aisle, I caught a glimpse of the dockworker Andras had possessed. He was chained in a corner of the cell, drenched in holy water.

Dimitri slipped on his sunglasses and held out his arm, stopping us. "Don't look the demon in the eye, whatever you do. That's how he jumps from one body to possess another. He needs to be close to make the switch, but if you don't know what you're doing, I wouldn't take any chances."

The demon thrashed against the chains, and Gabriel looped the bone whip around the demon's neck. Barbs jutted out from the dozens of vertebrae, teeth, claws, and other small bones that formed the whip. The moment the bones touched Andras, the barbs burrowed deeper into his skin, pulsing and twisting on their own.

The demon roared in pain.

I shuddered, and the tiny hairs on the back of my neck stood on end.

"Is that thing alive?" Priest watched, transfixed.

Gabriel jerked the whip, and Andras fell to his knees. "We don't have time for twenty questions."

The dockworker struggled to lift his head. "Help me." The raspy tone and the Russian accent sounded nothing like the voice the demon used earlier.

I grabbed Gabriel's arm. "He's trying to say something."

"I don't give a crap what he says, as long as he says it in hell." Gabriel shrugged me off.

The man's head lolled to the side as if he were drunk. "For the sins I have committed, I ask to be forgiven," he said in the same Russian accent.

"Why does his voice sound different?" Elle asked, keeping her distance.

"I think the guy Andras possessed is trying to break through," Lukas said.

Dimitri waved his arm. "Stay back."

Gabriel didn't even acknowledge Lukas. His attention was focused solely on Dimitri. "We need to kill Andras now."

"You mean exorcise him, right?" Priest asked.

Gabriel looked confused. "There's no way to exorcise a demon as powerful as Andras."

226

"Then how do you kill the demon without hurting the guy he possessed?" Elle asked.

Dimitri looked her in the eye. "You don't."

"You can't kill an innocent man," I said.

Dimitri strode over and yanked on the dockworker's shirt collar, exposing a tattoo on his neck. A knife—with drops of blood on the blade. "Do you know what this is? It's a Russian prison tattoo. It means this *innocent man* is a killer for hire. And those blood droplets represent the number of people he's killed. Do you want to count them?"

I shuddered.

Lukas stepped in front of me. "Why don't you take it down a notch? She missed the chapter on prison tats in criminal history class."

Alara glared at Dimitri. "Obviously you didn't."

Dimitri ran a hand through his sandy hair and lit a cigarette. "You don't understand the way this works. Right now, Andras needs to possess a body at all times."

"Which means if we kill the body, he dies with it," Gabriel added.

"The body you're talking about is a *person*," Alara said.

Dimitri crossed the room and bent down to pet Bear. The dog growled and Dimitri backed off. "Once Andras consumes enough souls, he'll be strong enough to take his true form."

"And then there will be no way to kill him," Gabriel

finished. He looked at Lukas, Jared, Priest, and Alara, one by one. "If you want to be Legion members so badly, you'd better start acting like it. Because none of your family members would ever let that guy walk out of here with that monster inside him."

Alara raised her chin. "My grandmother would figure out another way."

Dimitri put his hand on Gabriel's shoulder, a calming gesture, and Gabriel turned away.

❧ "Imani Sabatier would've killed Andras with her own bare hands if that was the only way to destroy him," Dimitri said.

"You don't know anything about my grandmother." Alara's voice cracked.

"I know more than you think, about all of your family members." He stubbed his cigarette out on the wall. "I'm not saying this is easy. But the Legion of the Black Dove and the Illuminati share one purpose above all others: to defend the world from a demon that is desperate to take it over. If one man's life—one murderer's life—is the sacrifice to save millions, I can live with that."

Which only left one question.

Could *we* live with it?

As much as I didn't agree with Dimitri, I'd seen what Andras was capable of on a small scale. I couldn't imagine what he might do if he grew any stronger.

If he opened the gates of hell, how many demons like him were waiting?

Hundreds?

Thousands?

We had barely stopped Andras, a demon temporarily weakened after being trapped for centuries. How would we stand a chance against him when he grew any stronger?

Jared crossed his arms and leaned against the wall. "Dimitri's right. We can't risk it."

"So you're okay with killing someone?" I couldn't believe what I was hearing.

"Haven't enough people died already?" Lukas asked him.

"That's not what I'm saying," Jared said.

"He's saying we don't have a choice," Alara said, sounding unsure.

"There's always a choice," I said, repeating the mantra my mom had drilled into my head since I was a kid. They sank like a rock in the pit of my stomach.

She chose to lie to me and my dad.

My mother had made the wrong choice, whether or not she knew it.

Just like I did.

"This is *so* not what I signed up for." Elle turned to Jared, her features hardening. "What are you gonna do? Whip out a buck knife and stab him in the heart?"

Seeing her standing there triggered a wave of guilt inside me. Elle should've been at a party, stringing along one of the guys desperate to get a date with her. Instead, she'd been attacked by a paranormal entity and chased by a demon. Now an unstable chain-smoker and a guy carrying a whip made from demon vertebrae were asking her to stand by and watch them kill someone.

Jared frowned. "I'm just trying to figure this out before anyone else gets hurt."

Dimitri took something out of his coat pocket and held it between his fingers.

A syringe.

"No one is cutting out any hearts. We aren't monsters." He depressed the plunger and a few drops of clear liquid squirted from the needle. "We're trying to stop one."

Andras, or the Russian criminal—it was hard to tell which one of them we were looking at—moaned in pain.

Lukas gestured at the needle. "That's not the way to do it."

"Please—" the criminal pleaded.

Gabriel cracked the whip, and the ivory bones coiled around the criminal's leg. "Shut your mouth." Gabriel yanked the handle, and the bones tightened.

The prisoner's head snapped up, and his body straightened. It began in his feet and traveled through his torso like a current was shooting up his back. The demon's midnight eyes stared back at us, the corners of his mouth curving in a wicked smile.

"Be careful, Gabriel," Andras said, the Russian accent gone now. "When I break free, I'm going to cut out your tongue."

Gabriel released the whip and cracked it again. This time, the narrow bones snaked around Andras' neck. "Hurts, doesn't it? Took four hundred and forty-seven demon bones to make Azazel."

Azazel? He named his whip?

Gabriel's mouth twisted into a cruel smile. He was enjoying this. "Want to know where I got them?"

"I know you are not the one who made it, Gabriel, Champion of God. I know your name and its meaning," the demon said.

"I paid for every bone, and watched while each was extracted from one of your kind—while the demons were still alive." Gabriel had a white-knuckled grip on the whip handle.

"What was the price?" The lilt in Andras' voice made it seem like he already knew the answer.

"We both know the price, and when I die, I'll pay it. And my name means 'strength of god.' Be sure to remember it so you can find me in hell."

Dimitri cringed. "Enough. He's buying time we don't have."

Gabriel flicked his wrist, and the whip slid from the demon's neck.

Dimitri's gaze fell on Jared, Lukas, Priest, and Alara. "Practice is over. You're the Legion now, and you vowed to protect the world from Andras." He held out the syringe to them. "Are you going to honor that vow or not?"

When no one responded, Dimitri bent down and placed the syringe on the floor in front of us. "It's easy to call yourself a hero. It's much harder to be one."

The syringe lay on the floor like a grenade. No one uttered a word. Speaking felt too much like volunteering. Bear sniffed it, then trotted over and lay at Alara's feet.

"I'll do it." My tone lacked any real conviction.

Priest swooped in and snatched it. "You can't. One of us should do it."

Us.

He was drawing a dividing line—the one I had always believed was separating me from the four of them. The line I wasn't sure existed. Until now.

Hearing Priest say the words destroyed me. He was the one person who accepted me from the beginning. Now he wouldn't even look at me.

"He's right," I said. "You don't want my Illuminati blood tainting your execution."

"He didn't mean it like that, Kennedy." Jared's hand slid underneath my tangled hair, and he rubbed the back of my neck with his thumb.

How long before he turned his back on me, too?

"Right, Priest?" Jared sounded confused.

Priest stared down at the cracked concrete floor, silent.

Lukas' shoulders stiffened. "Priest, what's your malfunction? It's Kennedy we're talking about."

Priest shoved his hands into the front pocket of his hoodie. "I'm not saying she's Illuminati, but she's not part of the Legion. That's all."

Jared's hand slipped from my neck. In the space of three strides, he was towering over Priest. "You weren't worried about whether or not she was one of us when she saved your life." He turned to Alara. "What about you? Do you agree with him?"

She had been unusually quiet, and I braced myself for the rejection headed my way.

Alara picked at the loose threads on her cargo pants. "My grandmother didn't trust the Illuminati."

"But I'm not one of them." Anger tore through me. It dulled the pain and the questions, the fear and the doubt. "I didn't know about any of this. My mom lied to me, and I can't even ask her why because she's dead."

Jared reached for me, but I twisted away.

Gabriel's cell phone chimed. He scanned the message and nodded to Dimitri. "The sanctuary's ready, and you owe me ten bucks."

"We weren't betting." Dimitri swept past us.

"I'm always betting." Gabriel walked over to Priest

and snatched the syringe. "Playtime's over, kids. It's time to move him."

"Move him where?" Alara followed Gabriel. "You said we had to kill him."

"We do, but not here," Gabriel said, with his back to Alara. "Andras can only be destroyed within the walls of a sanctuary, in the presence of a cross from a church altar."

She grabbed Gabriel's arm and jerked him around to face her. "Then what the hell was that crap you fed us about sticking a syringe in the guy and honoring our vow to the Legion?"

"A test." Gabriel looked down at her hand and brushed it off his arm. "In case you're wondering, you all failed."

22. GATES OF HELL

Dimitri slid his arms around the criminal's body, and Gabriel grabbed his legs.

Lukas stood between the shipping containers blocking the warehouse exit. "You're not taking Andras anywhere without us."

Dimitri shouldered his way past Lukas without much effort. "We assumed as much."

"Make yourself useful and get the door," Gabriel said.

Lukas rushed ahead of Dimitri and Gabriel without a word, with Priest, Alara, and Elle trailing after them, grabbing their duffel bags on the way.

"Come on, Kennedy." Jared took my hand. He held it

just as tight as he had before I told him the truth about my mom.

You're lucky.

But I didn't feel lucky. I felt like someone had punched a hole in me, and all my emotions had spilled out.

Outside, Lukas was unlocking the trunk of a silver SUV as Dimitri and Gabriel waited.

Every inch of the trunk's interior was lined with cold-iron grating.

The two men dumped the demon inside, and Dimitri rushed around to the front of the SUV and climbed into the driver's seat.

Bear ran back and forth behind the car, barking and growling.

"Get in if you're coming," Gabriel said to us. "Holy water isn't enough. Without other preemptive measures, those chains won't hold Andras much longer."

We piled in the back, before Gabriel could change his mind. It took Alara a few attempts to coax Bear into the car.

Andras banged against the grating.

Elle scooted forward to the edge of her seat. "He sounds really pissed off."

"There's an Illuminati safe house down by the stockyards. We'll be there soon." Dimitri turned on the radio and scanned through the stations, settling on the news.

I leaned my head against the window, watching the

traffic lights blur in the darkness. Everything looked different, and it took me a moment to realize why.

The rain and snow had stopped.

For the first time since the night I freed Andras, the sky was clear. But my thoughts were darker than the sky had ever been.

Why didn't Mom tell me the truth about her past? Was she ashamed? Maybe she thought I wouldn't forgive her... or maybe she didn't trust me with her secrets.

If my mom had lied about who she really was, she could've lied about anything.

Like the way she felt about my dad.

A radio newscaster's voice interrupted my thoughts: "In breaking news, the story of the seventeen missing girls has ended in tragedy. Seventeen bodies were found in the woods outside Topsfield, Massachusetts, earlier today. Initial reports from the coroner's office estimate the victims died between three o'clock and five o'clock this morning. The FBI has yet to make an official statement, but local law enforcement officers believe the bodies will be identified as the teenage girls who disappeared over the past seventeen days."

Topsfield. The location of the museum—thirty minutes from Faith's house and less than an hour from here.

Andras probably killed them before he killed Faith.

Alara leaned over the front seat, gripping Gabriel's headrest. "Turn it up."

"Alexa Sears, Lauren Richman, Kelly Emerson, Rebecca Turner, Cameron Anders, Mary Williams, Sarah Edelman, Julia Smith—"

I didn't listen to the rest of the names. I already knew them by heart.

Shannon O'Malley, Christine Redding, Karen York, Marie Dennings, Rachel Eames, Roxanne North, Catherine Nichols, Hailey Edwards, Lucy Klein—they're all dead. And it's my fault.

Dimitri guided the SUV through a wasteland of condemned buildings and rusted machinery before pulling up to an unmarked warehouse with a hazmat sign on the door. Gabriel jumped out of the car before it stopped and bolted to the door. He sorted through a ring of keys chained to his belt and systematically unlocked at least a dozen dead bolts.

Dimitri threw the SUV into park and dug through the glove box and took out a pile of ugly plastic sunglasses. "Put these on." He handed each of us a pair and waited for us to put them on before he climbed out. "Stay here."

"Nice try." Alara opened her door and followed him around to the back of the car ahead of everyone else.

Bear stalked in front of her protectively.

Gabriel emerged from the warehouse carrying a wide-barreled rifle and a fire hose. "Heads up." He tossed the gun to Dimitri, who caught it with one hand.

"Get back." Dimitri aimed the gun at the trunk.

"It's a tranquilizer gun like the ones they use at zoos," Priest whispered to Jared as he dropped a duffel bag full of weapons on the asphalt, and the Legion members grabbed their own.

I hung back with Elle, afraid of how Priest and Alara might react if I tried to help.

Dimitri nodded and Gabriel opened the trunk, pivoting to the side.

The criminal's muscular body lay crammed inside, motionless.

"He's still out. That should make it easier to move him." Dimitri lowered the gun.

As he did, Andras lunged from the trunk, knocking the tranquilizer gun out of Dimitri's hands in the process. The demon was still bound in chains, but they didn't slow him down. He pounced on Dimitri, snarling like an animal.

Jared, Lukas, and Priest opened fire, but the salt rounds had no effect on Andras. Alara dropped her paintball gun and dove for the tranquilizer gun. She scrambled onto her knees, aiming carefully.

A flurry of tranquilizer darts punctured Andras' back. He whipped around, his black eyes focused on Alara and his legs still pinning Dimitri to the ground.

Bear sprang and clamped his jaws around Andras' arm.

Gabriel turned on the hose, and a flood of water hit Andras. The force sent Bear rolling and threw the demon's body against the fender. Steam rose from his exposed skin, and he let out a piercing scream as he dropped to his knees on the asphalt.

Alara hit him with another dart.

Andras swayed for a moment, then collapsed.

Gabriel hauled the demon up by the chains around his wrists. A web of vicious burns marred his wet skin.

"That was enough ketamine to take down a grizzly," Dimitri said, trying to catch his breath.

Alara walked by and shoved the tranquilizer gun into his hands. "You're welcome."

Gabriel hoisted Andras over his shoulder and rushed toward the warehouse door. "We need to get him inside fast, before it wears off."

Inside, the warehouse was nothing like the one at the wharf. Instead of rusted paint and oil-stained floors, we followed Gabriel and Dimitri through a maze of hallways with shiny metal walls and fluorescent overhead lights. I looked for signs of whoever had been prepping the sanctuary, but the place seemed empty.

At the end of the hall, Gabriel led us down a narrow wooden staircase. At the bottom, Jared and Lukas had to duck under a low archway that opened into a claustrophobic tunnel. Portable construction lights hanging from nails illuminated wet stone walls.

Elle stepped closer to Lukas. "This place looks like a dungeon," she whispered.

Lukas grabbed her hand, his eyes fixed on the barred door a few yards ahead of us. "I think it is."

Elle stopped at the threshold of the cell, unwilling to go any farther. I understood why.

Aside from the stainless-steel toilet, the cell looked like something out of the Middle Ages—two hundred square feet at the most, with rough stone walls and a dirty mattress in the corner. A Devil's Trap was painted on the floor, and the Eye of Ever covered the ceiling. A huge silver crucifix was bolted to the wall like a relic in a church.

"I thought we were taking him to a sanctuary," Alara said.

Dimitri dumped Andras on the ground beneath two sets of shackles. "This is a sanctuary. It was blessed by a priest, and that cross"—he pointed to the silver monstrosity— "hung behind the altar of Our Lady of Saints."

"The clock is ticking, so you might want to step outside." Gabriel unchained Andras' wrists and ankles and replaced the chains with shackles. "I don't want to offend anyone's fragile sense of morality while we try to save the world."

"You're gonna kill him right now?" Priest asked.

Gabriel looked disgusted. "No. I thought I'd wait until he finds a way to open the gates of hell and invite all his friends over."

"The children of the Labyrinth do not need an invitation," the demon said, his head still bowed. "They will find a way, with or without me."

241

When he heard the demon's voice, Bear shot to his feet, a low growl building in his throat. Alara ran her hand along his back. "It's okay, boy."

Andras growled, sounding more feral than the dog.

Bear snapped at Andras, baring his teeth.

Alara reached down and grabbed his collar, just as the Doberman lunged. She didn't have time to pull her hand away, and the momentum hurled her body forward. Andras strained against the shackles, reaching for her.

"Alara!" Priest shouted.

Jared hurled himself at Andras, creating a wall between the demon and Alara. He slammed into Andras' chest, and his protective sunglasses clattered to the floor.

Andras raised his head, holy water running down his face.

"Don't look at him!" Gabriel yelled.

The demon's ebony eyes locked on Jared's pale blue ones.

"No!" The words tore from my throat, but it was already too late.

Jared hit the ground and fell forward onto his knees in front of Andras. With his arms bound in chains and Jared kneeling at his feet, Andras looked like a martyr from a Renaissance painting, staring down at one of his disciples. The demon tilted his head, and Jared mirrored his every movement, never once taking his eyes off the monster controlling him.

The criminal's body jerked forward, his arms straining against the chains, and an invisible force slammed into Jared's chest. The criminal's body went slack, and Jared's back straightened slowly, as if his spine was stretching one vertebra at a time.

We had witnessed the same scenario on the Boston streets, but this was different. It was happening to Jared. He was only a few feet away, but I couldn't get to him fast enough. I scrambled in front of him, blocking his view.

Maybe there's still time.

I grabbed his shoulders and shook him. "Jared, look at me."

The blank expression on his face didn't change. He stared straight ahead like a zombie, as if I wasn't even there.

I held his face in my hands. "Jared, you can fight this. You're stronger than he is."

I ignored everything else in the room. Bear barking. Someone crying. Voices shouting.

I'm losing him. If I haven't lost him already.

I took off my protective glasses and tossed them across the floor. "Look at me."

"Kennedy, no!" Gabriel shouted.

Jared's lashes fluttered, and his sleepy blue eyes focused on me. My heart leapt.

He's going to be all right.

Alara's hand closed around my arm. "Get away from him."

"Wait," Lukas said. "He's okay."

Jared reached up and curled his hands around my wrists, the first indication that I was breaking through. His icy touch sent goose bumps up my arms.

"I thought I'd lost you," I whispered, choking back tears.

Jared's pupils dilated, and the inky darkness spread, eclipsing his irises. "You did."

"Move!" Dimitri shouted from behind me.

A hand grabbed the back of my jacket and dragged me across the floor. "Close your eyes, and put your glasses on." Gabriel.

Jared lost interest in me and turned toward the door.

I put my sunglasses back on and followed his gaze to Dimitri, who stood just inside the cell, pointing the tranquilizer gun at Jared.

"If you kill me, you kill the boy, too," Jared said, in a voice that wasn't his own.

Gabriel rushed out into the hall and returned with a hose.

Andras' eyes flickered with amusement. "What will you do now, Champion of God?"

Gabriel unleashed the holy water and Dimitri fired.

Jared charged them, pushing through the flood of water. His body jerked each time a tranquilizer dart hit him.

By the time the third dart hit, Jared was soaked and his steps were sluggish. How much longer could he hold out?

Fall. Please. Just fall.

Jared staggered toward Gabriel, but he couldn't push past the pressure of the water. He dropped to his knees, coughing and sputtering. In one last effort to reach his attackers, Jared dragged his body across the wet concrete.

The fourth dart caught him in the shoulder, and Jared's cheek hit the floor. Even as he lay there with a demon inside him, I wanted to lift his head off the ground and cradle it in my lap.

Deep down, he was still the boy who made my stomach flutter every time he kissed me. The boy who fought for me, even when I didn't fight for myself.

He was still the boy who meant more to me than I could ever tell him.

Wasn't he?

Gabriel jammed his knee into Jared's back and looped a chain around his wrists.

"Stop. You're hurting him." I ran toward them, but Lukas grabbed me.

"It's okay," he said in a soothing voice.

There's nothing okay about this.

Jared lay motionless on the cell floor. With his lips parted and curls of dark hair stuck to his neck, he almost looked like he was sleeping.

Almost.

The burns marring his skin reminded me he wasn't.

Gabriel noticed me staring and threw me a pitying glance. "This isn't your boyfriend, kid. You'd better get that through your head."

"You don't know anything about him," I snapped. "Jared is stronger than you think, and he'll fight."

Dimitri looked away and lit a Dunhill, crushing the empty pack in his hand.

Gabriel secured the chains with a padlock, yanking harder than necessary to test them. He was probably doing it to make a point, which only made me hate him more. He looked up at me from where he knelt next to Jared. "He'd slit your throat without thinking twice about it if he had the chance."

"Don't try to scare me so you can justify what you're doing," I said.

Gabriel pulled down the collar of his shirt. A jagged scar ran across the front of his neck. "You should be scared."

Alara, who had barely moved since the attack, gasped.

"That's enough." Dimitri snapped.

Gabriel let go of his collar and the fabric slid back in place, covering the gruesome scar. "She needs to understand what we're dealing with before she gets herself killed."

Dimitri moved closer, until the two men were standing shoulder to shoulder. "I know how you felt about Elizabeth. But this is not helping."

Elizabeth. He was talking about my mom.

The thought of Gabriel having some kind of crush on my mother made my stomach turn.

"What are you gonna do with him?" Priest stared down at Jared.

My heart pounded in anticipation.

Dimitri passed Jared and walked toward the wall, where the Russian was shackled. He flicked his cigarette on the ground and dug a heavy key out of his pocket. He unlocked the first cuff.

The criminal's arm dropped and his body lurched forward, his other wrist still chained to the wall. Dimitri slid the key into the other cuff—the one keeping the criminal on his feet.

"Someone needs to catch him," Priest said, pacing.

"No need for that." Dimitri turned the key, and the Russian's body crashed to the floor in a heap. His lifeless eyes stared back at us, open and unblinking.

Lukas loosened his grip on me. "He's dead? But we saw Andras jump from body to body a half dozen times. The people he possessed were all fine afterward."

Dimitri shrugged, as if handling a dead body didn't faze him. "Jumping from one body to another takes a lot of energy. He probably wasn't strong enough to jump and kill the hosts. And every case is different, but the longer a demon possesses someone, the less likely it is for the victim to survive. Unless the demon chooses to stay."

Alara chucked the plastic bottle of holy water from her tool belt across the room and screamed. It sounded like rage and frustration and a hundred feelings I couldn't name, even though I was feeling them, too.

Gabriel bent down and hoisted Jared over his shoulder.

Jared's dark hair obscured his face, and his limp arms hung down Gabriel's back. He carried Jared to the wall, where the Russian's body had been a few minutes ago.

Don't chain him up. Please don't let them chain him up.

Every muscle in my body tensed.

Gabriel held Jared upright as Dimitri closed the cuffs around his burned wrists.

Something inside me snapped.

No! No! No! Get him down! Get him down!

"Get him down!" I screamed.

"I wish I could, Kennedy." Dimitri actually sounded apologetic.

"Then do it."

Dimitri's gaze flickered over my friends' faces, then back to mine. "I'm sorry. One screwup is enough." He looked down at the Russian's body before throwing it over his shoulder.

I wanted to blame Dimitri, but I couldn't. All this started long before he showed up. He wasn't what my World History teacher referred to as the first cause—the initial action that set a course of events in motion. The first domino to fall. The finger that pulled the trigger. The one thing responsible for destroying everything that came after it.

Dimitri wasn't the first cause, and he wasn't the reason Jared was chained up in a cell.

I was.

Dimitri waved his arm. "Clear this room. I want everyone out of here now."

"No," I yelled as Gabriel grabbed my wrist. "I'm not leaving him."

Jared was helpless—chained to the wall, burned and broken, with Andras inside him. Dimitri and Gabriel would do anything to destroy Andras.

What would stop them from killing Jared?

Nothing.

Gabriel dragged me a few feet, and I snatched my arm away. "Don't touch me."

Lukas crashed into Gabriel, plowing his shoulder into Gabriel's stomach. "Get your hands off her."

For a second, it looked like Lukas had a chance.

But Gabriel let his feet slide out from under him, taking Lukas to the ground with him. Once he had Lukas on the ground, Gabriel had the advantage. He fought like a seasoned soldier, flipping Lukas onto his back in one fluid maneuver. "I don't want to hurt you, kid. But I will."

I can't let him hurt Lukas, too.

I scrambled to my feet, scrolling through the images of the cell in my mind. Were there any weapons in here?

A flash of white caught my eye.

Gabriel knelt over Lukas, his knee between Lukas' shoulder blades. He cocked his arm, preparing to throw a punch.

I dove toward him and closed my hand around the whip and tore it from Gabriel's belt strap. The weapon was heavier than I imagined, and it took all my strength to raise it. My execution wasn't as smooth as Gabriel's, but the white vertebrae unhinged and sailed above my head in a wide arc.

Gabriel turned, his body still pinning Lukas'. "You'd better drop my whip yesterday."

"Then get off him."

"Kennedy—" Dimitri reached out toward me. "Hand me the whip. No one is going to hurt you or your friends."

My hand trembled violently. I could barely keep my shoulder raised. "I don't believe you." The words came out in ragged sobs. "You'd kill Jared to destroy Andras."

Dimitri's shoulders sagged and his forehead creased with what—worry? "No one is doing anything to anyone right now." He glared at Gabriel, until he eased off Lukas' chest.

"Give me my whip." Gabriel stalked toward me.

My shoulders relaxed, and the vertebrae fell against my back. The barbs bit through my shirt, cutting my skin like razors.

Gabriel's expression changed from anger to concern. "Don't move. You'll only make it worse."

I cried out in pain.

"K-Kennedy?" Jared rasped. This time, it was his own voice.

I spun around, whimpering as the barbs cut deeper than the razor wire.

Jared's head hung limp against his chest.

"He's still in there." My muscles seized with every breath.

Through the blur of my tears, I saw Jared's head move. He raised his chin in tiny jerks, until he found the strength to hold it upright.

Slowly, the malicious smile stretched across his lips.

"He's still in there." The demon mimicked my voice, capturing it perfectly. Then Andras reverted back to his own hollow tone. "But not for long."

24. BULLET WITH BUTTERFLY WINGS

I awoke to darkness and a damp cold seeping into my bones.

Where?

Images flashed through my mind like pictures in a flipbook.

Iron chains—

Raw, burned skin—

Metal cuffs—

The scar above Jared's eye—

The sound of my screams—

Swearing to kill Dimitri and Gabriel—

Calling out for Jared—

My eyes adjusted to the darkness slowly.

Jared pulled me against his shoulder. "You're okay. Everything's gonna be okay."

I breathed into his shirt. It smelled earthy and rich, like a campfire. Nothing like the combination of copper and salt that always lingered on Jared's skin.

The last few hours came flooding back, and I realized Lukas was the one reassuring me. Alara, Priest, and Elle were huddled around us, in the tunnel outside Jared's cell. Elle was scrunched under Lukas' other arm like she was freezing, and Priest and Alara were propped up against the wall, dead asleep.

Where were Dimitri and Gabriel?

"Jared." I shot up.

If they'd hurt him—

"He's all right." Lukas caught my arm. "I mean...he's not all right. But no one's been in the cell, if that's what you're worried about."

"Are you sure?"

Lukas nodded, rubbing the sleep from his eyes. "We've been here the whole time. Don't you remember?"

"Bits and pieces."

The horrible ones.

"You lost it." Lukas picked up his jacket and draped it over my shoulders. "You were threatening Andras, and begging Gabriel and Dimitri to get him out of Jared's body. Then you did a one-eighty and refused to leave Jared in there alone, because you thought Dimitri and Gabriel were going to kill him. Which is the reason for our fancy accommodations tonight."

"I'm sorry." I'd said it so many times now, but what else could I say? How do you apologize for destroying someone's life? Destroying their family? What can you say when words aren't enough?

"Don't be." Lukas nudged me with his shoulder. "You scared the crap out of Dimitri and Gabriel. They agreed to let us all sleep out here."

"That's a lot of trust for those two."

"Not really." Lukas smiled. "They took the keys to the cell."

The cell.

Were they burning Jared with holy water?

"We can't let them hurt him." I hadn't meant to yell.

Bear sprang to his feet, and Priest bolted upright, knocking off his headphones. "What happened?" The Smashing Pumpkins' "Bullet with Butterfly Wings" echoed through the tunnel.

Alara's eyes flew open. She yanked the paintball gun from her tool belt. "Is something in here?"

"Just us." Lukas put his hand on the barrel of the weapon, guiding her arm back down.

Elle rubbed her eyes and stretched. The way she unfolded her long limbs in the small space reminded me of the night she'd slept in the bathroom with me while I puked my guts out from drinking too many wine coolers.

Why didn't I send her home? What if something happened to her, too?

Elle ran her hands through her red hair. "What did I miss?" When she noticed I was awake, she dove over Lukas' lap and threw her arms around my neck. "Oh my god. I thought we were going to have to lock you up in a padded room or something."

"Not yet."

"That was some serious mother lion behavior in there." She gestured at the bars at the end of the tunnel. "I thought you were going to tear those two Freemasons apart."

"Illuminati," I said, returning the hug.

"Whatever." Elle pulled away and dismissed the mistake with a flick of her wrist. "The one with the baby demon whip needs to learn some manners."

We all stared at the floor. None of us wanted to look at the bars.

Priest looped his headphones around his neck. "What are we gonna do?"

"Dimitri says the only way to get Andras out of Jared's body is to find someone else for him to possess," Lukas said. "And there's still no guarantee the demon will leave."

Elle frowned. "I don't think I could do that to anyone."

Alara holstered her paintball gun and pointed at the text on her T-shirt: BY ANY MEANS NECESSARY. "This isn't a fashion statement. No one I care about gets hurt on my watch."

Lukas stared down the tunnel. "I don't know how much time we have."

"Then let's stop wasting it." Alara turned to me. "What's the plan?"

With Jared's life on the line, the margin for error was zero—the same number of viable ideas I had right now.

I walked to the end of the tunnel and forced myself to look through the bars, where the boy I cared about was chained to the wall like an animal. "We save him."

⊰ • ⊱

Alara and I waited in the hallway at the top of the stairs leading down to Jared's cell. Priest, Lukas, and Elle had taken off in search of Dimitri and Gabriel.

We were sitting on the floor with Bear stretched out in front of us. Alara hadn't said a word since we left the containment area, and without Elle's chatter, the silence between us had turned awkward.

"You never suspected anything?" she asked suddenly.

"What?" I glanced over at her.

Alara pulled at a loose thread on her cargo pants. "About your mom."

It felt like an accusation, not a question.

That my mom kept so many secrets it feels like she lied to me every day? That those secrets and lies were the reason my dad left?

I remembered every detail, every conversation, and every smile. The idea that all those memories were some kind of performance destroyed me.

"No." The admission made the truth feel even more painful. "The day my father left, he wrote my mom a note. It mentioned me." I couldn't bring myself to tell her what it said.

"I'm sorry. I didn't know." Alara's voice softened, and she sounded like the girl who had given me the protective medal around my neck.

"I may not be a member of the Legion, but I'm not Illuminati, Alara. I'm still the same person I was a few days ago."

Just miserable and broken and totally alone.

Alara didn't respond right away. "When my grandmother told stories about the Illuminati, they were always the bad guys. And the Legion was formed to stop them." She hesitated. "Now Dimitri is telling us the Order of the Enlightened is responsible for all the shady incidents since Priest's granddad was at Yale, and it turns out your mom was one of them. I'm just trying to get my head around this."

If Alara—the most confident member of the Legion—didn't know how she felt, how were Lukas and Priest feeling? I couldn't think of anything to say that didn't lead back to the fact that my mom was a member of the Illuminati and the Order—and a spy.

Dimitri lit one of his black cigarettes and shook out the match.

Elle pretended to cough. "Are you aware secondhand smoke is almost as dangerous as actually smoking?"

We weren't in the cell anymore. Gabriel and Dimitri had given us a brief tour of the safe house, a huge sci-fi compound of gleaming metal walls and white ceilings, hidden behind the warehouse's dilapidated exterior.

Now we were sitting in a room surrounded by glass dry-erase boards, covered in symbols and math equations, as if Dimitri and Gabriel were developing an Illuminati theory of relativity.

Dimitri took a drag and stubbed the cigarette out. "Everyone has a vice."

"I'm sure he has more than one," Alara muttered under her breath.

"Let's go over the rules again." Dimitri paced in front of us, while Gabriel sat at one of the black tables, cleaning his whip.

"Don't you mean for the tenth time?" Priest asked.

"If you're going to stay at the safe house until we figure out how to resolve the current situation, your safety is our responsibility," Dimitri said.

After our tour, Dimitri invited us to stay in two identical, sterile-looking rooms, which could've passed for sleeping chambers on the starship *Enterprise*. To his credit, he realized we weren't going to leave Jared alone with them.

"Never go downstairs alone." Elle was stretched across the table, with her head resting on her arm, as if she were listening to a lecture in class.

"Or without wearing your glasses." Lukas flicked the plastic sunglasses on the table in front of him, sounding bored.

Gabriel looked up. "This isn't a joke. If you make eye contact with Andras, he can jump out of your brother's body and into yours. Or he can mark your soul."

Elle rubbed her arms like she had goose bumps. "What does that mean?"

"If a demon marks your soul, he'll always be able to find you, no matter where you go," Gabriel said.

Priest held up his protective glasses, examining them. "There's gotta be a more effective way to keep him from making direct eye contact."

Him.

They were talking about Jared.

"Letting them stay here is a bad idea, Dimitri." Gabriel stopped cleaning the ivory bones. "They're untrained—"

Priest pushed his chair away from the table, the legs screeching across the floor. "I can make a weapon out of a soda can, or whatever you've got in that black bag of yours. So do your homework before you start talking about who's untrained."

Dimitri shot Gabriel a warning glance. If Gabriel was the storm, Dimitri was the eye. "I think Gabriel was referring to experience with demonic possession and containment."

Containment.

Jared soaked in holy water, probably freezing. Charred and covered in burns. That's what he meant.

Dimitri continued. "Our apologies, Owen."

Priest stood up, shoving his chair back. "Don't ever call me that again." He pointed at Dimitri. "No one called me that except my granddad."

Alara stopped sifting the powders in the bowl in front of her and smiled.

"I'm sorry, *Priest.*" Dimitri emphasized his name.

Priest grabbed his hoodie off the back of the chair. "I'm outta here. You wanna show me where I can do some work? Otherwise, I'm going to my room, or whatever you call those cryogenic chambers where you have us sleeping."

Elle stifled a laugh.

"Gabriel can take you to the mech room down the hall. You should find everything you need there. We might even have a soda can or two." Dimitri kept his voice light, as if making a stupid joke would win Priest over.

Alara stood up, adjusting her tool belt on the hips of her olive cargo pants. "I'm going with him."

Gabriel stormed out of the room and led them down the hall. Bear lifted his head and trotted after Alara.

Dimitri sighed. "This isn't going well."

Lukas flipped his coin over his knuckles a few times before he responded. "What did you expect?"

Dimitri rose and walked toward us. Even his black tactical gear couldn't offset the dark shadows under his eyes, like he hadn't slept in days.

"We locked Jared up to protect him from himself. Right now, he's the blade in the hand of a killer. How do you think he'd feel if he hurt someone—or one of you?"

"All I want to know is how we're going to get Andras out of my brother's body." Lukas looked Dimitri in the eye. "Find a way to do that, and I'll trust you."

Dimitri lit one of his black cigarettes, letting the match burn down to his fingertips. "I don't know if I can."

⊰ • ⊱

Lukas, Elle, and I spent the rest of the morning poring over the journals, searching for anything that might help us save Jared. We tossed out suggestions to Dimitri and Gabriel, who shot them down. At least *we* were sharing.

The Illuminati members spoke in low tones and didn't invite us to join their conversation, which only made Lukas more suspicious.

After lunch, Priest and Alara returned. Priest tossed a small, white plastic case across the table in front of Dimitri.

"A gift?" Dimitri raised an eyebrow.

Priest flipped up his hood. "You wish."

Dimitri picked up the case. "Contact lenses? Are you concerned about my vision?"

Priest pushed his blond bangs out of his eyes, his expression unreadable. "Hardly. Like I said, based on what happened to Jared, your wraparound anti-possession sunglasses obviously aren't effective. And they definitely aren't my style." Priest pointed at the contact case. "My granddad used to say if the trap doesn't catch the mouse, you've gotta build a better mousetrap."

Alara stood behind him with a smug smile on her face. "Tell them how they work."

"Those babies are soaked in holy water, with some of Alara's Haitian mojo thrown in for good measure."

"He means herbs and wards," she said.

Dimitri examined them cautiously.

Priest stifled a smile. "I thought you Illuminati guys were badass, with your SWAT gear and bone whip."

"I value my eyesight," Dimitri said.

Alara rolled her eyes. "I'm wearing a pair right now. So is Priest." She tossed Lukas, Elle, and me plastic cases of our own.

I caught mine. "Thanks."

Dimitri held his eyelid open and positioned his finger in front of his eye, with the contact lens balanced on the end. "You're positive these will work?"

Priest slipped on his huge headphones. "Only one way to find out."

25. LOST BOY

Dimitri wasn't willing to take Priest at his word without some evidence the contact lenses worked, so everyone followed Priest down to the mech room to see how he'd made them.

I stayed behind, staring out the warehouse window. I missed the rain—my rain—because that's the way I thought about it now. It was comforting, the only constant in my life since the night I assembled the Shift.

Where was the Shift now? Buried in the mud under the prison rubble?

I imagined taking it apart. Going back and undoing all the damage it had caused.

Some things wouldn't change—my mother's death and the secrets she'd kept from me; a world full of angels and demons, vengeance spirits and secret societies, and my place within it.

But the rain would never have started.

Faith wouldn't be dead.

The human race wouldn't be on the brink of destruction or enslavement.

Jared wouldn't be possessed by a demon.

I heard footsteps in the hallway, and when I turned around, Gabriel was leaning in the doorway.

"Need something?" I pulled my hair into a ponytail to avoid making eye contact with him.

"If you want to go down to the containment area, I'll take you."

My eyes flicked from his face to the tail of the whip curled behind him. "Why?"

"Because I know you want to see him, and I'd rather you go with me than sneak down there alone."

He was smarter than I thought.

"Why?" I asked again.

"I just told you."

"I mean, why do you care?" It was a fair question. Gabriel hadn't shown any interest in helping us until now.

He didn't respond right away, and I could almost see him weighing the pros and cons between lying and telling the truth. "Your mother and I were friends for a long time. And she loved you more than anything in the world, even if she hid her past from you."

"My mom hid more than her past. If she was a spy from some rogue order of the Illuminati, then she wasn't the person I thought she was." I tried to sound indifferent, but I was failing miserably.

"I don't know why she lied to you. But I know she'd want me to keep you safe."

"What was the deal between you and my mom, Gabriel? Because you're way too worried about what my mom would want for a guy who was just her *friend*."

Gabriel started to say something, then stopped. After a moment, he cleared his throat and tried again. "Our relationship is none of your business. But since you seem to think it is, I'll say it again. Your mom was my friend. She saved me when I wasn't strong enough to save myself. And I owed her for that, a debt I never had a chance to repay." He walked toward me. "So I'm not going to let Elizabeth's only daughter get herself killed."

"Fine." I stormed past him and stood in the doorway. "Take me down there."

Gabriel didn't say a word until we reached the metal door that led into the tunnel. A row of winter jackets hung on pegs next to the door. He slipped one off a nail and handed it to me. "Put this on."

"Are we going outside?"

"Do you ever cooperate?" He held the jacket between us.

"No."

Not with you.

He sighed. "Are you wearing the contacts your friend made?"

I nodded.

"Remember, Kennedy. That isn't the boy you know in there. Andras is one of the most powerful demons in hell. He might look like your boyfriend and sound like him, but he's not Jared."

A knot formed in my throat.

My boyfriend.

Did Jared think of himself that way? Would I ever get the chance to find out?

"One more thing." Gabriel took a glass baby food jar out of his pocket and unscrewed the lid. He dipped his finger in the jar and scooped out a thick black paste. "I need to spread some of this on your cheeks."

I stepped back. "Excuse me?"

"I'm going to draw protective sigils on our faces. It's ash."

I tucked my hair behind my ears and turned my face toward him. "From a fire?"

"You could say that." Gabriel drew a circle on my cheek. "Incinerated demon bones."

I jerked away, disgusted. "I feel sick."

He grabbed my chin. "You'll feel sicker if Andras possesses you."

"How do you know about this stuff?" The jar of ash

seemed like the kind of thing Alara might stash in one of her pockets.

"Metaspiritual warfare is my specialty, to use Legion terminology." Gabriel worked fast, drawing what felt like circles and swirls on my cheeks. When he finished, he traced the sigils on his own skin.

Gabriel opened the iron door, and a blast of freezing air burst from the tunnel. I knew that a sudden drop in temperature was a sign of demonic activity, but it felt like a meat locker down here. It wasn't nearly this cold last night. I zipped the coat and followed Gabriel, my breath coming out in white puffs.

"There are gloves in the jacket pockets," he said.

"I'm fine." I didn't need Gabriel treating me like a child.

All I could think about was how close we were to the cell door. The gray metal glistened in the dim light, and a layer of frost coated the bars.

The chains that ran from the wall to the shackles binding Jared's wrists and ankles were longer now—long enough to allow him to walk around the tiny cell, but short enough to keep him from escaping.

Words were scrawled across the back wall in chalk, some horizontal, while others were vertical, diagonal, or backward.

Not words. Names.

The names of the dead girls.

Gabriel shook his head. "Great. Our last guest must've left the chalk. Now he's got a hobby."

Jared sat on the floor with his back against the wall, wearing jeans and a white undershirt. His clothes were soaked.

"He's going to freeze to death," I said.

"Demons don't get cold."

At the sound of Gabriel's voice, Jared lowered his chin, his eyes still closed. "He's right." The voice wasn't Jared's or the demon's but a blend of the two.

My hands trembled as they closed around the bars, and the icy metal burned my palms.

"Ow." I winced and pulled away.

"You should be careful. You could get hurt down here." The demon's voice was softer now, more like Jared's. Hope swelled inside me. Then he opened his eyes and Jared's blue ones stared back at me. "But it's the people around you who always get hurt, isn't it?"

Gabriel pointed between the bars. "Shut your mouth, or I'll show you what it feels like to get hurt."

Andras rose and cocked his head to the side. His movements were slow and deliberate, like he was trying out a new body that didn't quite fit. "Are you going to take out your whip, Gabriel? Beat me with the bones of my soldiers?"

"Maybe I'll add your bones to them." Gabriel

unhooked the whip from his belt and let it pool around his feet like an ivory snake.

"You're wearing your war paint. Are we going to war today?"

"I'm ready whenever you are," Gabriel said.

The demon stepped closer. His feet were bare, and holy water dripped onto the floor around him. "Are you certain, Champion of God? The only man ready to face the Maker of Nightmares is a man with no fears. You are *not* one of those men."

"Gabriel, stop." I knew where this was going.

Andras yanked on the chains, his hands still shackled in front of him. "You would be wise to listen to her, Gabriel. After all, she is Elizabeth's daughter."

At the mention of my mother's name, she appeared on the other side of the bars. Wearing a white button-down shirt and jeans, my mom looked every bit as alive as she had in life—from her long, wavy brown hair and beautiful features to her warm chocolate eyes and playful smile.

"Elizabeth?" Gabriel whispered.

It felt like the world around me had stopped. I couldn't see anything except my mother—because now that I was staring at her, I realized that's who she would always be to me. Not a rogue Illuminati member or the woman who had betrayed my father and lied to me.

She gasped, her eyes shining. "Kennedy?" Her gaze

drifted to Gabriel. "What are you two—? Why am I in a cell?"

As she turned, Andras clamped his hand around her throat.

"No!" Gabriel shouted, pounding on the bars.

I grabbed his arm. "It's not real. Your mind is playing tricks on you. Andras is manifesting one of your fears. I've seen him do it before."

Gabriel ignored me, his gaze fixed on my mom.

Andras stood behind her and lifted her off the ground, his hand still locked around her neck.

"Are you fearless now, Gabriel?" Andras roared. "Is the magic painted on your skin protecting you from the Maker of Nightmares?"

Gabriel turned his pockets inside out. I realized he was searching for the keys.

"Don't open it." I pressed my back against the cell door, blocking Gabriel's access. "I swear it's not her."

His eyes were wild. "Kennedy, move!"

I heard choking noises behind me and my mom's voice. "Please—"

Don't look.

"I'm going to tear your heart out!" Gabriel yelled, pushing me aside.

The hiss of the sprinklers sputtered above us. As Gabriel slid the key into the first lock, freezing water, spiked with rock salt, showered from the ceiling.

Steam rose from Andras' skin, and he staggered back and fell against the wall. The holy water's effect on my mother was worse. The water droplets punched holes in her, eating away at her form. Gabriel dropped to his knees and gripped the bars, while I watched the last pieces of my mom disappear.

The demon gritted his teeth. "That's the way I prefer to see you, Gabriel. On your knees."

Gabriel dragged himself to his feet and stared at the keys in his hand, black ash from his cheeks running down his face. "I almost..."

"But you didn't," I said.

Andras clapped, his movements slower, as if he'd expended too much energy. "You're smarter than Jared thinks you are, Kennedy Waters."

"You have no idea what Jared thinks." I tried to sound confident, but I was still reeling from seeing my mother, even if it was only an illusion.

"I'm inside his body. Do you believe it's any harder for me to get into his head?"

Was it possible?

I shuddered.

The demon smiled. "I know what happened at Hearts of Mercy. Jared regrets it. He cares about you, but he only kissed you because he thought you were one of them—the missing member of the Legion he was searching for."

The words ripped through me. If Andras knew about

the first kiss we'd shared while we were trapped in the wall...

He really can get inside Jared's head.

The demon wasn't finished. "Instead he learns you're Illuminati. Can you imagine the disappointment?"

My cheeks burned.

"What does that leave you with, Kennedy Waters? A dead mother. A father who didn't want you. Friends who don't trust you." Andras paused, savoring the moment. "And a boy who doesn't love you."

My heart felt like it stopped beating.

Gabriel finally snapped out of his haze. "He's trying to get under your skin, Kennedy. He doesn't know anything."

Then how did he know about Hearts of Mercy and the kiss?

"I want to talk to Jared," I said.

The demon laughed. "I'm sorry. Jared's not home right now. But he asked me to give you a message."

"Don't listen to a word that comes out of his filthy mouth," Gabriel said.

What if Jared really was trying to break free and communicate with me? How could I walk away without knowing?

"What's the message?"

The demon rose and walked toward the bars, dragging the chains along with him.

274

"What's the message?" I repeated.

He's not going to tell you.

Jared's body rocketed toward me, faster than any human being could possibly move. He stopped just inches from the bars—and me.

Gabriel raised his whip, and I caught his arm. "No." I turned back to Andras. "What's the message?"

The slow, insidious smile spread across his lips. "Good-bye. That's all he said." The demon's body sped backward, like someone had hit Rewind, until he was leaning against the wall on the other side of the cell.

Gabriel grabbed my arm. "Come on."

"Leaving so soon, Champion of God?" Andras asked.

"Don't worry." Gabriel forced a smile. "I'll be back."

As I turned away from the bars, Andras called out, "Alexa Sears, Lauren Richman, Kelly Emerson, Rebecca Turner, Cameron Anders, Mary Williams, Sarah Edelman, Julia Smith, Shannon O'Malley, Christine Redding, Karen York, Marie Dennings, Rachel Eames, Roxanne North, Catherine Nichols, Hailey Edwards, Lucy Klein." He taunted me with their names, as if I didn't already know them by heart. "They're all dead, Kennedy. Because of you."

"You killed them, not me." I kept my voice even.

The demon tilted his head to the side. "But I did it for you."

"He's lying. Let's get out of here." Gabriel touched my shoulder, but I couldn't make my legs work.

"Am I? Jared was sure his brother, the great code breaker, would have figured it out by now."

I stared at the names scrawled on the wall like a schizophrenic crossword puzzle: Anders, Klein, Edwards, Turner, Nichols, Eames, York, North, Dennings, Williams, Redding, Smith, O'Malley, Edelman, Richman, Sears, Emerson. My mind took snapshots as I scanned the letters, searching for patterns in the girls' names.

Within a few moments, random letters caught my attention, arranging and rearranging themselves in my mind's eye. Then the first letter of each girl's last name jumped out at me.

A. T. E. R. S.

No.

R. O. S. E. W. A. T. E. R. S.

My stomach lurched.

K. E. N. N. E. D. Y. R. O. S. E. W. A. T. E. R. S.

"Why?" I barely got the word out.

Andras looked right at me. "I wanted to know how it would feel to be inside your skin. The other girls were substitutes. Souls to tide me over until I found yours. The one that set me free."

My knees buckled and I hit the floor, icy water seeping through my jeans. Tiny pinpricks stabbed at the wet skin underneath, but I didn't move. I wanted the numbness to spread until I couldn't feel anything.

"Let's get you out of here." Gabriel pulled me up.

A familiar melody floated through the tunnel as Gabriel led me away. I recognized the lyrics. "Cry Little Sister," Jared's favorite song.

"Kennedy? Are you listening to me?" Gabriel grabbed my shoulders. "That wasn't Jared. Demons prey on your insecurities. The things you feel guilty about."

But he knew other things, like details about my relationship with Jared. How could he know those things unless Jared was thinking them?

When we reached the door, Jared's voice drifted up the stairs, singing "Cry Little Sister."

26. ATHENAEUM

The maze of steel hallways in the warehouse all looked the same, and within three turns, I was lost. For once, I didn't care. I had been lost for so long now—running from memories I couldn't escape, wounds I couldn't heal, and mistakes I couldn't erase. It had started the night my mom died and led right up to the moment Andras confirmed my worst fears a few minutes ago.

I'd ditched Gabriel the second we made it back upstairs, and retreated to my room. But I wasn't ready to face Alara or Elle. Instead, I had grabbed Faith's journal and taken off, and now I was lost.

Technically, I wasn't alone. Bear had followed me, unwilling to stay cooped up in our room any longer. I reached down and scratched between his ears.

My mind kept replaying the demon's words.

Friends who don't trust you...and a boy who doesn't love you.

All the doors in the hallway were identical sheets of reflective steel.

Except one.

At the end of the corridor, an intricately carved wooden door dwarfed the metal ones. Symbols were etched into every inch—a Gothic cross, the Devil's Trap, a Celtic knot, a pentagram, the evil eye, and others I didn't recognize. The Eye of Providence stared back from the center of the triangular brass knob.

Bear sat in front of the door, watching me.

If it's unlocked, I'll go in.

I turned the knob, and the hinges creaked. A soft light spilled into the hall from inside. It was probably a study.

Or Dimitri's or Gabriel's room.

The thought stopped me cold. As I started to turn around, Bear slipped through the door.

Guess I'm going in.

Inside, endless rows of books lined the walls of the circular room. The shelves were lit from behind, illuminating the books like the stars glowing on the ceiling above me. A huge opalescent sphere on a crazy-looking metal stand projected dozens of constellations onto the black ceiling, like a planetarium. Protective symbols and summoning circles like the ones from the journals covered the pale stone floors.

Six identical glass-front bookcases cut through the center of the shelves. It was difficult to see inside them, and I stepped closer to one. Instead of books, the case held a disturbing collection of objects: pristine vertebrae and bones suspended in apothecary jars; silver dishes filled with skeleton keys; a Venus flytrap inside a terrarium; exotic butterfly wings housed in individual glass bottles; a framed black widow spider; and stranger things I couldn't identify.

Bear barked at a fluffy taxidermied chick with two heads, on the bottom shelf. Next to the chick, less identifiable creatures floated in containers of formaldehyde like carnival oddities.

I drifted past the case, examining the cracked spines of the older books: *The Book of Secrets*, *Le Dragon Rouge*, *The Grand Grimoire*, *Heptameron of Darkness*, and *The Sketchbooks of Leonardo da Vinci*. I slid one of the smaller books off the shelf and leafed through pages of architectural drawings depicting tunnels and passageways with hidden entrances and concealed chambers.

Would Dimitri let us read them? Maybe there was information in one of those books that could help Jared.

Bear raced past the sphere-shaped projector and through an archway, across the room.

Perfect. It probably leads to another dungeon.

I was relieved to find a spiral staircase that led up, not down.

Bear peered at me from the top, where the black railing enclosed a second level of the circular room that blended perfectly into the dark walls. As I climbed the steps, the entire room was spread out below me. An inscription ran along the circumference of the room, the words alternating in Latin and English.

CONFUSA EST, INVENITUR ORDO.
IN CHAOS WE FIND ORDER.

"The Creed of Chaos," someone said from behind me. I jumped, even though I recognized Dimitri's voice.

"I didn't mean to startle you." He rose from a threadbare armchair tucked into an alcove.

"You didn't. It's fine." I stepped back, hoping to put a little distance between us, and my shoulder bumped into something hard. Another glass-front bookcase—filled with severed doll heads.

Cracked porcelain and shiny plastic faces peered out from behind the glass. "I don't know what you guys are into, but these are even weirder than the little alien embryos downstairs."

Dimitri pointed at the mountain of heads and lit a cigarette. "Charity work. Every one of those dolls was haunted. Gabriel and I exorcised the spirits."

"So they're souvenirs?"

"Gabriel likes to keep an eye on them." The more I learned about Gabriel, the stranger he seemed.

"That's not creepy or anything."

Dimitri studied the dolls for a moment and smiled. "I see your point."

"Do you guys live at the safe house?" I asked.

"Our work takes us all over the world, so we don't have permanent residences. This is the closest thing we have to a home."

I couldn't imagine living in one of the impersonal rooms I'd seen earlier. At least doll heads and a mummy gave this weird museum-library hybrid some character. "So what is this place?"

"An athenaeum," Dimitri said. "In addition to some of Gabriel's collections, this room houses our library and Illuminati records."

"Records of what, exactly?" I asked.

"Anecdotes, case studies, observations—"

"Your spy diaries?"

Dimitri frowned. "We're not the Order. We don't employ spies in the way you're suggesting."

Which means they employ them in some other way.

"The Illuminati has a long history of observing and recording paranormal and unexplained phenomena. You'd be shocked if you knew how many of the world's greatest thinkers were members of the Illuminati."

I pointed at the linen-wrapped mummy. "Like him?"

Dimitri laughed without even looking. He obviously knew every inch of this place by heart. He glanced up at the stars on the ceiling. "How about Galileo?"

"And you know this because?"

"Like I said, we keep great records." Dimitri switched on a crystal floor lamp, illuminating the alcove. It gave me a clearer view of the mummified guy—who I hoped wasn't a former Illuminati member they were preserving. A broken piece of a Renaissance-style fresco was mounted on the wall behind the mummy.

Dimitri pointed at the fresco. "The missing section of Raphael Santi's *La disputa del sacremento*, Disputation of the Sacrament. Painted inside the Vatican and commissioned by the pope himself. Of course, Raphael was only one of many Renaissance painters who were members of the Illuminati."

Dimitri made the Illuminati sound like an average, run-of-the-mill organization, like the Red Cross.

I turned around and caught a glimpse of another canvas. But I recognized this one. "That can't be what I think it is...."

Dimitri walked over to the surrealistic painting of an enormous polar bear hanging over the bow of a ship as it sailed over a building. "Of course. I forgot your mother was a fan of Chris Berens."

"That's an understatement," I said, stepping closer

to the canvas. "I know the name of every piece he's ever painted."

Dimitri ran his hand down the frame. "Except this one. It's untitled, but they call it—"

"*The Lost Painting.* Some people don't even believe it exists." I could hardly believe I was standing in front of it.

"Well, those people would be wrong." Dimitri smiled. "You know, he painted it for us."

"Us?"

"The Illuminati. Chris Berens heads the Order of the White Bear in Amsterdam. He's a curator, responsible for hiding and protecting the irreplaceable Illuminati works of art." Dimitri pointed at the section of *La disputa.* "Which is exactly how we ended up with a piece of Santi's fresco. I hope as you learn more about the Illuminati, you'll see that we aren't the enemy."

I nodded. "Maybe."

He gestured at the silver-plated journal under my arm. "Were you looking for a place to read?"

I shrugged. "More like a place to be alone."

"We don't generally allow anyone in here, but I can make an exception." He patted Bear on the head. "I'll leave you to it."

"I didn't mean—"

"I'm not offended," he said. "I come here to be alone, too." He glanced up at the ceiling. "And to look at the stars."

The Lost Painting by Chris Berens

Once Dimitri left, I settled into the armchair farthest from the mummy, with Bear curled up at my feet. I had skimmed Faith's journal this morning, but I didn't have time to read it carefully. Maybe I missed something that could help Jared. I read the first few pages again.

Anarel's words still gave me the chills: *Soon enough, the sins of man will rival those of the demons in hell.... There are no innocents among you.*

I flipped past pages filled with drawings of summoning circles and demon seals, exorcism rites and ciphers, until I reached an incantation I hadn't paid much attention to before.

> *An angel's blood.*
> *A demon's bone.*
> *A passing shadow.*
> *A dragon stone.*
> *Heaven and hell, darkness and light.*
> *Caged in the Vessel, waging their*
> *eternal fight.*

The Vessel—that's how Faith had referred to the Shift.

Did we give up looking for it too easily? What if the answer had been right in front of us all along, but we'd missed it because we were so busy looking for another one?

A prison to hold a demon.

The Shift was the one thing we needed to save Jared, and we had lost it.

⊰ • ⊱

Lukas opened the door to the room he and Priest shared, holding a slice of pizza. An open box lay on his bed next to his journal and laptop. "Hey. I'm reading everything I can find on demonic possession and exorcism. I can access source documents from libraries all over Europe."

"Did you find anything?"

He finished the slice and wiped his hands on his jeans. "Not yet."

"I need to show you something." I ducked under his arm impatiently and sat down on the end of the bed across from him. I'd rushed to their room straight from the athenaeum, hoping to find them both. "Where's Priest?"

"I think he's in the mech room. It's a metal shop on steroids. If everything didn't completely suck right now, he'd be having the time of his life." He gestured at the half-eaten pizza. "Want a slice? I was so hungry I couldn't think straight. I conned Gabriel into picking it up when he went on a supply run. He almost had a heart attack when I suggested delivery."

"No, thanks." I handed Lukas my aunt's journal and pointed at the page. "Remember when Faith mentioned the Vessel? There's something about it in here." I rambled on without giving him time to read. "Faith said the Vessel is the only prison that can hold Andras. This is how we're going to save Jared."

Lukas held up his hand. "Back up. I think I missed something."

"We can use the Shift to trap Andras." I waited while he read the passage.

"That would require actually knowing where to find it. Not to mention the part about an angel's blood, a demon's bone, and a dragon stone—whatever that means."

"Maybe the Shift is still at the penitentiary."

He shook his head and handed me the journal. "We already searched what was left of that place."

"Like your brother's life depended on it?"

Lukas grabbed a hoodie and pulled it on over his T-shirt. "Let's track down Priest and Alara."

I knew this was a long shot. Even if we found the Shift, how did the angel's blood, demon's bone, and dragon stone fit in? Gabriel and Dimitri probably knew, but I didn't trust them enough to put Jared's life in their hands.

But those details didn't matter unless we found the Shift.

Still, this was the first time it felt like there was a real chance to save Jared—one that didn't involve trying to persuade a demon to leave his body and take up residence in someone else's. And that possibility changed everything. It stirred something in the deepest part of me—a feeling I'd almost forgotten.

Hope.

27. MASTER OF BONES

The next day was New Year's Eve, a subject my friends avoided like the plague. We were holed up in Lukas and Priest's room trying to come up with a plan. Every once in a while, someone almost made the mistake of mentioning the holiday, and the room fell into an awkward silence.

After the third time, I couldn't take it anymore. "I know it's New Year's Eve. You don't have to tiptoe around it."

Priest and Lukas exchanged worried looks.

"As far as I'm concerned, it's a totally overrated holiday," Elle said, tossing her hair over her shoulder.

We both knew she was lying. A night dedicated to dressing up, flirting shamelessly, and kissing some heartsick guy at the end of the night was Elle's definition

289

of the perfect holiday—which only made me love her more for pretending it wasn't.

Lukas gave me one of his crooked smiles. "No one's really in the mood to celebrate."

Alara fed Bear one of the oatmeal cookies she'd saved for him. "And I'm completely against celebrations in any and all forms."

"The only thing we have time for right now is figuring out how to get back to the prison so we can find the Shift," Priest said, turning up Linkin Park in the background. His music was our insurance policy—the sole reason Dimitri and Gabriel refused to set foot in here.

Alara sighed. "There's no way we'll be able to get out of this place without Dimitri and Gabriel asking a million questions. Like where we're going."

"And I don't want them looking for the Shift without us," Lukas said.

No one argued. We needed to get to West Virginia State Penitentiary without Dimitri and Gabriel, and we had to do it fast.

"We'll have to sneak out during the day," Priest said. "Gabriel stays awake all night like a vampire."

"If we disappear, they'll come looking for us," Lukas said.

Bear slept by the door, but I knew his ears would perk up if he heard anyone in the hallway.

"I'm not leaving Jared alone with Gabriel and Dimitri."

Even if I trusted them—which I wasn't sure I did—Gabriel couldn't see past the demon when he looked at Jared, and Andras manifesting my mother had only made it worse.

Priest turned up "Castle of Glass." "Two of us go, and everyone else stays to make sure Dimitri and Gabriel don't do anything crazy."

"That still leaves one problem," Lukas said. "We left the Jeep parked on the street in Boston. It probably has a boot on it by now, and I doubt Dimitri and Gabriel are going to give us a ride unless we tell them what we're looking for."

A mischievous smile tugged at the corner of Elle's lips. She was stretched out on Lukas' bed, propped on one elbow. "Maybe they won't give us a ride to the prison, but I can get them to take us into town."

"Then what? Moundsville is ten hours from here," Lukas said.

Priest perked up. "I can steal a car."

"No one is stealing anything," I said.

"I can get us a car." Alara was swapping the black laces in her tactical boots with white ones covered in bleeding ex-*voto* hearts.

"How?" Priest still hadn't figured out where Alara had gotten the Jeep, a detail she refused to divulge.

"Stick to designing weapons to save our asses and keep us from being possessed." Alara smiled. "Leave serious stuff like auto theft and saving the world to the girls."

Even after we explained Elle's plan twice, Priest was still having a hard time grasping the genius of it. "It'll never work. Gabriel and Dimitri won't care about buying that kinda stuff."

Lukas flipped his coin. He didn't seem interested in discussing the details any more than we were hoping Dimitri and Gabriel would.

Alara checked the supplies in her tool belt: plastic soda bottle filled with holy water, paintball gun, ammo, pouches of herbs and rock salt, an EMF, a multi-tool. "You obviously don't have any sisters."

"What does that have to do with anything?" Priest asked.

Alara winked at him. "Watch and learn."

⊣ • ⊢

We found Gabriel camped out in the room with the glass dry-erase boards. Azazel was stretched across the ebony table in front of him.

"Can I help you with something?" Gabriel didn't look up from the barbed demon vertebrae he was polishing.

Alara and I fidgeted uncomfortably for his benefit. "I need to go to the store," I said.

"I'm sure we've got whatever you want here." He moved on to a hooked claw.

Alara cleared her throat. "Um...not everything."

Gabriel rubbed the dark stubble on his chin.

"Doubtful. But tell me what you need. If we don't have it, I'll go out and pick it up for you."

I gave Alara a questioning glance.

She shrugged. "If you're sure. It's girl stuff. It's in a special aisle. There are lots of different kinds."

Gabriel's cheeks flushed.

"I have a picture on my phone." Alara pressed a few buttons, pretending to look for something.

He held up his hand. "I'll take you. But we can't be gone too long."

Priest, Lukas, and Elle were hanging out in the hallway, listening. I imagined the look on Priest's face and smiled.

Gabriel wound the whip around his arm and hooked it behind him. "Do you both need to come?"

Alara gave him an innocent look. "Well, we both—"

Gabriel cut her off. "Let's go." He obviously didn't want the details, which was exactly what we had counted on.

⇥ • ⇤

When we pulled up in front of the drugstore, Alara hopped out first. "Sure you don't want to come in?"

Gabriel gave her a hard stare and opened a tattered issue of *Soldier of Fortune*. "I'll wait here."

Alara sauntered through the automatic doors in her cargos like she owned the place, and the world along with it.

I followed her through the aisles toward the back of the store. "You're really going to do this?"

She stopped in the makeup section and glanced in the mirror, smudging her black eyeliner a little. "Just give me a head start. Hang out in here for fifteen minutes before you go back to the car."

That's the part I was dreading, but it was worth it if she found the Shift.

Alara pushed open the swinging doors at the end of the freezer aisle, marked EMPLOYEES ONLY. "There's always an exit in the back of these stores." She stopped and took a deep breath. "How do I look?"

It was the last thing I expected her to ask. "Are you serious?"

She zipped her hooded leather jacket and tightened her tool belt. "Of course I am. Do I look like the kind of girl a guy would mess with on the subway?"

For a second, I thought she was joking. But she was waiting for an answer. "No."

"Perfect." Alara strode through the back door and straight toward the jet-black Dodge Challenger parked in the alley.

A broad-shouldered guy with black hair and sun-kissed skin leaned against the car, his arms folded in front of him. Everything about him was rough around the edges, but he was gorgeous.

The moment he saw Alara, his bad boy demeanor

vanished and his face broke into a wide smile. He didn't wait for her to make it all the way to the car. Instead, he met her halfway and hooked an arm around her neck, pulling her in for a hug. "I knew you'd miss me."

She pretended to push him away, but he only held on tighter. "What if I said I just needed a ride?"

He grinned. "I'd ask you what you did with the last ride I lent you. Then I'd say you were lying." He held out his hand. "You're Kennedy, right? Alara talks about you all the time. I'm Anthony D'Amore."

I couldn't decide what surprised me more—that I was about to shake hands with Alara's mystery guy or that she'd told him about me.

"Nice to meet you. Alara's told me—"

"Nothing about me, right?" He took her hand and interlaced his fingers with hers. "That's my girl."

His girl?

Priest and Lukas would've killed to see this.

"How do you two know each other?" I had to ask.

"We met at one of those junior high mixers. Alara went to our sister school."

A mixer? I had enough trouble imagining Alara in a club, let alone a school dance.

"I used to get into a lot of trouble, and Alara was always the one who got me out of it."

"Now it's your turn to return the favor," she said, nudging him playfully.

"You're lucky I'm on break, or I'd be training. I have a big match coming up."

"Are you a boxer?" I asked.

Anthony laughed. "No, Alara's the fighter. I design BattleBots for the team at MIT."

He was a nerd. Alara's gorgeous, tough-looking secret boyfriend was a robot-battling geek from MIT. It was like Clark Kent had just told me he was Superman.

"We'd better go," Alara said.

I gave her a quick hug. "You just became exponentially cooler in my eyes."

"Just don't tell Priest and Lukas." Her smile faded. "If the Shift is there, I'll find it."

"I know."

As I turned back to the store, Anthony opened the car door for her. "So, where are we going anyway?"

"How do you feel about haunted prisons?"

⊣ • ⊢

I underestimated exactly how angry Gabriel would be when I showed up at the car without Alara. Enraged was more accurate. The only thing that infuriated him more was the fact that I wouldn't tell him where she'd gone.

The car ride back to the safe house was miserable, a Jekyll-and-Hyde meltdown on Gabriel's part. But his reaction was nothing compared to Dimitri's.

After he'd forced Gabriel to account for every second of the trip, it was my turn. "Where is she, Kennedy?" Dimitri sounded too calm, which only proved he wasn't.

He chose the athenaeum for our little chat, otherwise known as an interrogation. Dimitri leaned forward in the chair across from the one I was sitting in, next to the mummy. "I'm not angry—"

"Yes, you are."

He took a deep breath and dug through his pockets until he found a cigarette. "All right. I am angry. But only because Alara is out there alone, and I don't want anything to happen to her."

Tell him and get it over with.

"She's not exactly alone."

Gabriel looked up from where he stood at the railing. "Who's with her?"

"A friend."

Dimitri rubbed his hand over his face. "This isn't a game. There are already seventeen dead girls, and we have no idea what Andras is capable of, even from in here."

Dead girls.

I'd never heard anyone call them that before. Usually, they were the *missing girls* or the *abducted girls*, or, more recently, *the bodies*. Hearing Dimitri refer to them that way made the possibility of Alara getting hurt feel more real.

What if he was right, and there were vengeance spirits hunting us—or possessing people who were under Andras' control, like my aunt's black-eyed neighbors?

Could Andras control people and spirits from in here?

"I still don't understand why she ran off." Gabriel shook his head. "You aren't prisoners. I thought you all wanted to be here to help your friend."

"She is trying to help him."

Gabriel dropped into the chair next to Dimitri's and closed his eyes. "But who's going to help her?"

Maybe he had a point. Alara *was* at the site of a haunted prison with a mechanical engineer who built BattleBots in his spare time. How much help would he be if they encountered vengeance spirits like the ones that tried to kill us the last time we were there?

"She went back to Moundsville."

Dimitri tensed. "The prison? Why?"

I couldn't tell them, and Alara wouldn't want me to. She and Priest didn't trust Dimitri and Gabriel, and Lukas and I were still on the fence. We didn't know enough about them, or how much of what they'd told us was true.

Gabriel jumped out of his chair. "I'm going to find her."

"You can't be gone that long." Dimitri snatched his coat, his expression grim. "Andras is getting stronger every day. At this point, if we lose control of him, Azazel is our strongest weapon."

The whip coiled tighter, as if the demonic weapon recognized its name.

"You're the only one who can command it." Dimitri swept past him and down the stairs. "I'll find her."

Gabriel stood at the railing until the tails of Dimitri's black coat disappeared through the doors.

"Can I ask you a question?" It was something I'd wanted to ask him the last time we were alone, but I was afraid to hear the answer. "The Order sounds like it was full of monsters. Was my mom hurting people?"

"The Order was working against the Illuminati from the inside for a long time. They believed the best way to protect the world from demons was to learn to control them." He took a deep breath. "They were conducting experiments—summoning weaker demons and trying to train them like pets. But what they were actually doing was letting demons into our world and giving them a chance to learn about us."

"They didn't see that coming?" I asked. When Dimitri and Gabriel told us about the Order, I imagined a group of Illuminati extremists, not a bunch of misguided scientists secretly training demons.

"I guess it's like being the guys who invented the atomic bomb. You think about all the ways your invention can help people. But in the wrong hands, that same invention can destroy the world." Gabriel hunched over the railing, staring at his hands. "It took me a long time to figure out the truth about their *research*."

"What gave them away?" I asked.

"I started spending time in the labs. I thought we were using the demons to make weapons." Gabriel unhooked the whip and let it roll out across the floor, the ivory bones unhinging one by one. He looked over at me, his eyes full of sadness and shame.

"How do you think I made Azazel?"

28. NIGHTMARES AND ASH

After Gabriel and Dimitri finished lecturing me, I relayed the details to Lukas, Priest, and Elle. Everyone agreed with my decision to tell them that Alara had gone back to the prison. She still had a few hours' head start on Dimitri. Maybe she'd find the Shift before he made it there.

The possibility of finding the Shift sent me down to the containment area. I needed to see Jared. The walk through the tunnel alone was the worst part—wondering whether I'd find Jared or Andras on the other side of the bars.

I always held my breath until I knew, the way I was holding it now.

Jared sat on the mattress, wringing his hands in front of him. The names of the dead girls were still on the wall. But now there was something new. Circles and strange symbols that looked like they belonged in an old alchemy book, some repeated over and over in manic sequences.

Dimitri had left sticks of chalk and charcoal in the cell, hoping to see if Andras would write anything else. Maybe he'd know what the symbols meant, but I didn't want to. The sight of anything written by the demon's hand made me sick.

Jared looked up when he heard my footsteps, his pale eyes sad and heavy.

It's him.

Relief washed over me, and for a long moment, neither one of us spoke. There was too much to say and no way to say it.

I wrapped my hands around the bars, longing to be closer to him. "Are you okay?"

Is the demon hurting you?

Jared adjusted his ripped thermal to cover the worst of the burns on his neck. "Yeah. How about you?"

"Me? I—" My voice cracked, and I pressed my fingers against my eyes.

Don't cry. You can't do that to him.

When I moved my hands, Jared was standing in front of me, a few feet away from the cell door. His expression was full of concern—for me, instead of himself.

"I'm fine. I'm just worried about you." I kept my voice even, so the lie would sound like the truth.

I miss you and I need you and I want you back.

"What's that stuff on your face?" He pointed at the black marks on my cheeks.

"Sigils. Gabriel taught me how to paint them."

Pain flickered in his eyes. "What are they for?"

"Don't do this," I whispered.

"What are they for?" he repeated.

"Protection." I couldn't look at him.

"From me." When Andras was in control, Jared's eyes never expressed any emotion. But now they betrayed everything he was feeling. "I want to hear you say it, Kennedy."

"Why?"

Jared lifted his hands, letting the chains hang between his wrists. "I'm chained up like this for a reason. I'm a monster, and you can't save me."

My heart hammered in my chest. "Andras is the monster."

"Don't you get it?" Jared shook his shackled wrists in front of him. "He's *inside* me."

"We're going to figure out a way—"

He didn't wait for me to finish. "I don't want you to come down here anymore. I can feel him getting stronger. Sometimes I can even hear him thinking, like we're the same person. His thoughts, the things he wants to do to you..." Jared turned around, hiding his face. "You can't ever come down here again. Promise me."

I couldn't stay away. Knowing he was hurting and not being able to hold him or comfort him was hard enough. "That's not a promise I can make."

Jared slammed his palms against the wall, then pushed off and walked toward the bars. "I'm not going to make it out of this alive. If the strain of the possession doesn't kill me, Andras will once he doesn't need my body anymore. That's his plan. By then, he'll be stronger and impossible to stop."

"Did you hear something in his thoughts?" It could be the break we needed.

Jared shook his head. "There's only one way. We both know that. If you won't kill me, I need you to help me do it myself."

For a second, I was speechless. "No. There has to be another—"

"There's no other way." He pulled his arms over his head until the shackles were resting behind his neck. "If I'm going to die, I want to take him with me."

My throat burned, and tears rolled down my face. "We have an idea. Just give us a little more time." I couldn't risk telling him the details, not with Andras reading his thoughts.

Jared's gaze trailed from the wet cell walls to the burns covering his chest and up to the Eye of Ever on the ceiling. Finally, he looked at me, his face marked with pain I could see as easily as the scars. "I don't know how much time I have left."

I stared back at him, trying to make sense of the words. My stomach clenched, and every part of me felt numb.

He moved closer, and I stepped back too fast.

"I'm sorry," I said, realizing what I'd done.

He walked up to the bars, his movements tentative. "I just wanted to—" His blue eyes were full of pain and confusion.

It's Jared. He won't hurt me.

If I was wrong, he could kill me.

As long as I don't have to kill him.

I took a step closer, then another, until we were only a foot apart.

"I just wanted to say good-bye." He reached through the bars, and I didn't move. "There are so many things I wish I'd told you. The way I feel about you..."

My heart pounded. "Tell me now."

He wiped a tear from the corner of my eye with his thumb. I shut my eyes. I wanted him to know I trusted him, even if it was stupid or reckless.

Jared's fingers curled in and touched my jaw, and he traced the path of my tears with his thumb.

My eyes flew open and I caught his wrist, pulling it away from my face. "Don't. The sigils will burn you."

His pulse thundered against my skin. "I've been burned before."

"Not like this," I said.

"I don't care."

"But I do," I whispered.

Jared let his finger trail down my cheek until it reached my lips. I kept my eyes locked on his as the ash burned him. He didn't flinch. Then he pulled his fingers back inside the bars and held up his palm.

I raised my own, until our hands were almost touching—like a reflection in the broken mirror that had become our lives.

Our palms met against the iron, and he closed his hand around mine. "Every person has one thing that defines them. A truth they believe in above everything else. You are my truth."

⊰ • ⊱

When I opened the door to our room, Elle was sitting on her bed with a book. She jumped and shoved it under her blanket.

"What are you reading?"

She didn't respond right away, a strange expression passing over her face. Then she slid the frayed volume out from underneath the blanket and held it up.

"*Summoning Circles in Demonology: Doorways to Darkness*? Where did you get that?" I asked.

Elle shrugged. "Dimitri lent it to me. I wanted to learn more about paranormal entities."

Paranormal entities?

"When did you start using ghost-hunting terminology?" A few days ago, she thought *EMF* was an acronym for *electromagnified ghost finder*.

She stiffened, which wasn't like her. Elle never got uncomfortable; her specialty was making other people feel that way.

"Does this have anything to do with Lukas?"

Her shoulders relaxed a little. "Maybe."

"Maybe? That's all I get?" Usually, Elle spilled every detail about a guy she liked, and plenty about the ones she didn't like.

"I've done enough reading for tonight." She dropped the book on the floor. "Do you care if I turn off the lights?"

"Not if you're tired." I barely had time to crawl into bed before she flicked the switch. Part of me expected her to turn them back on and tell me everything. But she didn't.

Instead, I replayed my visit with Jared, focusing on the happy moments.

His voice.

Touching his skin.

You are my truth.

Thoughts of him lulled me to sleep and filled my dreams.

⊰ • ⊱

The chains are gone.

Jared is standing in front of me, shirtless in his frayed

307

jeans. He's soaking wet and barefoot. His coffee-colored hair is wet, too—messy and curling at his neck.

My eyes sweep over the scars on his chest and up to his face.

He smiles at me, and his pale blue eyes light up beneath long black eyelashes.

He's still in the cell, but the door is open, and I'm in there, too.

Together.

"Come here," he says.

I walk toward him, unable to speak.

The nightmare is finally over.

I can feel it in my bones—in my heart. It's the way he's looking at me, and the fact that the chains are gone.

When I'm close enough, he hooks a finger through the belt loop of my jeans and pulls me closer.

We're a foot apart, and he holds me there. "I want to look at you." He tucks my hair behind my ear, and the moment his fingers touch my skin, I shiver. "I never thought I'd be able to touch you again."

I don't try to hold back my tears. I feel happy in a way I've never experienced before. "Me too."

Jared slides his hand behind my neck and steps closer. Our lips are touching, but he hasn't kissed me yet. "I dreamed about this," he whispers. "All those nights I spent locked in this cell. This is what I thought about."

I push up on my toes because he's so much taller than

me, holding his shoulders for balance. I kiss him, and he relaxes against me.

Everything is going to be okay now.

He pulls back and looks at me, cradling my face. "On the worst nights—when I slept on the floor because it hurt to move, from Gabriel's whip digging into my flesh and holy water burning every inch of my body—I thought about this moment."

Jared's hands drift down to my neck, and his grip tightens. "And what it would feel like to be inside your skin."

His blue eyes are lost in shadow, the black ink filling them until every trace of the boy I am falling in love with is gone.

⇥ • ⇤

The nightmare jolted me awake, and it took me a moment to realize it was a dream. I caught a glimpse of Bear curled up in Alara's bed without her, and I turned on my cell.

One new text.

I opened it and my last text to Alara appeared: did u find it???

One word followed my question: no.

In a single moment, the last scrap of hope I'd been holding on to vanished.

29. UNCAGED

I waited until the next morning to visit Jared again.

Today was New Year's Day, and the idea of seeing him chained up killed me. But I couldn't leave him down there alone all day either.

Even though he probably doesn't know today is any different from yesterday.

With no way to track the days, how could he?

It was also time to tell him the truth about the Shift—that it was the key to saving him, but we had no idea where to find it.

If Andras knew what happened to it, maybe Jared knew, too. More evidence of their horrific mind meld was the last thing I wanted. But Jared was running out of time.

One of the bulbs had burned out at the end of the

tunnel, leaving parts of the cell in shadow—along with Jared. Even in the darkness, he looked broken, and I felt myself breaking, too.

He doesn't deserve this.

Iron bars were the only things separating us.

He didn't look up from where he sat on the cell floor, leaning against the wall, in nothing but a pair of jeans. I glanced at the chain binding his wrists. With his head bowed, he looked exactly the same.

But he's not.

I let my fingers curl around the wet metal bars, and I fought the urge to unlock the door and let him out.

"I told you not to come down here anymore." He hadn't moved, but I knew he didn't need to see me to sense my presence. "No one else will."

He meant Lukas, Priest, and Alara.

"Everyone's trying to figure this out. They don't know what to do about—" The words caught in my throat.

"About me." He rose from the floor and walked toward me—and the bars separating us.

As he drew closer, I counted the links in the chain hanging between his wrists. Anything to keep from looking him in the eye. But instead of moving away, I gripped the bars tighter.

He reached out and wrapped his hands around the metal above mine. Close but not touching.

"Don't!"

Steam rose from the cold-iron bars as the holy water seared his scarred skin. He held on too long, intentionally letting his palms burn.

"You shouldn't be here," he whispered. "It's not safe."

Hot tears ran down my cheeks. Every decision we'd made up to this point felt wrong now: the chains coiled around his wrists, the cell soaked in holy water, the bars keeping him caged like an animal.

"I know you'd never hurt me," I whispered.

The words had barely left my lips when Jared lunged at the bars. He grabbed at my throat and I jumped back, his cold fingers grazing my skin as I slipped out of reach.

"You're wrong about that, little dove." His voice sounded different, cruel and soulless.

Laughter echoed off the walls and chills rippled through me. I realized what everyone else had known all along.

The boy I knew was gone.

The one caged before me now was a monster.

And I was the one who would have to kill him.

Unless I could find a way to save him.

30. MARKED

Alara and Dimitri returned the next day—frustrated, exhausted, and barely speaking. Dimitri had dealt out an excessive number of disappointed looks before disappearing into his room with a fresh carton of cigarettes. After a lecture from Gabriel, Alara recounted what sounded like a painstaking search for the Shift. But I already knew how that story ended, and hearing it again made Jared's situation seem even more hopeless.

I retreated to the athenaeum with Faith's journal, trying not to think about the way Jared's hand had felt around my neck. I knew he wasn't the one who tried to strangle me, but it was his voice that kept replaying in my head.

I lost myself in the journal, skimming over the older,

more damaged entries until I reached what had to be Faith's handwriting. The word *nightmares* jumped out at me.

The nightmares are getting worse. Sometimes I don't sleep for days, hoping to outrun them. But when I finally close my eyes, they're waiting for me. I've started painting them. Once I complete a painting, the nightmare stops. But a new one always begins. I keep thinking one day, I'll paint something and it will be over. I will fall asleep that night and I won't even dream.

I flipped a few pages until I reached another entry.

My dad told me the truth about my specialty today. He saw one of my paintings—a little boy in khaki shorts and a red blazer, lying dead in the street. There's a symbol carved into the boy's forehead, and a shadowy figure hovering above him. In my dream, I knew it was a demon. I even knew his name. Azazel.

My hand shook when I saw the demon's name.

Azazel.

The name of Gabriel's whip.

At first, Dad seemed shocked by the painting. But he looked proud, as if I'd painted the Mona Lisa instead of a dead kid. Then he showed me the picture in the newspaper. It was my painting—every detail except the shadowy figure.

Apparently, invocation and precognition is my specialty.

Dad says invocation is something he can teach me, not that I want to learn to summon and command demons or angels. They seem equally alien, and I don't want to face either one. But precognition is scarier. It's a gift, he says. Which means it cannot be taught. If you're one of the "lucky ones," as he calls them, images come to you. Images of the future. If he could see them, he'd know there was nothing lucky about it.

I tried to imagine seeing a child's death before it happened—finding a photograph of a scene from one of my paintings. It was a miracle Faith didn't lose her mind and go completely crazy, carrying that kind of burden. I remembered when Lukas, Jared, Priest, and Alara first told me that invocation was my specialty.

When they thought I was one of them.

Faith and I had such similar reactions. The ability to summon, and supposedly command, angels and demons hadn't seemed "special" to me either.

It doesn't matter. You don't have a specialty.

I turned back to the journal, pushing the thought away.

Last night's dream was strange. The words came first, which has never happened before. And I even saw a date.

*Under the wings of a hawk, a dove
will be born.
Not a black dove bound by the ties
of centuries past.
But a white dove, born in this one
to break the ties that bind us.
And set us free.
July 30*

I recognized the date.

I must've read it wrong.

July 30. My birthday.

The images came later. Alex holding a baby with a tiny hospital bracelet around her wrist. He's in the nursery, and I know it's his baby because I can see the card taped to the Isolette: Kennedy Rose Waters. July 30.

Below the entry, Faith had drawn a girl with the snow-white wings of a dove, standing at the edge of a cliff. It reminded me of the painting I was working on when my mom died. A girl standing on a ledge, with swallow wings growing out of her back—who was too scared to fly.

But instead of painful, unwanted wings, the girl's wings in Faith's drawing were breathtaking and full—the kind of wings that could carry her.

I'm not sure how many times I reread the page or what shocked me more: knowing Faith predicted my birth down to my name and the day, or the idea that I was the white dove.

Faith's entry made it sound important, as if I had a special destiny. Maybe there was still room for me somewhere in my friends' story.

317

KENNEDY'S PAINTING

Later that night, I went to see Jared. But this time, I didn't go alone.

Elle hugged her parka tighter around her thin frame. "It's freezing down here."

Lukas pulled her against his shoulder and rubbed his hand up and down her arm. "The more powerful the demon, the colder it gets."

Even subzero temperatures couldn't have prepared me for what waited at the end of the tunnel.

The demon stood in the center of the Devil's Trap, his arms outstretched like he was soaking in the sun. New scars mixed with the old ones to create a map of pain he didn't seem to feel. Behind him, every inch of the cell was covered in frenzied writing—letters, characters, words, and symbols overlapping or spiraling in circles.

Priest pointed at the script scrawled across the mattress. "That's Assyrian, for sure."

Gabriel stood at the bars, speechless. "Sumerian. Ammonite. Minoan. Aramaic. We need to know what it says."

Distorted drawings of monstrous creatures marred the floor: falcon-headed wolves with human limbs, and masked creatures morphing from equestrian bodies, their claws clutching swords and battle-axes.

"Was there anything like this in the book you were reading?" I asked Elle.

Elle looked at me like I was crazy. "What book?"

"The one Dimitri lent you," I said.

She frowned. "I don't know what you're talking about. Are you okay?"

I glanced at Lukas. Maybe she didn't want him to know.

Alara gasped, pointing at what looked like demonic Morse code.

"Enochian, the language of light and darkness," Alara said. "Of angels and demons."

Andras turned his head slowly toward Alara. "Only a witch would use those words to describe the tongue of the Labyrinth."

She pulled back her shoulders and stepped closer to the bars. "I am not a witch."

The demon laughed. "You deal in spells and wards, elements and earth. Your kind met their end in flames, in both our worlds. But in the Labyrinth, we don't burn witches at the stake. You set fire to one another. And when your souls have burned to ash, the Dark Prince resurrects them so they can be burned again." Andras smiled at Alara. "Your grandmother is probably there right now, burning as we speak. I can almost smell the stench of her soul."

"My grandmother is not in hell," Alara snapped.

He cocked his head. "Are you sure?"

Alara slipped the paintball gun from her tool belt, her delicate features contorted with rage.

Priest grabbed her arm, guiding it back down to her side. "He's just trying to get under your skin."

She pointed a shaky finger at Andras. "I'm gonna be the one who kills your miserable ass, you hear me?"

"You're talking about Jared," I said softly. A fact that didn't seem to register with her at all.

Alara spun around, her face only inches from mine, and she pointed at the bars. "That *thing* is not Jared."

"Let's calm down." Gabriel scanned the tunnel for Dimitri. "Andras is the Author of Discords. He incites anger and dissension. We're giving him what he wants."

"Shut up, Gabriel," Alara said.

The demon walked toward the writing on the wall. As he turned, Jared's back came into view. Every inch of his skin was covered in the same indecipherable symbols. The drawings themselves weren't as disturbing as their placement: Jared's lower back, between his shoulder blades—spots he couldn't possibly reach with his wrists chained in front of him.

My mind flashed on one of Faith's apocalyptic canvases—the painting of the guy in the cell with the symbols on his back. Looking at Jared now was like seeing it in the flesh.

Elle inched closer to Lukas. "We have officially entered *The Exorcist* territory."

Footsteps echoed behind us, and Dimitri emerged from the mouth of the tunnel.

Autor de Discordiaz

321

"What the hell took so long?" Gabriel demanded.

"I had to add rock salt to the tank. The concentration isn't strong enough anymore." Dimitri unzipped a cracked leather bag and tossed a stack of dusty journals and books with crumbling spines on the floor.

"Did you bring the bells?"

Dimitri unearthed a dozen chipped, widemouthed bells, suspended from thick loops of rope.

"Bells?" Priest stared at Dimitri. "That's your plan?"

Dimitri shoved one into his hands. "These are altar bells, used in some of the most famous churches in history, including the Vatican. Andras is getting stronger, and we need to counteract that. The sound will weaken him."

The bell ripped from Priest's hands and clattered across the tunnel floor. The remaining bells flew from the bag as if they were being pulled by a magnet. They rolled across the stone and piled themselves up, climbing over one another like rats scaling a wall.

Once the bells laddered their way to the ceiling, they separated and spread through the tunnel above our heads.

"Oh my god." Elle backed away.

The deafening sound of clanging metal erupted in the small space, and everyone covered their ears.

Except Andras.

He had returned to the center of the Devil's Trap, waving his chained arms together as one, like a maestro conducting a demonic orchestra. He closed his eyes, reveling in the sound that was supposed to bring him to his knees.

The sprinklers whirled on, and more salt rained down on the demon's body. Pillars of steam rolled off his skin, and without warning, the bells stopped ringing.

"Cover your heads," Dimitri yelled.

The bells hung in the air for a moment, then dropped. One hit my shoulder, while others crashed to the floor around me.

Gabriel stumbled to his feet and unhooked Azazel. The bones screeched and writhed as he cracked the whip against the bars.

Andras narrowed his eyes. "You cannot control me with your toy, Gabriel."

The demon cupped his shackled hands, letting them fill with holy water. Steam rose from his palms as he lifted his hands to his lips and drank.

Alara gasped, and Dimitri and Gabriel looked stunned.

When Andras finished, his eyes turned black. "Who is your champion now, Gabriel?" The demon held out his shackled wrists. "This boy's soul feeds me, like the souls of the girls I killed before I found you, Kennedy." He pointed at me and smiled. "The girl both of us want to possess."

A shudder ran through me.

Soaked in holy water, Andras moved closer to the bars.

"Who do you think will win your soul?" His eyes turned the same pale shade of blue as Jared's. The demon's body jerked, and he seemed disoriented for a moment.

"Run," Jared whispered.

I stood perfectly still, afraid the slightest movement might snap the thread between us.

Jared shook his head in quick jerks, and the ink seeped back into his eyes.

Priest backed down the tunnel, with Elle stumbling after him. "We should get out of here. That monster isn't Jared."

Andras whipped around. "I agree, Owen. I am *not* Jared. He is an entirely different kind of monster." He stared at Lukas with a vicious look in his eye. "Isn't that right, Lukas? Why don't you tell Owen who was really responsible for his grandfather's death?"

The color drained from Lukas' face.

Gabriel studied Lukas, watching his reaction.

"Save it," Alara said. "No one believes your lies."

Lukas' eyes darted from the demon hiding behind his brother's face to Alara. He flipped his silver coin between his fingers.

The demon jerked the chain shackled to his ankle and stepped closer to the bars. "Am I lying, Lukas? Tell your witch the truth."

The coin slipped from Lukas' fingers and dropped on

the floor. Alara watched it clatter to a stop between their boots.

"Lukas?" A hint of fear lurked in Alara's tone.

He frowned, and a deep line cut between his brows. He didn't take his eyes off the coin, as if he were letting it decide his fate. Heads or tails. The truth or a lie. But both sides of Lukas' coin were the same.

"Let's talk about this upstairs," Dimitri said.

"No," Alara snapped. "I'm not going anywhere until I get an answer."

"It was an accident," Lukas said finally.

Priest shook his head, confused. "Wait, what are we talking about?"

"He didn't mean it," Lukas mumbled.

Priest stiffened. "Didn't mean *what*? You're not making any sense."

The demon threw his head back and laughed. "In the <ins>hell</ins> Labyrinth, we lie to our enemies. Only humans lie to their friends."

Lukas lunged at the bars. "Shut your mouth. Or I swear to god, I'll kill you myself!"

Andras smiled. "I'm sorry. God is busy performing miracles at the moment."

Alara grabbed Lukas' arm and jerked him around to face her. "What's he talking about?"

"Our uncle wanted to find the missing member of the

Legion. Like I told Faith, he thought the Legion would be stronger if all five members were together." The words tumbled out, the same way they had when Jared first told me the story inside the wall, at Hearts of Mercy. "Jared figured out the names of all the Legion members. He made a list—"

"A list?" Rage flashed in Alara's brown eyes.

Gabriel stared at the floor as if he knew where the story was going.

"Jared was trying to help. So we could destroy *him*." Lukas pointed at the cell, and the demon that looked exactly like his brother.

Alara slumped against the wall. "That's how Andras found them."

"It was an accident," I said.

"Breaking something is an accident." Priest's voice grew louder with every word. "Killing five people is something else."

"Owen does have a point." Andras smiled.

I ignored him and plowed ahead. "Jared didn't know Andras would find them."

"He knew the rules." Priest pointed at me, seething. "And you'd say anything to protect him."

I'd never seen Priest this angry, and I didn't think it had anything to do with the demon's proximity. "That's not true. My mom died that night, too."

"Your mother was a spy."

I stared back at him, speechless.

"That's enough." Gabriel stepped between us.

Alara looked up from where she was leaning against the wall. She'd been strangely quiet until now. "Wait. How do you know it was an accident?" She stared at me as if we were the only two people in the room. "You knew this whole time?"

I swallowed hard. "Jared wanted to tell you himself."

"That's a lie," Andras said casually, as he moved closer to the bars. "I should know. I spend all day in his head."

"No." Lukas backed away.

Priest gave Andras one last look, then turned and stormed down the tunnel. "I'm getting my stuff, and I'm outta here."

"Where are you going?" Elle asked, rushing after him. "You can't leave."

Dimitri hesitated for a second, then flicked his cigarette against the wall and followed them.

Gabriel looked to us. "Priest isn't serious, is he?"

"I've never seen him that upset," Alara said softly. "If he says he's leaving, he means it."

"We don't need this right now." Gabriel stormed down the tunnel.

Alara didn't say anything until he was gone, but when she finally looked at me, tears glittered in her eyes. "You should've told me, Kennedy."

"I'm sorry." My voice faltered.

"It's too late for sorry," she said, turning away from Luke and me.

"Alara," Lukas called after her.

Alara spun around and pointed at him, her cheeks streaked with tears. "Don't."

Her footsteps echoed through the passage as she walked away, but there was nothing I could say. If anyone understood how it felt to be lied to by someone you trusted, it was me.

"Jared never would've told them," Lukas said finally. "He was too ashamed."

"He's right," Andras said. "And I didn't need to read your boyfriend's thoughts to know. Jared's soul was branded with guilt the first time I saw him, at your aunt's house."

The first time he saw him.

Memories slid together in blurry flashes, like black splotches clouding my vision.

Jared standing in front of the shattered bay window at my aunt's house.

The child's pupil-less black eyes staring back at him.

Gabriel's voice replayed in my mind: *If a demon marks your soul, he'll always be able to find you.*

The realization crystalized in my mind with chilling clarity. "That's how you found us. When Jared looked at you from the window...you marked him."

We never stood a chance.

Andras took a step forward, but I didn't move. There was something about the way he was looking at me.

"I didn't need Jared to find you. His soul isn't the one I marked that day at Faith's." A trail of holy water burned its way down the demon's cheek. "It was yours."

⊰ • ⊱

Lukas dragged me down the dark tunnel. "You can't let him get in your head. It's just another one of his lies."

What if it wasn't? What if my soul was the one marked by a demon? I had stared out the window at the little girl, too.

He'll always be able to find you....

I had assembled the Shift and released Andras, and now he'd left his demonic fingerprint on my soul? Maybe this was my punishment. House arrest at the hands of one of hell's soldiers. A soldier who was slowly killing the boy I—

Love.

I felt it every time I looked at Jared, every time he touched me.

I'm in love with him.

At the top of the stairs, the fluorescent glare against the steel walls made me dizzy. I reached for the closest wall to steady myself, but it was too far away. Or I was.

Lukas caught me as my knees buckled, and wrapped his arm around me. "It's gonna be okay."

"You're wrong. It's my fault Andras found us in Boston. My fault Jared's possessed." I could barely choke out the words. "I'm the one he marked."

How many times had I prayed to be marked as a Legion member?

"I wish it were me. Jared doesn't deserve this," I said.

Lukas took a shaky breath. "None of us do."

I wiped my face, and Lukas loosened his grip, his arms still around me. "There's something I need to tell you," he said.

"Hey, I've been looking for you—" Elle said from behind me.

Lukas dropped his arms and took an awkward step away from me.

"We were talking about Jared," I said, wiping my nose on my sleeve.

"Whatever," she snapped. I recognized the anger in her voice, but I wasn't prepared for the expression on her face. My best friend looked like she wanted to kill me. "I didn't mean to interrupt."

"It's not like that." Lukas skirted his way around me like I had the plague.

Elle took off down the hall in a flash of red hair and black leather.

I leaned against the cold metal behind me and slid to

the floor. I wanted to scream and pound on the walls and cry—do anything to avoid feeling the way I did right now.

Broken, battered, and beaten.

This was a war we couldn't win. Or one we'd already lost.

31. FEAR ME

Hours later, I stood outside the mech room, working up the courage to face Priest. Dimitri and Alara had persuaded him to stay for now, but I hadn't seen him since he'd threatened to leave.

Priest didn't hear me when I stepped inside. He was wearing his headphones, nodding in time with the music, his attention focused on a long silver pipe in front of him. On any other day, standing behind a lab table surrounded by scrap metal and power tools would've cheered him up. But as he searched the wall of hammers, screwdrivers, and drills behind him, the frown never left his face.

I watched as he attached a propane tank to one end of the pipe and drilled a row of holes along the top. Usually, his oversized hoodie and long blond bangs reminded me of the skaters from my old high school in Georgetown—the misfit band of freshmen and sophomores who traveled in swarms, with their skateboards sticking out of the top of their backpacks. The boyish quality that had always made Priest seem like one of them was gone now.

I recognized the look on his face; it belonged to someone who knew what it felt like to be betrayed, and I hated myself for being part of the reason.

"How long have you known?" he asked, without glancing in my direction. He pushed his safety goggles up on his head and secured a speaker to the opposite end of the pipe with a roll of silver duct tape.

I stared at the floor, letting my hair create a curtain between us. "Jared told me when we were trapped in the wall at Hearts of Mercy."

"And you didn't think Alara and I had a right to know?"

"I thought Jared should tell you himself, and he wanted to," I said.

"Except he didn't, did he?" Priest turned on the speaker and flames flared from the holes in the pipe, rising and falling to the intensity of the music.

"That's amazing."

He didn't look at me. "It's a Rubens tube. Physics 101. Any idiot can make one."

Except an idiot like me, who would lie to her friend—that was the message.

"I'm so sorry."

Priest slammed his fist against the table. "Sorry won't bring my grandfather back. I'm not like the rest of them. Jared and Lukas have each other, and Alara still has a family, even if she doesn't wanna live with them. My granddad was all I had. I thought you of all people would understand that."

"I do."

He shook his head. "No, you don't. You went to a regular school. You have a best friend who took off with a bunch of strangers because she wanted to find you. I lived in the same broken-down house with my granddad for as long as I can remember. I was homeschooled. That means no teachers, no friends, no enemies. No one except the two of us. He was my best friend." Priest's voice cracked. "My *only* friend."

I tried to imagine a life without school and Elle. A life that only existed within the four walls of my house. "You're right. I should've told you."

Priest unhooked his headphones from around his neck and hurled them across the room. The plastic smashed against one of the shiny silver walls.

"Jared should've told me!" he shouted. "He was supposed to be my friend. I followed him around like a puppy. And the whole time, he knew my granddad was dead because of him."

I bit the inside of my cheek to keep from crying. "He is your friend."

Priest turned his back on me and stalked down the hall. "We have a different definition of friendship."

After my conversation with Priest, I wanted to find an empty room and hide, but it would only delay the inevitable. Facing Alara.

I took a deep breath and opened the door to our room. The only sign of her was a box of shotgun cartridges and a bottle of rock salt.

"She's not here," Elle said.

I sat on the end of Elle's bed, the way I had a million times back in her room at home. "What's going on with you? You're acting weird."

Her eyes narrowed. "Why? Because I don't want to watch you hang all over Lukas?"

For a second, I thought she was joking. Elle had never been jealous of another girl in her life, at least not over a guy. Amazing hair, a cool pair of vintage shoes, maybe. The idea of Elle being jealous of me was even more ridiculous.

"Lukas and I are just friends. Anyone who spends more than five minutes with the two of you can tell how he feels about you. Trust me, you have nothing to worry about." A sob caught in my throat, and my voice cracked. "The only guy who ever cared about me is sharing a body with a demon."

"I'm sorry," Elle said, but she didn't sound convincing. "I'm acting stupid."

What's wrong with her?

Maybe she was having a hard time dealing with this world I'd dragged her into and I hadn't noticed. "It's okay."

"Don't worry." She draped an arm over my shoulders. "We're going to find that thing to save Jared."

"The Shift."

I didn't have the energy to look for Alara. Instead, I fell asleep thinking about another person I couldn't save.

⇥ • ⇤

A scream pierced the darkness and my eyes flew open.

Elle.

I shoved myself off the bed, struggling to reach her.

"Don't touch me!" she screamed.

Bear barked in the darkness.

The door burst open, and someone turned on the lights. Lukas and Priest stood in the doorway, weapons drawn. Alara must've come in after we fell asleep, and she jumped out of bed. "What happened?"

"I don't know." I scanned the room, but no one else was there.

Elle clawed at her arms, hysterical and sobbing. Lukas

ran to the bed and pulled her into his lap. She was covered in dark bruises, as if someone had hit her.

Footfalls echoed through the hallway, and Gabriel and Dimitri appeared in the doorway, out of breath. Gabriel noticed Elle's bruises. "Who did this?"

The lights flickered, and Priest pushed our half-open door closed. "Not who...what."

On the back of the door, a message was scratched into the metal over and over:

WHEN THE NIGHTMARES COME, FEAR ME.

Lukas hugged Elle tighter. "He's getting stronger."

I didn't wait to hear the rest.

I grabbed the contact lens case next to my bed and took off. My bare feet slapped against the cold concrete floor as I ran toward the door to the containment area. Priest was behind me, shouting my name, asking me if I remembered something or had a theory. I didn't have either, just a feeling something was very wrong.

When I reached the bottom of the stairs, I popped in the contacts. Voices drifted through the tunnel—the demon's and a girl's voice.

The cell door was still closed, but Andras wasn't alone.

A girl stood in front of him, picking the locks on his

wrist shackles with a wire. Even with her back to me, I recognized her immediately.

"Am I hallucinating again?" Priest asked.

The girl turned slowly, long brown waves grazing her neck.

My neck.

The girl in the cell looked exactly like me.

"Oh my god," I whispered.

She noticed us and tried to work faster, but the shackles held. Her eyes darted to Andras for guidance. He spoke to her in a strange language, and reluctantly she gave up.

She brought a finger to her lips and blew me a kiss, the same way Andras had on the street in Boston.

Gabriel caught up with us. "What the—"

He struggled to unlock the cell, but the girl was already transforming. Her body—what looked like *my* body—spiraled into a ribbon of particles that glittered in the air like dust in the sun.

The wire slipped out of her hand and fell to the floor.

Gabriel cracked Azazel, and the whip hit her dusty form. She cried out in pain, confirming what I had already known. She wasn't one of Andras' illusions—because this scenario *wasn't* one of my fears.

The girl-who-wasn't-me was real—whatever she was.

Gabriel jerked the whip back as if he was trying to drag her toward the bars. But Azazel's barbs didn't hold, and the ribbon of particles twisted through the bars and shot down the tunnel.

Gabriel slammed his hands against the wall. "We lost her."

"What the hell *was* she?" Priest asked him.

I was already trying to figure that out for myself.

My eyes darted to the wall behind Andras. Every inch was still covered with writing and symbols—new ones overlapping the protective and binding symbols that were already in the cell when Gabriel and Dimitri locked him inside.

Dimitri had been tracking the demon's writing. It had seemed random, like the scribbling of a madman.

But as I studied the wall more carefully, something looked different today. Behind the symbol and the sadistic Scrabble pattern Andras had created from the dead girls' names, another image jumped out at me, as clearly as if I had drawn it myself.

A summoning circle from *The Goetia*, a seventeenth-century grimorie that provided instructions for summoning and commanding demons.

Andras had used the circumference of an existing symbol to hide it, his cryptic writing hugging the black lines of the drawing.

The letters, which meant so little before, created a hidden message. A name was written over and over within it.

Bastiel.

How did he do it without us noticing?

I hit Rewind, and my mind searched the mental snapshots of the wall, separating the layers of recorded images.

Layer one: the day Alara left to search for the Shift—

Strange alchemical symbols drawn in repeated sequences over the names of the dead girls—

Layer two: last night when Andras revealed Jared's secret to everyone and Elle got jealous when she saw Lukas hugging me—

The inner circles and the name *Bastiel* written seven times, the letters hidden among other words—

Layer three: today—

The outer circle and the looping characters of a forgotten language—

"I know what he did," I said. "He drew a summoning circle using the symbols that were already in the cell. It's hidden underneath a ton of meaningless characters I don't recognize. He summoned another demon—Bastiel."

Andras roared like an animal, and the muscles tensed and rippled up his arms. "She will be my vengeance and rain hell upon you all." He curled his hands into fists, pulling against the chain attached to his shackles.

The iron snapped, and the links fell to the floor.

Gabriel shoved me behind him, even though Andras was still locked inside the cell. "I don't know how you figured that out, but nice job." Gabriel held Azazel in his hands, whispering:

"From the bones of my enemies and the blood of my allies,
The bargains with devils and the truces with angels,
With the promise of my soul,
I call you to come together as one."

The whip reared and lunged through the air, curling and twisting. Azazel cracked against the demon's back. Andras cried out, but he was stronger now and quickly recovered.

Andras looked at Gabriel. "You make promises you cannot keep, Gabriel. And for that, I won't harvest your soul. I'll make you my slave."

Dimitri rushed through the tunnel carrying an armload of books, with Lukas, Alara, and Elle behind him. He slid a heavy book across the floor to Priest. "The *Rituale Romanum*. Quickly."

The Rite of Exorcism.

"The pages are marked," Dimitri yelled. "Read."

Priest had the book open in seconds, and he and Alara began reading. Dimitri and I were the only ones faster, having committed the rite to memory.

"I cast you out, unclean spirit,
along with every Satanic power of the enemy,

every spectre from hell, and all your fell companions.
In the name of our Lord."

Lukas and Elle joined in, Elle's voice shaking so badly
I could barely understand her.

"Begone. And stay far from this creature of God.
For it is He who commands you,
He who flung you headlong from the heights of heaven
and into the depths of hell.

"He who commands you,
He who once stilled the sea and the wind
and the storm.
Harken, therefore, and tremble in fear."

Gabriel cracked the whip again and Azazel snaked
through the bars, biting into Andras' flesh. The demon
cried out, but he didn't fall. Instead, he focused his gaze on
me, and I felt a surge of energy hit me. A heavy sensation
spread through my limbs, paralyzing me.

"Kennedy?" Dimitri called my name, but I couldn't
answer. My muscles had stopped working, the heaviness
in my arms and legs replaced by the sting of numbness.

My body rose from the ground. Silence spun around
me, cocooning me inside it. Hands reached for me. The

others called out, soundlessly. My arms were stretched out at my sides, the crumbling ceiling above me.

Azazel's barbs snapped in the air, but I couldn't hear the tiny demon bones wailing. The whip caught Andras, slamming him into the bars.

I kept rising.

The metal door flew open at the end of the tunnel, and someone stepped into the dim light.

A man carrying an open book, larger than any of the volumes Dimitri had carried down with him. His lips moved as his eyes darted from Andras to the book, then finally to me.

Those eyes.

The whip snapped again, the vertebrae and claws unhinging in the air beside me. This time, I heard the bones scream.

Andras cried out. I couldn't be sure if it was a result of Azazel's attack, or of the *Rituale Romanum* rite my friends were still chanting, or of the words the stranger was reading.

I was falling—

Air and light. Sounds and screams.

My body fell into someone's arms, and Priest stared down at me.

Gabriel had Andras against the wall, chaining his hands as the demon thrashed against him. Azazel was wrapped around him, pulsing like a heartbeat each time he strained against the barbs.

Alara charged into the cell, throwing handfuls of ash over Andras' wet body. Dimitri stood in the middle of the tunnel, with his back to me, staring at the man approaching us.

Clean-shaven, wearing jeans and a rough canvas work jacket, he could've been anyone. But the moment his green eyes had found me, I knew exactly who he was.

My father.

32. DIARIO DI DEMONI

Stay away from him," I called out. "Bastiel could be shape-shifting again."

I remembered when Elle acted jealous after seeing Lukas and me talking, and the night I found her reading the book about summoning demons. When I mentioned the book the next day, she acted like she had no idea what I was talking about.

Because she didn't.

Dimitri's eyes narrowed. "He's not Bastiel. A demon can't touch the *Diario di Demoni*."

The battered leather-bound book in my father's hands was the diary of the Vatican exorcists, the one thing the original Legion members had taken the night they fled. My dad held it in front of him and recited the words. He looked different than I remembered, worn out in a way that had nothing to do with age.

"I exorcise you, unholy spirits,
servants of darkness,
infernal legions of the Labyrinth.

"Heavenly warriors, protectors of light,
free us from this shadow;
destroy this unblessed deception.

"I call on Gabriel, Raphael, Michael,
and their celestial soldiers.
Darkness trembles before you."

Andras twisted and jerked, as if the words were more painful than Azazel's barbs. His body swayed to one side, and he hit the floor.

Dimitri rushed to clamp the shackles around his wrists, the whip still wrapped around Andras' neck. But the demon didn't move. His chest rose and fell, the only real indication he was still alive.

My father closed the book without a word.

When Dimitri dropped the chain on the cell floor, it startled us both. "Alex. You're the last person I expected to see here."

My father turned toward Dimitri. "And you're the second-to-last person I want to see." My dad's eyes fell on Gabriel. "But based on what I just witnessed, you two aren't capable of cleaning up the mess you've made—not without help."

Dimitri fished a Dunhill out of his pocket. "The demon is the Legion's mess, not ours."

"It's my fault," I said, my heart pounding. "I'm the reason Andras is free."

A worried crease formed between my father's deep-set eyes. "You shouldn't be involved in any of this, Kennedy."

A shiver ran up my spine when he said my name.

My dad turned away and joined Gabriel and Dimitri in the cell, circling around them like they were infected with a deadly virus. "I assume this is Andras, the demon responsible for killing my sister?" He rested his boot against Jared's side and pushed his body over. "I didn't realize the Illuminati were keeping demons as pets these days. Which is the only reason I can come up with to explain why he's still alive."

"We're trying to save my brother," Lukas said, from where he stood outside the cell. "And they're helping us."

When my dad saw Lukas, a troubled look passed across his face.

"It's a delicate situation." Dimitri flicked the cigarette against the wall and walked toward my father. "One that just became even more complicated before you showed up."

"There's a second demon," Gabriel said.

My dad whipped around at the sound of his voice. "Gabriel Archer. I thought you crawled back into your hole after the last time I saw you."

Gabriel stiffened, and he looked at the floor.

"If I find out you had anything to do with Faith's death, after what you did to her, I swear I'll kill you with that aberration in your hand."

Gabriel Archer.

"You're the one who spied on my aunt? The one who used her and broke her heart?" I waited for Gabriel to deny it.

"Your mom and I were mixed up with the wrong people, Kennedy." Gabriel raised his eyes to meet mine. "We thought we were doing the right thing."

"Shut your mouth." My dad pointed at him. "Don't talk to her. When this is over, I'm going to bury you."

"How did you find us?" Priest asked my father.

"Bear." My dad said the Doberman's name, and the dog trotted over to him and sat at his feet. "He has a chip. I went to check on Faith and found the grave." He swallowed hard. "When I realized she was gone, and I saw that crap all over her bedroom walls, I tracked Bear here."

"What's the radius on the GPS?" Priest asked. "In square miles."

Alara elbowed him.

"Ouch." He rubbed his arm. "It was a scientific question."

My dad ignored him and stared at Dimitri. "You're serious? There's another demon? Want to explain how you superheroes let this happen?"

I pointed at the summoning circle hidden within the writing and the symbols on the walls. "Andras summoned her. He hid the circle in the drawings."

"Which means the gate is at least partially open," Dimitri said.

"Nice work." My dad's voice was full of contempt. "Where is the other demon now?"

"She turned herself into dust or some kind of particles and took off," Priest said, his eyes flickering over each of us. "I mean, it looked like she did. But she's a shape-shifter, so she could be any one of us."

My father took a carved wooden cross out of his jacket and tossed it to Priest. "Recite the Lord's Prayer...or any prayer, for that matter."

Priest looked confused. "Our Father, who art in heaven—"

"That's enough." My dad gestured at Elle. "Pass the cross to your friend."

She's my friend. Something you'd know if you hadn't left.

We took turns passing the cross around to prove that

a shape-shifting demon wasn't in the room, disguised as one of us.

"The gate's partially opened, so what's your plan?" my dad asked.

"After we figure out how to get Andras under control, we'll go after the other demon. But we can't leave while he's this strong." Dimitri studied my father. "Does that mean you're in?"

Gabriel watched my dad from lowered eyes.

"Do I have a choice?" my dad asked.

⫞ • ⫟

"Kennedy, can I have a minute?" My father caught me as I came up the stairs from the containment area.

You could've had thousands of minutes if you had bothered to stick around.

I stood in the sterile steel hallway. I had imagined this moment—the one where he'd finally come back and tell me how much he regretted leaving, and promise that he'd spend the rest of his life making it up to me. Those were the fantasies of my eight-year-old and twelve-year-old selves.

By the time I was fourteen, I started thinking about what I'd say to him. How I'd find a way to emotionally destroy him the way he had destroyed me.

It was only when I'd seen him standing at the other end of the tunnel that something else occurred to me— something that could bring me even more pain.

What if I threw every hateful thought I'd been saving at him, and he didn't care?

"I don't know what your mother told you—" he began.

"She didn't tell me anything. I memorized the note you left, even though I couldn't read it." All the pain I'd bottled up inside for so long poured out. "Mom wouldn't tell me what it said. She cried herself to sleep at night for years after you left."

"It wasn't your fault." His emerald eyes seemed even greener than I remembered.

"That's not what I thought when I was old enough to understand what it meant." I pictured the lined sheet of paper, ripped on the corner.

Elizabeth

You're the first woman I ever loved, and I know you'll be the last. But I can't stay. All I ever wanted for us—and for Kennedy—was a normal life. I think we both know that's impossible.

Alex

"'All I ever wanted for us—and for Kennedy—was a normal life. I think we both know that's impossible.' What part of that doesn't sound like it's about me?" I asked.

My dad raked a hand through his salt and pepper hair.

"When I found out about your mother, I had to leave. Faith didn't know how to protect herself. I'm not sure how much she told you, but the Illuminati hunted her for years."

"Dimitri and Gabriel?" I had to know.

"No. But Gabriel had already ruined Faith. She never trusted anyone except me after what happened. She's my younger sister, and our parents were dead. It was my responsibility to protect her."

"What about your responsibility to your daughter?" I demanded.

He leaned against the wall, shoulders sagging. "I couldn't take you from your mom. You would've hated me, and she loved you. She never would've done anything to hurt you."

My father dug in his pocket and held out a stack of photographs. "But I made sure you were okay."

He fanned out the photos, and my childhood unfolded like a deck of cards: a shot of me sitting on the slide with pigtails in my hair and my OshKosh overalls; wearing my second-grade Little Red Riding Hood Halloween costume with the stuffed wolf puppet my mom sewed over the shoulder; me and Elle eating ice cream cones in front of Baskin-Robbins a block from our junior high school; last year, carrying a canvas to the art fair in a pair of baggy overalls, with charcoal smudged on my cheek.

There were at least a half dozen more.

"Did you take all these?" I couldn't look away from the photos.

"I've always kept track of you, Kennedy. But I didn't want to put you or Faith in danger. She was kidnapped by the Order once. They wanted information about her paintings. Faith had what they call prophetic dreams, and she painted her visions of the future."

I thought about the entry in Faith's journal that predicted my birth and called me the white dove. "She told me about the kidnapping."

He gave me an incredulous look.

"Are you the fifth member of the Legion now?" As much as I hated to ask him, I needed to know for sure.

My father put the photos back in his pocket. "I'm afraid so."

I closed my eyes and nodded, trying to swallow the knot in my throat. "Guess I'll never be a black dove, after all. Glad I didn't rush out and get the tattoo."

"Faith used to say black doves fight the battles that need fighting, but the white dove ends them and sets us all free. For what it's worth, she always said you were our white dove."

It wasn't worth anything coming from him. He obviously didn't know I'd read the entry in Faith's journal. She was the one I believed.

"It didn't stop you from leaving." I sounded heartless and cold, but he deserved every word.

"I hope you'll be able to forgive me one day. I've always loved you."

Too little too late.

"One day I might forgive you, but it won't be today." I walked by him, letting all the missed birthdays and Christmases, all the nights I was afraid and he wasn't there, rebuild the walls around me, one broken promise at a time.

And I'll never forget.

33. SERPENT OF BONES

"**C**an I touch one of the bones?" Priest asked.

We were is the athenaeum, examining Azazel.

Gabriel cracked the whip against the ground, and Azazel's bones uncoiled, rippling forward like a dragon's tail. "Be careful. Demon bones are almost as unpredictable as demons themselves."

Bear ran back and forth in front of the whip like he didn't know what to make of it.

Priest poked at a claw with his finger, and the bone recoiled, drawing itself closer to the hooked claw behind it.

After four hours of sleep—for those who had actually slept—I woke everyone up. We didn't have time to sleep, not until we figured out how to save Jared.

"I think we're approaching this the wrong way." Priest

355

stood up and started pacing. "Andras is so strong now, he's practically showering in holy water. Your whip is one of the only things that still weakens him."

"Go on." Gabriel sat on the edge of the table, listening.

I couldn't stand to look at him now that I knew he was the one who betrayed Faith.

"What if there was a way to expose Andras to Azazel's power constantly? Would it weaken him enough to buy us some time?" Priest asked.

Gabriel looped the bones around his arm. "In theory. But a demon whip can only be commanded by its maker."

"Can I borrow the black marker for a minute?" Priest asked Alara.

It wasn't that long ago when I used to carry one, too. Not that I needed it anymore.

She handed it to him and watched as he drew a diagram on the back of an old receipt.

"Is that a necklace?" I asked.

"No." Priest shook his head. "A collar."

Everyone crowded around to get a better look.

"Azazel needs a whip master because, by nature, a whip requires someone to handle it," Priest explained. "A collar just needs someone to wear it."

Lukas nodded. "Someone the collar will weaken."

"Where do we get a bunch of demon bones?" Elle asked.

My eyes darted to the ivory serpent of bones coiled around Gabriel's arm. My dad stalked over from where he was leaning against one of the glass cases. He was the only person I hated seeing more than Gabriel.

"This entire conversation is insane, not to mention dangerous." My dad turned to Gabriel. "I don't know how you created this monstrosity in the first place, but you aren't going to involve these kids in your Frankenstein project."

"No one asked your opinion," I snapped.

Priest crossed his arms, squaring off against my father. "Actually, it's my project."

My dad ignored him.

"As much as it pains me to say this, I agree with Alex." Dimitri leaned forward in the armchair, next to the mummy. "Assuming we find a way to disassemble Azazel and make a collar, how do you plan to put it on Andras? Gabriel wields Azazel from a distance. Snapping a dog collar around the neck of one of Lucifer's soldiers will require someone to get close."

Alara toyed with her eyebrow ring. "My grandmother used to tell me stories about growing up in Haiti, when she was a kid. The bokors in her village used this stuff called *coup de poudre* to turn people into zombies."

"Zombies?" Priest raised an eyebrow.

"Hear me out," she said. "It was made from puffer fish venom and caused temporary paralysis so severe that it slowed down a person's heart rate. What if we used it to paralyze Andras long enough to put the collar on him?"

"Please tell me you don't carry fish venom around with

you," Elle said, examining the severed doll heads in the case.

"I can buy it from a voodoo shop." She looked at Gabriel and Dimitri. "Or one of you can bribe a fancy sushi bar to sell you some."

Dimitri and Gabriel exchanged glances.

"The concoction might not paralyze Andras, but it should sedate him if we use enough," Dimitri said.

"Stop." My dad held up his hand. "Demon collars and zombies? Does this sound rational to you?"

I hurled a salt round at the shelves, and it exploded, white crystals peppering the air like snow. "Jared doesn't have time for rational."

My father's expression softened. "I know you think you're in love with this boy, but he isn't worth risking your life for."

Alara and Elle stared at my father in shock. In the short time Alara and I had known each other, she understood me better than my own father did. Even Gabriel shifted uncomfortably, as if he sensed the rage coming my dad's way.

"You have *no* idea what I think because you don't know anything about me."

"Kennedy—" he began.

"Do you know how I met Jared and Lukas? They saved me from a vengeance spirit that tried to suffocate me. Where were you?"

"It's complicated."

"Save it. I'm not interested." I shook my head in disgust. "But don't show up here and try to play the concerned father with me now. It's too late."

He looked away.

"There's still the issue of the bones." Dimitri rose from the chair. "Gabriel would never take Azazel apart, not after what it involved to acquire the bones and assemble the whip."

Gabriel's eyes flickered from the whip in his hand to Priest. "You really think it could work?"

Dimitri looked stunned. "Gabriel, this is a mistake. One that could get them all killed. Don't let them use your weapon to do it."

"I'm not even sure if I *can* take Azazel apart." Gabriel looked right at me. "But I'll try."

⇥ • ⇤

Dimitri drove Alara into Boston to hunt down an authentic voodoo shop. He didn't trust anyone else to take her, after she already slipped away from Gabriel once. Between the last name Alara shared with her grandmother—one of the most respected practitioners on the East Coast—and her impeccable Haitian Creole, it took her less than three hours to find the venom we needed.

Priest and Gabriel's job proved more challenging. Azazel didn't want to be taken apart. Gabriel had to separate the bones himself using surgical instruments, while the rest of us listened to the bones scream.

When he finished, the ivory collar resembled something a tribal warrior might wear into battle. The vertebrae, teeth, and claws were lined up in a jagged pattern, and Gabriel had fused two interlocking spinal bones to form a clasp.

After Dimitri and Alara returned, she spent hours prepping the serum. Then we spent at least that long reviewing the plan a dozen times. By the time we made it down the stairs to the containment area, it was dinnertime.

Birds pummeled the roof, and the sound of their bodies thudding against the building made me shudder.

The portable construction lights had shorted out, and a thin layer of frost coated the walls. It stung my fingertips as I dragged them across the stone to guide me.

Jared's voice drifted toward us, filling the tunnel with "Cry Little Sister" like an eerie lullaby. When we reached the cell door, he stopped singing. "Is that you, Gabriel? I can smell the ash on you. And the fear."

Gabriel clutched the ivory collar of bones, with what was left of Azazel hanging from his back. "I fear no man or beast, Andras. Only God."

The demon laughed. "God? What do you know about God? You're a man destined to spend eternity in the Labyrinth. You should be thanking me for opening the gates."

Priest and Alara worked quickly, positioning the projectors.

"The gates aren't open yet," Gabriel said.

"Ready," Priest whispered.

Water splashed into the cell, and Andras laughed. "Pouring holy water through the ceiling grate? You have fallen on hard times, Gabriel. But I am thirsty."

Please let this work.

I listened to the demon drink. How would we know if he'd consumed enough of the venom-laced water? What if it didn't have the same effect on a demon?

Alara tapped my leg, signaling me to get ready.

One. Two. Three.

We hit the power buttons on our projectors at almost the same time.

Andras heard the buzz of the machines and padded around the cell. "What are you up to out there, Champion of God? Did you bring your Legion and exorcist? I want them to be here when I break free of these chains and tear out your throat."

Bear snarled.

Priest turned on the wand in his hand. The black light inside made the flecks of white lint on his jeans glow. He stepped in front of the bars, holding the wand against his chest. As the fluorescent beam hit the walls, four symbols revealed themselves like the points on a compass. The Wall, the Devil's Trap, the Eye of Ever, and the most recent addition to our arsenal—a winding symbol Dimitri referred to as the Devil's Staircase, designed to confuse demons.

Alara nodded at me. "Now."

I envisioned the invocation in my mind, as clearly as if the lines were written on a page, and recited them with Alara.

"From the depths of despair and the world beyond, claim the soulless among us and call him home."

"Your spell can't control me, stupid girl," Andras growled.

We didn't stop.

"Through blood, prayer, and battle we ask, for Darkness remembers his name."

Andras flew into a rage, pacing manically one moment, then lashing his chains against the glowing symbols the next.

As we recited the lines for the second time, the demon staggered.

"It's working," Elle whispered.

Andras' movements slowed as the venom took effect. "What are you doing, witch?" he called out, reaching for the wall to brace himself.

Dimitri signaled Lukas, and the two of them joined Priest in front of the cell. Dimitri held open a gilded leather book, and the three of them read from a set of exorcism rites that weren't part of the *Rituale Romanum*.

> "Depart then, transgressor.
> Depart, seducer, full of lies and cunning.
> foe of virtue, persecutor of the innocent.
> give place, abominable creature,
> give way, you monster."

Andras' spine jerked.

Then he froze, his limbs immobile.

Gabriel unlocked the cell and stepped inside, carrying the collar made from Azazel.

Andras focused his black eyes on the door, and it slammed behind Gabriel.

"Stay back," Dimitri called out. "He's still too strong." He turned to my father. "Alex, use the *Diario di Demoni* to exorcise him."

My father shook his head. "It will never work."

"You don't have to fully exorcise him," Dimitri said. "Just weaken him enough for Gabriel to get the collar around his neck."

"I'll do my best." My dad flipped through the book until he found the right page, then he started to read.

"I invoke the power of light.
Restore this besieged soul
from the Labyrinth's terrible hold.
Raise this tormented soul from perdition,
release it from imprisonment;
return it to the safety of your wings."

Dimitri, Priest, and Lukas continued the rites from the *Rituale Romanum*, their voices overlapping with my father's.

Andras' spine stiffened, and his eyes widened in shock. A pale gray form rose above Jared's immobile body, while Jared's limbs remained paralyzed. Only the form hovering half in—and half out—of his body moved.

He had the hazy gray arms and torso of a man. But the extended jaw, long snout, and black eyes belonged to an animal.

Andras—in his true form.

"Now!" Dimitri yelled.

Gabriel sprang forward, with the demon bones wailing in his hands. Andras snarled as he raised the collar. The bones recoiled, pulling away from the demon's throat.

"I can't get it on." Gabriel fumbled with the collar.

Without thinking, I bolted into the cell.

"Get out of here, Kennedy."

"Give me the other side." I reached for the collar, ignoring him. "We have to get it on now."

The bones screamed, the sound piercing my eardrums.

"They don't want to be linked to him." Gabriel strained to hold his side of the collar open. "It's like another death."

I struggled against the vertebrae as the jagged edges cut my hands.

Another death.

Maybe there was something worse than being linked to a demon. I wiped the ash off my face and smeared it onto the bones, covering them in the ashes of other dead demons.

The bones shrieked and shrank away from me and into Gabriel's hands. He forced the ends around the back of Jared's neck. The moment he snapped them together, the bones stopped moving.

The demon's blurry torso bucked one last time before it slipped back into Jared's body.

Everyone stopped reading, and the tunnel fell silent.

Jared dropped to the ground, with the demon somewhere inside him again.

Gabriel dragged me out of the cell and bolted the door behind us.

Elle grabbed my shoulders. "Are you okay?"

The lights flickered, and the power came back on.

I stared at Jared's body on the floor, picturing the demon inside him. How much longer until the demon was the only one left?

34. BASTIEL

Less than an hour ago, we had wrestled Jared into the collar made from what was left of Azazel. Now we were back in the athenaeum discussing another demon.

"The collar is on, and Bastiel already has a head start." Dimitri was ransacking the contents of the glass-front bookcase. He tossed a leather-bound book titled *A Classification of Demons* into a nylon bag at his feet.

Gabriel threw a set of dental extraction tools into a second bag. "If she gets strong enough to summon another demon, they'll start multiplying like rats. We need to track weather anomalies and unusual crimes to try and find her."

"When are you leaving?" My father hadn't let Gabriel or Dimitri out of his sight since we left the containment area.

"Sorry to disappoint you, Waters," Gabriel said. "But one of us is staying."

"I can handle the situation here," my dad said.

Gabriel handed Dimitri vials filled with powders and metal filings. "You expect us to trust you with the fate of the world?"

"Trust?" My dad laughed. "That's a big word for you, Gabriel. I'm not sure you should be using it."

"Enough." Dimitri glared at them and zipped the bag. "Trust is earned, Alex. And you haven't earned mine. Gabriel stays. If that thought is too unpleasant for you, feel free to come with me."

"I'm not leaving Kennedy with him." My dad glanced at Gabriel with disgust.

"Why not?" I snapped. "You left me alone in a house with a poltergeist after Mom died. I'm sure Gabriel can't be any worse."

"He betrayed my sister."

The hypocrisy was lost on my father. "And you abandoned your daughter," I countered.

"I'm going with Dimitri." Priest walked toward him.

Lukas let go of Elle's hand and caught Priest's arm. "What are you talking about?"

Priest pulled away. "Andras is collared now. It won't take seven people to babysit him. We have to find Bastiel and the Shift. Dimitri is gonna need help."

Lukas looked at me. We both knew Priest's decision was about more than his unfailing sense of logic.

Ever since the night Priest learned the truth about how Andras had located our family members, he'd been distant. He couldn't seem to get past Jared's mistake, or the fact that Lukas and I had kept it a secret.

"I think the six of us should stay together," Lukas said.

"Noted." Priest picked up one of Dimitri's bags, ignoring Lukas.

Alara stood up from where she was sitting on the floor, and Bear followed her. "I'll go with them."

Dimitri closed the bookcase. "Get your things. We leave in thirty minutes."

Priest took off before any of us had a chance to catch up with him. But Alara was waiting for me in the hallway.

"Are you going because I didn't tell you about the list?" I asked.

"I joined the Legion and left with my grandmother to protect my sister. Now I'm leaving with the Illuminati for another kid I love. I can't let Priest go alone."

"He's never going to forgive us, is he?" I swallowed hard, but the lump in my throat didn't budge.

"Never is a long time."

"I'm so sorry, Alara. If I could take it back—"

She touched the medal around my neck, the one she'd

given to me. "You remind me of Maya. Did I ever tell you that?"

I shook my head.

"She believes in people the way you do—a hundred and fifty percent. All or nothing. It's my favorite thing about her. That and her gorgeous curly hair, which you *don't* have. But you're stronger than my sister, and me. Promise to remember that when I'm not here to remind you."

"I'll try." I threw my arms around her.

"That's what people say when they aren't willing to fight," she said.

"I'm willing to fight." I released her from my death grip.

Wasn't I?

Alara walked backward down the hall, watching me. "Prove it."

⊰ • ⊱

Priest stood by the warehouse door in his orange hoodie, with a new pair of headphones around his neck and a duffel bag at his feet. Alara stood next to Dimitri, wearing her black eyeliner like war paint.

Dimitri and Gabriel were talking in low tones, a cigarette balancing between Dimitri's lips.

"I can't stay," Priest said finally.

I nodded as the familiar tightness spread through my chest. "I should've told you."

"You said that before." He looked everywhere except at me. "What's done is done. There's no going back."

"Sometimes moving forward changes what's behind you."

He shifted his weight, avoiding my eyes. "Maybe. I don't know."

I rushed over and hugged him. "I do."

He wrapped a reluctant arm around me.

"Be safe," I said, before I let go.

Dimitri and Alara came up behind me, with Lukas, Elle, and my father trailing after them. To his credit, my dad kept his distance. I wasn't ready to forgive him, but he was the fifth member of the Legion, which meant he was staying—whether I liked it or not.

Alara drew Elle and me in for a group hug. "Kick ass and take names while I'm gone." I nodded, and Elle sniffled. Alara stepped back, a mischievous smile tugging at the corners of her mouth. "Is someone sad to see me go?"

Elle waved her hand in the air, dismissing the idea. "Hardly. I have allergies."

Alara shoved Lukas in the arm, playfully, and looked at Elle. "Take care of him, too."

Dimitri hefted the bag of supplies over his shoulder and then patted his long coat pockets for the cigarettes that would probably end up killing him. "Take care of each other. We'll be back as soon as we can. Hopefully, with a shape-shifting demon, or what's left of her."

I held Elle's hand as they filed out the door, wondering if I'd ever see them again.

⊰ • ⊱

I sat on the floor under the stars of the athenaeum's painted sky. I couldn't stand to watch Priest and Alara drive away. Bear rested his head in my lap, whimpering, as if he knew everything had changed. Open books were strewn on the floor around me, none of them holding any answers.

"I figured you would be in here." Lukas closed the heavy wooden door behind him.

"I didn't realize I was so predictable."

Lukas leaned against the wall, his silver coin flying between his fingers. A deep line was etched between his eyebrows from frowning.

"Is it Priest?" I asked.

"What about him?" He started pacing.

"Is that what's bothering you?" I gestured at his hand. "Because if you flip that thing any faster, you're going to lose a finger."

Lukas caught the coin, trapping it in his fist. "That obvious, huh?"

"You'd suck at poker." I hugged my legs against my chest. "It's too easy to tell when you're lying."

The worried lines in his face grew deeper. "There's something I need to tell you."

For the first time, I noticed how dark the shadows beneath his eyes had become. "Okay."

Lukas shoved his hands in his pockets, the way Jared always did when he was nervous. "Jared and I were competitive growing up. My dad thought it was the whole twin thing—fighting to form our individual identities and all that crap—but that wasn't it." He studied the creed written on the floor between us. "Jared was my dad's favorite, and everyone knew it, including me."

"Maybe it just felt that way." It was a stupid comment. I'd spent enough time at Elle's house to see the way some parents favored one child over another, and how poorly they disguised it.

"Dad never missed an opportunity to point out the similarities between Jared and him. Both of them liked the icing but not the cake, they threw a punch the same way, had the same score on the range. Jared downplayed it, but I still wanted to prove I was better than him—stronger, faster, smarter—it didn't matter." Lukas scrubbed his hands over his face. "So when I figured out Jared was searching for the other Legion members, it seemed like the perfect way to make him look bad."

"Are you saying you knew?"

He nodded. "But I didn't think Jared was putting anyone in danger. I swear. To our dad, things were either right or wrong; there was no gray. He did everything by the book, no exceptions. Jared and I both thought all that stuff about the Legion members not being allowed to meet was just Dad being Dad—especially since nothing bad ever happened as a result of him and our uncle working together. I wanted Jared to dig his own grave with my dad, that's all. I never thought anyone would get hurt."

Andras used the list to kill Jared and Lukas' father and their uncle . . . and Alara's grandmother, Priest's granddad, and my mom. Jared hated himself because of it.

I stood up, my legs like rubber beneath me. "You knew how guilty he felt, that it was eating him alive, and you never said a word."

"I would've stopped him if I'd known what was going to happen." Lukas pressed the heels of his hands against his forehead.

"Priest left here hating him."

"I know," he whispered. "If I could take it back—"

"You can't."

Lukas stared at the floor. "I'll find a way to make this right, I swear. But it won't matter unless we figure out how to get that demon out of my brother." Lukas' voice wavered, and he swallowed hard. "Jared's my other half. In a lot of ways, the better part. I can't lose him, Kennedy."

I reached out and lifted his chin, forcing him to look me in the eye. "Then help me save him."

35. THE VESSEL

After Lukas' confession, I needed to see Jared, even if he didn't know I was there. He sat on the floor propped up like a rag doll, with the demon bones rippling around his neck.

Gabriel had painted over the summoning circle Andras had used to call Bastiel. Nothing more than a black halo of paint remained.

"Kennedy?" Jared whispered, his voice raw.

I kept my distance, painfully aware of how many times I'd misjudged Andras.

Jared's eyelids fluttered as he struggled to keep his eyes open. "There's something I need to tell you." His back went rigid, and he sucked in a sharp breath.

"Is it the collar? Are you in pain?"

He shuddered and exhaled slowly; his breathing evened out again. "Not any more than usual. Whatever you do, don't take it off. Promise me."

"I promise." My throat burned as I choked out the words. "What do you need to tell me?"

I didn't know how long the collar could keep Andras at bay.

He studied me through heavy-lidded eyes, the color of a faded sky. "There are only three people I've ever loved in my whole life—my dad, my uncle, and Lukas." He paused. "Now there are four."

Is he saying he loves me?

Nothing existed in the moment except the two of us, and the meaning behind his words. It was as if they erased the bars between us. I reached my hand through, offering it to him.

He swallowed hard, his eyes flicking from my face to my outstretched hand. "I want to touch you. Just for a second. But I can't, Kennedy. I'm terrified I'm going to hurt you." His eyes found my neck. "Again."

"I trust you."

I trust you with my life, my body, my mind—even my heart.

"I don't trust myself, or the monster inside me." His eyes glistened and he looked down at my hand. "He wants to hurt you."

"You are *not* him." I opened my hand wider. "You're

not a monster, Jared. Because if you are, then I must be crazy because I'm falling in—" I stopped, realizing what I was about to say.

I bit the inside of my cheek and looked up at him. I didn't know what to expect after an admission like that, but the expression on his face wasn't it.

Jared watched me, lips slightly parted and eyes wide, in what I could only describe as awe. "What were you going to say, Kennedy? Tell me. Please."

He reached out and touched my palm with his fingertips. He traced circles in the center with his index finger, and I shivered.

"I shouldn't have said it." The heat rushed to my cheeks.

Jared's face fell and he let his shackled hands fall in front of him. "Because you didn't mean it?" The pain in his voice made my heart ache.

I brought my hand back up to the bars, gripping the cold iron.

He looked so broken.

"No. Because I did." I gathered all the courage I had left. "And it scares me. I'm terrified of losing you."

Jared approached the cell door slowly and placed his hands on top of mine. His fingers curled around the bars, mine creating a barrier between his skin and the wet bars.

"I just want to hear you say it one time," he whispered.

I loved him, but I didn't know if I could say it out loud.

"Please. Just once before I die."

It felt like someone sucked all the air out of the room.

Before I die…

Jared caught my wrists and rubbed the smooth skin with his thumbs.

Without warning, his body seized. He stumbled back, grabbing at the collar. The bones screamed, and I covered my ears. His neck jerked, and when he opened his eyes, they had turned to coal.

"Your boyfriend is dying. And you're next, you little bitch. When I open the gates, this world is going to be my playground. My legions will use your body like a puppet, and I will become the maker of all your nightmares."

I didn't need Andras to bring any of my nightmares to life. This was my nightmare—losing the boy I loved.

And I can't even tell him.

Jared was in there somewhere, waiting for me. "Jared, listen to me. You can fight him."

"There are"—Jared's body twitched and slid to the floor. He reached toward me, the wings of the black dove tattoo on his arm spreading open—"some battles you can't win."

This was not how things were going to end for us, or for him. "But you still fight. You still hope. Because there's a chance you *might* win. And even if you don't—you fight for the people you love, especially when they can't fight for themselves." I took a deep breath. I had to be strong for him. "You can do this. Don't let him win."

"Shut your mouth, or I'll—" Jared's neck jerked. The blackness of the demon's eyes pulled in toward Jared's pupils, as though they were sucking Andras in along with them. Jared's chest heaved, and he struggled to catch his breath.

"Don't have much time." Jared winced and squeezed his eyes shut. "Something he doesn't want you to know. A secret."

The cell door rattled by itself.

Jared's eyes flew open. His back slid up the wall, while the rest of his body remained completely still. I reached for his leg.

No, he mouthed. His body continued to rise.

"What doesn't he want us to know?"

"He thinks you'll never figure it out. The—" All of a sudden, the invisible hand that had been holding him let go. Jared's body dropped, the chain acting like an anchor. He hit the ground hard, and crumpled into a heap on the floor.

Jared opened his eyes and stared back at me. "The white dove is the Vessel."

36. WHITE DOVE

SEP.19.18

I wanted to be a black dove, but it turns out I'm a white one.

I'm also the Vessel.

A cage for a demon.

The only person capable of holding Andras.

I should've been shocked or terrified—emotionally devastated and changed in some irrevocable way. Instead, an overwhelming sense of calm settled over me.

I am the Vessel.

The only person capable of saving Jared. I wasn't ready to think about what that entailed—not yet. The verses in Faith's journal were cryptic at best.

An angel's blood.
A demon's bone.
A passing shadow.
A dragon stone.
Heaven and hell, darkness and light.
Caged in the Vessel, as they wage their
eternal fight.

I didn't know how to make sense of them yet, but I understood what they *meant*—there was still a chance to save Jared's life and stop Andras. The possibility existed, and for today, that was enough.

It was too late for Faith and the seventeen dead girls, and for all the other people who were dead because of Andras—including our family members. I couldn't take any of that back, but maybe I could finally make it right.

I took a crumpled piece of paper out of my pocket and unfolded it carefully. It was the ripped piece of *Lady Day*. Her dome was still split in half—like the girl herself. As I smoothed out the creases, I realized that sometimes we have to step outside the walls and fight. Sometimes the armor we thought was protecting us was actually weighing us down.

I remembered the night at the penitentiary, lying in the mud with my legs tangled in razor wire. After I forced

Jared to leave me behind in the rain, I made him a silent promise: *I'll find you.*

Instead of keeping my promise, I lost myself in a storm of emotions that had almost destroyed me. But now I would need all of them—heartbreak and loneliness, pain and rejection, rage and sorrow—to survive what lay ahead.

The white dove is the Vessel.

I stood outside the cell door, watching Jared's chest rise and fall. The boy I loved was lost somewhere inside the body he was sharing with a demon.

I'll find you.

This time I would keep that promise, not only to Jared but to myself.

I was the white dove, and I would find a way to carry the people I loved. And set myself free.

DRAWING FROM FAITH'S JOURNAL

ACKNOWLEDGMENTS

This book truly took a Legion. From listening, plotting, hand-holding, and cheerleading to reading, editing, designing, and shepherding this book into the world—these are the people who made it happen.

Jodi Reamer, my agent, who is so much more than an agent—for answering millions of e-mails and thousands of phone calls and solving hundreds of problems (all mine). Your brilliance and unwavering belief in this series—and in me—enabled me to write this book. I am so grateful to have you in my corner.

Erin Stein, my editor at Little, Brown—for your creativity, insight, and never-ending patience. This book took forever, but you kept nudging me along to the finish line. (Okay, maybe you gave me a piggyback ride part of the way.)

Julie Scheina, my consulting editor—for finding all the things I could've done better and convincing me I *could* do them. A thousand thank-yous would never be enough.

The Legion at Little, Brown Books for Young Readers—Dave Caplan, for designing this heart-stopping cover; Jennifer Corcoran, for your publicity genius; Hallie Patterson, for telling the world about my books; Rachel Poloski, for all your help; Barbara Bakowski, for tolerating all my ridiculous commas (and fixing them); Adrian Palacios, for the gorgeous digital content; Victoria Stapleton, for making your authors feel like rock stars and giving us a personal avatar; Melanie Chang, for leading the PR & marketing charge; LBYR's amazing sales team, for convincing booksellers to join the Legion; Andrew Smith, for your energy and creativity; and Megan Tingley, for believing in this series.

Jacqui Daniels and SallyAnne McCartin of McCartin-Daniels PR—for thinking outside the box and telling anyone and everyone about *Unmarked* and the Legion series. You are forces to be reckoned with, in the very best way.

Writers House, my literary agency—for representing me and the Legion out in the world. Special thanks to Cecilia de la Campa, my foreign-rights agent, for sharing your enthusiasm for *Unmarked* with so many different time zones; and Alec Shane, for dealing with all my crazy requests and the Nerf guns. I still owe you that sword.

Kassie Evashevski, my film agent at UTA—for your intelligence and passion, and your belief in this series; and Johnny Pariseau, for your enthusiasm and hard work.

My foreign publishers—for making the Legion series your own. *Merci. Grazie. Danke. Obrigado....*

Chris Berens—for the beautiful and haunting artwork you created for *Unmarked*. Your work was woven into Kennedy's story before we became friends, but what your imagination and generosity have brought to this series is impossible to define. If there is a magical athenaeum anywhere in this world, it exists in your studio.

Tahereh Mafi, Ransom Riggs, and Holly Black—for reading my draft, giving me amazing revision notes, and plot twisting and untwisting with me. Thank you for talking me off those ledges.

Margaret Stohl, my friend and Beautiful Creatures and Dangerous Creatures coauthor—for the endless encouragement and cheerleading.

Erin Gross—for your social media genius, tireless work ethic, and unparalleled creativity and honesty, and for keeping me together even when I'm coming apart at the seams. Most of all, for your friendship.

Chloe Palka—for moving across the country to help me finish this book, for doing hundreds of hours of typing and dictation, and for the creativity you brought to this project. You are made of fire and blood.

Yvette Vasquez—for creating the playlists that kept me writing and that captured the heart of the book and the characters. You are one of my favorite people in the world.

Ransom Riggs, Marie Lu, and Jonathan Maberry—for offering quotes for *Unmarked* that truly blew me away.

Robin Quick—for knowing the difference between the Illuminati, the Freemasons, and the Sons of Liberty, and for sharing your knowledge with me. The cornerstone in this book is for you.

Lauren Billings—for giving me a summer-school science lesson when I needed it.

Vania Stoyanova—for the author photo on this book, which I love.

Lorissa Shepstone of Being Wicked—for designing the most gorgeous author and novel websites, and a million other things.

May Peterson—for translating my sad excuse for Latin into the real thing.

Eric Harbert and Nick Montano, attorney and brand manager, and my heroes—for being the two guys outside of my family who I can always count on. I value your friendship more than you know.

Alan Weinberger—for making sure my knees hold up on tour and for always taking my calls.

Readers, librarians, teachers, booksellers, bloggers, and everyone who supported *Unbreakable*—for being the *real* Legion and the reason I write.

Mom, Dad, Celeste, John, Derek, Hannah, Alex, Hans, Sara, and Erin—for your love, support, and encouragement. You always make the impossible seem possible.

Alex, Nick, and Stella—for giving me stories to tell and listening to me tell them. Everything begins with you. I love you.

Return to the haunting world of the *New York Times* bestselling Beautiful Creatures series with *Dangerous Creatures*, the first book in Kami Garcia and Margaret Stohl's brand-new series featuring fan favorites Link and Ridley!

Available now

Ridley

There are only two kinds of Mortals in the backwater town of Gatlin, South Carolina—the stupid and the stuck. At least, that's what they say.

As if there are other kinds of Mortals anywhere else.

Please.

Luckily, there's only one kind of Siren, no matter where you go in this world or the Otherworld.

Stuck, no.

Stuck-*up*? Maybe.

Stupid?

It's all a matter of perspective. Here's mine: I've been called a lot of things, but what I really am is a survivor—and while there are more than a few stupid Sirens, there are zero stupid survivors.

Consider my record. I outlasted some of the Darkest Casters

and creatures alive. I withstood whole *months* of Stonewall Jackson High School. Beyond that, I survived a thousand terrible love songs written by one Wesley Lincoln, a clueless Mortal boy who became an equally clueless quarter Incubus. And who, by the way, is not the most gifted musician.

For a while, I survived wanting to write him a love song of my own.

That was harder.

This Siren gig is meant to be a one-way street. Ask Odysseus and two thousand years' worth of dead sailors if you don't believe me.

We didn't choose for it to be that way. It's the hand we were dealt, and you won't hear me whining about it. I'm not my cousin Lena.

Let's get something straight: I'm *supposed* to be the bad guy. I will always disappoint you. Your parents will hate me. You should not root for me. I am not your role model.

I don't know why everyone seems to forget that. I never do.

No matter what she says, Lena was meant to be Light. I was meant to be Dark. Respect the teams, people. At least learn the rules.

My own parents disowned me after the Dark Claimed me as a Siren on my Sixteenth Moon. Since then, nothing rattles me—nothing and no one.

I always knew my incarceration in the sanitarium that my Uncle Macon called Ravenwood Manor was a temporary pit stop on the way to *bigger* and *better*, my two favorite words. Actually, that's a lie.

My two favorite words are my name, *Ridley Duchannes*.

Why wouldn't they be?

Sure, Lena gets the credit for being the most powerful Caster of all time.

Whatever. It doesn't make *me* any less excellent. Neither does her too-good-to-be-true Mortal boyfriend, Ethan "the Wayward" Wate, who defeats Darkness in the name of true love every day of the week.

So what?

I was never going for perfect. I think that should be clear by now.

I've done my part, played my hand, even thrown in my cards when I had to. I've bet what I didn't have and bluffed until I had it. Link once said: *Ridley Duchannes is always playing a game.* I never told him, but he was right.

What's so bad about that? I always knew I'd rather play than watch from the sidelines.

Except once.

There was one game I regretted. At least, one that I regretted losing. And one Dark Caster I regretted losing to.

Lennox Gates.

Two markers. That's all I owed him, and it was enough to change everything. But I'm getting ahead of myself.

It all started long before that. There were blood debts to be paid—though this time it wasn't up to my cousin and her boyfriend to pay them.

Ethan and Lena? Liv and John? Macon and Marian? This wasn't about them anymore.

This was about Link and me.

I should've known we wouldn't get off easy. No Caster goes

down without a fight, even when you think the fight is over. No Caster lets you ride off into the sunset on some lame white unicorn or in your boyfriend's beat-up excuse for a car.

What's a Caster fairy-tale ending?

I don't know, because Casters don't get to have fairy tales—especially not Dark Casters. Forget the sunset—the whole castle burns to the ground, taking Prince Charming down with it. Then the seven dwarves go all ninja and drop-kick your butt straight out of the kingdom.

That's what a Dark Caster fairy tale looks like.

What can I say? Payback's a bitch.

But here's the thing:

So am I.

CHAPTER 1

Home Sweet Home

It was their last night of summer, their last night of freedom, their last night of being frozen in time together in Gatlin, South Carolina—and technically speaking, Ridley Duchannes and Wesley Lincoln were in a fight.

When are we ever not? Ridley wondered. But this wasn't just any fight. It was the knockdown, drag-out, mother-of-all supernatural takedowns—*Siren Predator versus Hybrid Incubus Alien.* That was what Link had called it, behind her back. Which was about the same as saying it to her face, at least in Gatlin.

It had started right after graduation, and three months later, it was still going strong. Not that you'd know from looking at them.

If Link and Ridley openly admitted that they were still fighting, it would mean openly admitting that they still cared. If they openly admitted that they still cared, it would mean openly admitting to things like feelings. Feelings implied all sorts of gushy, messy, fuzzy complications.

Feelings were how they'd gotten into this fight in the first place.

Disgusting.

Ridley would rather have Link stab her through the heart with a pair of gardening shears than admit to any of those things. She'd rather fall on her face like Abraham Ravenwood did, in His Garden of Perpetual Peace, drawing his last breath unloved and alone—a far fall for the most powerful Blood Incubus in the Caster world.

At least Ridley understood Abraham Ravenwood. She was an expert on being unloved and alone.

Worshipped and obeyed? Great. Feared and hated? She'd take it.

But loved and together? That was harder.

That was Lena's territory.

So Ridley wasn't about to admit that she and Link were still fighting. Not tonight, or any other night. You couldn't hit one relationship domino without toppling all the others. And if they couldn't discuss whether they were in a fight, she didn't even want to *think* about what else might come toppling down.

It wasn't worth the risk.

Which was the reason Ridley didn't mention anything she was thinking as she trudged through Gatlin's stickiest marsh, heading for Lake Moultrie in her mile-high snakeskin platforms.

"I should have worn kitten heels," Rid lamented.

"Pretty sure kittens don't have heels." Link grinned.

Rid had caved and asked him for a ride to the stupid farewell party her cousin had organized. It was the first time the two of them had been alone together for longer than five minutes, ever since that night at the beginning of the summer when Link made the mistake of telling Rid he loved her at the Dar-ee Keen.

"Meow," Ridley said, annoyed.

Link looked amused. "I don't really think a you as a cat person, Rid."

"I love cats," she said, wrenching one foot out of a patch of drying mud. "Half my closet is leopard." Her shoe made a gross sucking sound that reminded Ridley of her little sister, Ryan, slurping on an ICEE.

"And the rest is leather, Greenpeace." Link's spiky hair stood straight up, as usual—more bed head than boy band. But you could see what he was going for. His faded T-shirt said GRANNY BROKE BOTH HIPSTERS, and the chain hanging from his wallet made him sound like a puppy on a leash. In other words, Link looked like he'd looked every day of his life, hybrid Incubus or not. Gaining supernatural powers had done nothing to improve his sense of style.

Just like the boy I fell for, Ridley thought. *Even if everything else between us is different.*

She yanked her foot up out of the muck again and went toppling over backward. Link caught her on her way to a full-body mud bath. Before Rid could say a word, he hoisted her over his shoulder and bounded across the marsh, all the way to the edge of the lake.

"Put me down." Rid squirmed, tugging her miniskirt back into place.

"Fine. You're a real brat sometimes." Link laughed. "Want me to put you down again? 'Cause I gotta whole lotta blond jokes…"

"Oh my god, stop it—" She hit his back, kneeing his chest in the process, but deep down, she didn't mind the ride. Or the jokes. Or the superstrength. There were some perks to having a quarter Incubus for an ex-boyfriend. Hanging upside down wasn't one of them, though, and Rid tried to push her way back upright in his arms.

Lena waved them over from her spot at the campsite, a makeshift fire pit at the water's edge. Macon's massive black dog, Boo Radley, was curled at her feet. Ethan and John were still working on the fire itself, the Mortal way, under Liv's direction—not that she'd ever made a fire before. Which was probably why it was still only smoking.

"Hey, Rid." Lena smiled. "Nice ride."

"I have a name," Link said, holding Ridley with one arm.

"Hey, Link." Lena's black curls were pulled up into a loose knot, and her familiar charm necklace hung from her neck. Even her old black Chucks never changed. Ridley noticed that the ornament from Lena's graduation had already joined her charm collection. *Meaningless Mortal ceremonies.* Rid smirked at the memory of Emily Asher's diploma turning into a live snake, right as Emily shook Principal Harper's hand. *Some of my better work,* Ridley thought. *Nothing like a few snakes to end a boring graduation, and fast.* But Lena looked a thousand times happier now that Ethan was back.

"Down. Now." Ridley gave Link one last kick for good measure.

Link dumped Ridley back on her feet, grinning. "Don't ever say I didn't do anything for you."

"Aw, Shrinky Dink. If it's the thought that counts, you didn't." She smiled sweetly back at him. She reached up and patted his head. "That thing's like an air mattress."

"My mom says balloon." Link was unfazed.

"Pound it, Pudding Head." Ethan dropped a last log on the smoking pile of sticks. He bumped fists with Link.

Liv sighed. "There's plenty of oxygen going to all the logs. I used a classic tepee structure. Unless the laws of physics have changed, I don't know why—"

"Do we have to do this the Mortal way?" Ethan looked at Lena.

She nodded. "More fun."

John struck another match. "For who?"

Ridley held up her hand. "Hold on. That sounds like camping. Is this camping? Am I *camping*?"

Link moved across the fire pit. "You may not know this, but Rid is not a happy camper."

"Sit." Lena gave her the Look. "Because I'm about to make you all very happy. Camping or not." She fluttered her fingers, and the fire ignited.

"Are you kidding me?" Liv looked from Lena to the crackling fire, insulted, while the boys laughed.

"You want me to put it out?" Lena raised an eyebrow. Liv sighed but reached for the marshmallows, chocolate, and graham crackers. Between her love of snack foods, her faded Grateful Dead T-shirts, and her messy braids, Liv seemed like she should be heading back to high school, not college. Once Liv opened her mouth, though, she seemed like she should be one of the professors.

"I'd pay serious money to see Rid campin' for real." Link flopped down next to Ethan.

"Your allowance isn't serious enough to get me to go camping, Shrinky Dink." Rid tried to figure out a way to sit down on a stone near the fire pit without ripping the thin black spandex skirt she was rocking.

"Havin' a little trouble with your nano-skirt, there?" Link patted the makeshift seat next to him.

"No." Ridley twirled the pink stripe in her hair. Lena speared a marshmallow on a stick, laughing as Ridley took another pass at sitting on the rock.

"Can't rest your dogs while you're strapped in that butt Band-Aid?" Link was enjoying himself.

Ridley was not. "It's a micro-mini. From Miu Miu. And what would you know? You can't even dress a salad."

"I've got my own kind of flair, Babe. And I don't need to buy mine at Meow Meow."

Ridley gave up on the rock, squatting instead at the edge of a log just down from Link. "Flair? You? You wash your face with shampoo and brush your teeth with a washcloth."

"What's your point?" Link raised an eyebrow.

Lena looked up. "Enough. Don't tell me you two are still going at it. This has to be some kind of record, even for you." She waved her stick and her marshmallow caught on fire.

"I mean, if you're referring to that one night—" Rid began.

"It was more of a conversation," Link said. "And she did blow me off—"

"I said I was sorry," Rid countered. "But you know what they say. Once a Mortal…"

Link snorted. "Mortal? I wouldn't believe a Siren if she—"

Lena held up her hand. "I said not to tell me." Ridley and Link looked away from each other, embarrassed.

"It's all good," Link said stiffly.

"Camping." Ridley changed the subject.

Lena shook her head. "No, this is not camping. This is...I don't actually know the verb for it. S'moring?" Lena caught a glop of brown and white goo between two graham crackers, shoving the whole thing into Ethan's mouth.

Ethan made a sound like he was trying to say something, but he couldn't open his mouth enough to make any actual words.

"I take it you like my s'moring?" Lena smiled at him.

Ethan nodded. Tonight, in his oldest Harley-Davidson T-shirt and ratty jeans, he looked the same as he had the day Ridley first met him, after basketball practice at the Stop & Steal. Which was crazy, if you thought about everything that had happened to him since then. *The things that boy has been through in the name of my cousin. And people think Sirens are hard on the opposite sex. He'd do anything for her.*

A little voice in Ridley's head pointed out the obvious: *Loved and together is the opposite of unloved and alone.* Ridley could barely stand to watch a relationship that functional.

She shuddered and shook her head, recovering. "S'moring? Don't you mean snoring? Because this is no way to spend our last night together. There are enemies to be made. Laws to be broken. Cheerleaders to—"

"Not tonight." Lena shook her head, spearing another marshmallow.

Rid gave up, grabbing a bag of chocolate bars to console herself. Sirens loved their sugar, especially this one.

"Speak for yourself. I think this is brilliant," said Liv, stuffing her face with a gooey chocolate–marshmallow–graham cracker mess. "Melted chocolate and warm marshmallow coming together as one—on the same graham cracker? That's democracy at its best. This is why I love America. S'mores."

"Is that the only reason?" John nudged her.

"The only reason? Yes. No," Liv teased, licking a finger. "S'mores, the Dar-ee Keen, and the CW." She shot him a playful look and he smiled, tossing a marshmallow into Boo Radley's open mouth. Boo thumped his tail appreciatively.

Twenty-five marshmallows later, Boo was a little less appreciative and the fire was burning down to embers, but the night was far from over.

"See? No tears. No good-byes," Lena said, breaking up the ash with her burnt-black stick. "And when we go, no one is allowed to say anything you'd read in a cheesy greeting card."

Ethan drew his arm around her. Lena was trying, but all the sugar in the world wasn't going to make this good-bye go down any easier.

Not for the six of them.

Ridley made a face. "If you want to boss people around, Cuz, start a sorority." She rummaged through a bag of empty chocolate wrappers. "It's our last night together. So what? Accept it and move on. Tough love, people." Ridley talked a good game, but deep down she knew her own tough love wasn't all that much tougher than her cousin's marshmallow meltdown.

They just had different ways of showing it.

Lena grew still, gazing into the dying fire. "I can't." She shook her head. "I've left too many people behind too many times. I won't do it again. Not to you guys. I don't want everything to change." She reached for Boo, burying her hands deep in his dark fur. His head dropped down to his paws.

The six friends fell silent, until only the crackling remnants of the campfire could be heard.

Ridley was uncomfortable with the silence, but more uncomfortable with all the feelings talk that had preceded it, so she kept her mouth shut.

It was finally Link who spoke up. "Yeah, well, change happens. I used to really love these things," he said, squeezing a marshmallow between his fingers. He shoved John, who was sitting on a rock between Link and Liv. "Dude. When you turned me into an Incubus, you shoulda warned me about the whole we-don't-need-to-eat-and-everything-tastes-like-crap thing. I would've eaten a bunch a stuff for my last meal."

John held up a fist. "You're only a quarter Incubus, you big stud, and I did you a favor. No one would've ever called you a big stud if you'd kept eating those things."

"No one calls him that now," Ethan said.

"What are you saying?" Link was indignant.

"I'm saying, you used to be kinda sorry, Stay Puft, and now the chicks are lining up. You're welcome." John sat back.

"Oh, please," Ridley said. "As if his head could get any bigger."

"That's not the only thing that's bigger." Link winked, and everyone groaned. Ridley rolled her eyes, but he didn't care. "Oh, come on. Like you didn't see that one comin'."

Lena sat up straight, looking over the fire at the faces of her five closest friends in the world.

"All right. Forget this. Forget good-bye. So what if we're going to college tomorrow?" Lena glanced at Ethan.

"And England." Liv sighed, taking John's hand.

"And Hell," Link added, "if you ask my mother."

"Which no one is," Rid said.

"What I mean is, we don't have to do this the Mortal way," Lena said. Ethan stared at her strangely, but Lena kept going. "Let's make a pact instead."

"Just no blood oaths," John said. "Which would be the Blood Incubus way."

Link perked up at the thought. "Is that another camp thing? 'Cause we definitely didn't get to do that at church camp."

Lena shook her head. "Not blood."

"Maybe like a spit promise?" Link looked hopeful.

"Eww," Rid said, shoving him off his log.

"Not a spit promise." Lena leaned in, holding her hand over the fire. The flames reflected against her palm, turning orange and red and even blue.

Rid shivered. Her cousin was up to something, and with powers as unpredictable as Lena's, that wasn't always a good idea.

The embers glowed under Lena's fingertips. "We need to mark this occasion with something a little stronger than s'mores. We don't need to say good-bye. We just need a Cast."

KAMI GARCIA is the #1 *New York Times* bestselling coauthor of *Beautiful Creatures*, which is now a major motion picture, and the instant bestseller *Dangerous Creatures*. *Unbreakable*, her solo novel and first book in the Legion series, was an instant *New York Times* bestseller and was nominated for a 2013 Bram Stoker Award. Kami lives in Maryland with her family and her dogs, Spike and Oz, named after characters from *Buffy the Vampire Slayer*. You can find her online at kamigarcia.com and on Twitter @kamigarcia.